Christmas at Grey Sage

Phyllis Clark Nichols

GILEAD
PUBLISHING

Acclaim for
Christmas at Grey Sage

Christmas at Grey Sage by Phyllis Clark Nichols is a heartwarming, comical frolic from the first page. I fell in love with Maude and Silas and the Unlikely Christmas Party entourage. Forced to stay together at the Grey Sage Inn in New Mexico one snowy Christmas, a ban of eclectic travelers trying to escape Christmas find the joy and peace of the season once again and help inn-owners Maude and Silas heal from a long-ago tragedy.

This book is what Christmas is all about. I didn't want to leave the inn. But the recipes included at the end of this story will make me feel as if I'm there once again, sitting by the fire on a snowy night. Curl up with some hot chocolate and enjoy your stay at the Grey Sage Inn. You will have a blast!

—*Lenora Worth, NY Times, USA Today and PW Bestselling Author*

Christmas at Grey Sage is a beautifully gentle story about grief, friendship, and the unlikely companionship of strangers that will leave you smiling and singing carols as you close its pages. Phyllis Nichols has a knack of creating an enchanting storyworld, populated by diverse and quirky characters you can't help but root for. A satisfying and fun holiday read.

—*Mary DeMuth, author of over 30 books, including The Muir House*

*P*hyllis Clark Nichols has done it once more! In this new book, she deals again, masterfully, with the topic of Christmas. In an accessible but deep way, her narrative connects the readers with a collective human wealth of experiences, feelings, senses, symbols, and relationships, inviting them to reflect on their own wounds, in order to emerge with a new sense of joy and hope, not only for Christmas, but for life.

—*Nora O. Lozano, Ph.D., Executive Director, Latina Leadership Institute, Professor of Theological Studies, Baptist University of the Américas*

Christmas at Grey Sage by Phyllis Clark Nichols
Published by Gilead Publishing, Grand Rapids, Michigan
www.gileadpublishing.com

 GILEAD
PUBLISHING

ISBN: 978-1-68370-1286 (paper)
ISBN: 978-1-68370-1293 (eBook)

Edited by Leslie Peterson
Cover designed by Larry Taylor
Interior designed by Amy Shock

Printed in the United States of America

*For Bill, who makes every day seem like
Christmas morning*

Christmas Longtime Past

Grey Sage in Santa Fe,
the Christmas of 1973

*W*hen Maude opened the door to the Christmas closet in early December that year, she had no reason to think there would only be nine more Christmases celebrated at Grey Sage.

She pulled boxes off shelves and hauled cartons to the gathering room, the keeping room, and the front hallway. Dressing Grey Sage for Christmas took weeks of artistic planning and three days of hard work. Maude and Lita, her neighbor and friend of Hopi descent, always made ten fresh pine wreaths for the front windows; decorated four Christmas trees with homemade ornaments; arranged pine boughs and hung stockings on three mantles; encircled all the exterior door knobs with jingle bells; gathered pine cones to fill red baskets next to each fireplace; tied miles of red velvet ribbon; and placed too many candles in too many places to count. When the house smelled of conifers and the rooms glowed from the inside out, then the cooking started. And then Maude McClane Thornhill declared it was *almost* Christmas.

Christmas always moved in and took up residence in early December, but for Maude, the season did not truly fill the house until the family arrived and "the unveiling" was done. All year long, every day, Grey Sage landscapes begged to be painted, and every year she painted a new one to be revealed on Christmas. But this year's painting was more than a landscape, and she marked the days until she could drop the green velvet drape for the family to see.

When Elan had squatted at the edge of the creek looking for

smooth stones on an afternoon in May, he'd had no notion that his mother was studying the way the sun's rays darted through the pines to highlight his face and his swirling blond curls. For months, trees grew greener, water danced over stones playing with the light, and Elan came to life on her canvas. She spent hours painting the delight in his smile and the curiosity in his eyes, and she cherished every one of those hours. This painting would take center stage over the fireplace in her office as soon as the Christmas decorations were back in the closet.

Maude treasured family assemblages during the Christmas season, and this year would be no exception. She always stuffed the days leading up to Christmas as tight with memory-making activities as she stuffed the children's Christmas stockings with surprises. Never was there a shortage of laughter, food, and storytelling.

Usually, a couple of days before Christmas, the ladies of the family enjoyed last-minute shopping in the Plaza and on Canyon Road while their husbands minded the boys. Evenings meant a steaming, spicy bowl of green chili with Indian flatbread in front of the fireplace and a sampling of the sweets from Maude's favorite bakery in town, or a morsel of the homemade candy her mother always brought. Somewhere in the mix of activities were board games, a bonfire with marshmallows, stringing popcorn for the birds, and the Thornhill siblings taking turns playing their favorite Christmas tunes on the piano.

She made certain Elan had everything he needed for spectacular Christmas memories. Although Maude and Silas had wanted other children, that was not to be. Christmas gave Elan and his cousins several days together for walks in the woods and snowball fights and sled races.

By this time, enough years had passed that Thornhill traditions were firmly tied to Santa Fe. Alo and Lita Loloma—neighbors who were more like family—always insisted on hosting a traditional Christmas Eve dinner. Lita would take over Maude's kitchen and prepare a traditional Hopi dinner of venison rump roast with her secret spices; a Christmas salad of prickly pears, jalapeños, red lettuce, red onions, sliced avocados, and pine nuts; an array of roasted root vegetables with polenta; and her ancestral Cold Christmas Cake. She proudly served her Christmas Eve dinner on the dining table Maude had designed. Alo had scoured the pine brake down the hill for the perfect tree to build Maude's table. He surrounded it with handmade chairs and a pine bench sufficient to seat eighteen of the Thornhill clan and four of the Lolomas every Christmas.

After the last bite of the Cold Christmas Cake, everyone would load up the vehicles and drive to Santa Fe to attend the Christmas Eve service at the cathedral. Afterward, if the temperatures cooperated, they'd enjoy a walk around the Plaza and wander onto residential streets and avenues to see the luminaria-lined neighborhood sidewalks. The lights, the sounds, the smells, the feel—Santa Fe was nothing short of enchanting at Christmas.

But neither was Grey Sage. Not one complaint was ever heard when Silas suggested they load up and head home for that last cup of hot chocolate and a treat before bedtime. The day had been full, and not even the adults lingered in front of the fire after putting the children to bed. The house was always warm and quiet—nothing to be heard except an occasional whir of the wind through the pines.

That Christmas morning, Maude and Silas rose early and walked through the gathering room. Silas had spent hours last night assembling Elan's Christmas present and needed one last look at his masterpiece before heading to the kitchen to make the urn of coffee. Maude's job was to move the cinnamon buns from the fridge to the counter to let them rise and to build the fire in the keeping-room fireplace. She had always been better with wood and matches than with coffee scoops and coffeepots.

Although it was still dark, they looked out the kitchen window and determined by moonlight that they'd had at least a two-inch blanketing of snow during the night. Fresh snow and the smell of coffee and cinnamon buns made for a perfect Christmas morning as far as they were concerned.

Just before daybreak, when Maude could stand no longer stand the fact that she and Silas were the only ones awake, she went into the gathering room to build another fire. Alo had stacked the firewood in the box last night, so all she needed to do was put it on the grate and strike the match. When the fire blazed, she pulled Handel's *Messiah* from the shelf and placed the album on the turntable. She turned the volume up so high that when she dropped the needle at the beginning of the "Hallelujah Chorus," the rattling windows shook away the overnight dusting of snow on the outside wreaths.

Maude replaced Handel with the silky voice of Perry Como singing "I'll Be Home for Christmas" only when she was certain no one could still be asleep.

In a matter of moments, all the seats in the living room were taken by coffee-sipping adults in red-and-green plaid and monogrammed Christmas robes, all awaiting the sideshow of five little boys who were about to see what Santa had been able to get through the chimney.

Within minutes, the sounds of laughter, chatter, Christmas carols coming from the stereo, and the humming of an electric train filled the living room at Grey Sage.

Six-year-old Elan lay on the Saltillo tile floor, his eyes following the train under and around the Christmas tree. "Look, Dad, it has an engine and a caboose just like the one that goes by Pop's house in Texas. I think Santa had to stay here a long time last night to lay this track and build this train."

Silas, always the careful one, was on his knees next to Elan, making sure the cord was safe. "Sure did, son. I can imagine it was a really difficult job, and Santa must have been grateful for the Feast Day cookies you left under the Christmas tree."

Maude sputtered into her coffee and laughed. She stepped nearer to her husband and needled his leg with her bedroom slipper. "Oh, yes, Elan. I wonder if Santa followed the instructions like your dad does when he puts things together." She looked down at her husband and winked. "I'm just glad Santa didn't find the rest of Lita's cookies in the butler's pantry, or else we'd have none for our Christmas celebration today."

Elan scooted across the floor and hugged his father. "This is the best Christmas ever, Dad. A train—a real electric train! And you think Santa will bring me new cars every year?"

Silas ruffled Elan's blond curls and hugged him. "Maybe, if you write him a letter."

After breakfast and cleanup, Maude returned to the family in the gathering room. Elan was still on the floor by himself, flipping switches and examining train cars. "Elan, you need to get your clothes on. Your cousins are all dressed and ready for sled rides. Besides, no self-respecting engineer would still be in his pajamas at ten o'clock in the morning."

Elan hopped up. "Okay, Mom. But don't turn the train off, Dad. I'll be right back, and I like to hear it running."

As he walked by on the way to his room, she handed him a box wrapped in red foil. "Here, Elan. See if you might like to wear this today."

"Thanks, Mom." Elan took the box and ran down the hall to his room. In only a few moments, he returned in gray-striped overalls, a red shirt, and an engineer's cap. "Look, Dad. I'm an engineer. A real engineer!" His face glowed with excitement.

"Hmm ... A barefooted engineer."

"Dad!" Elan squealed as Silas scooped him up and then tickled his feet until he dissolved into giggles.

Watching them, Maude laughed. Her heart was full. This—this was what she lived for. It was Christmas morning. Her house was filled with family, all laughing and telling stories, enjoying good food and good cheer. And the contentment she saw on Silas's face and the joy she heard in Elan's voice were all she needed for the holiday—and for all time.

Christmas was just as it should be.

Chapter One

Monday, December 19, 2005

Maude stood at the kitchen window and rubbed her hands, especially the fingers of her left hand. Seems the cold made them ache a bit more with every winter, making it painful to hold her palette now. But she wasn't painting today. She and Lita would spend the day preparing for the arrival of the ten guests who would occupy the inn for the next couple of nights.

She turned from the window to see Silas in the keeping room just off the kitchen, sitting in his favorite chair.

Reason says I should have used that ratty chair for firewood years ago, but somehow seeing Silas this morning, sitting, reading, and drinking his second cup of coffee, makes me glad I kept it.

Making Silas comfortable these days was higher on her list of priorities than replacing a worn-out chair.

Seeing her look, Silas grumbled from across the room, "Lita doing the grocery shopping? Did you tell her not to buy eggnog? I don't like that store-bought eggnog. It's too sweet. We'll be making our own."

"I'm certain Lita knows you don't like eggnog from a carton since she's been drinking your homemade eggnog for about forty years." Maude continued looking over the guest list Lily had sent.

"Did you tell her to buy real cream and lots of it?"

"Yes, Silas. She's getting extra cream and extra eggs, and we're counting on you for the extra *nog*. In any case, she and Alo should be here shortly. She'll be preparing food, and I'm sure Alo will be cutting wood."

"Good, we wouldn't want our guests to arrive to a cold house, now would we, Maude?"

It was strange to be thinking of food and fires and guests this time of year. It had been an age since Grey Sage had housed people during the Christmas season.

Not so the rest of the year. Several years ago, Lita had persuaded Maude and Silas to open their home as an inn.

Lita had pleaded. *"But Maude, you know how many times the tourists see the sign on the gate and drive in. They already think it's an inn, and they're looking for a cup of coffee and something to eat."* She also convinced Maude they could easily sleep and feed twenty on the weekends. *"I'll do the cooking and cleaning, and you can host retreats."*

Maude had given in to the idea of hosting artists' and writers' retreats, and it wasn't long before Grey Sage developed quite a reputation across the Southwest and in the East, where Silas and Maude still had many friends.

But even as life returned to the house with so many guests, the one thing Silas and Maude could never manage was Christmas at home. They closed Grey Sage for two weeks during the holidays and took a trip.

Until now. This year Lily Mayfield had persuaded Maude to open Grey Sage for a couple of nights for a group of her travelers. Maude agreed—with the condition they'd be out by Thursday, with Silas and her on a flight by Friday morning.

Maude felt the wind gust as Lita came through the back door. "Getting colder out there?"

"Oh, yes." Lita plopped several bags on the counter. "The sky's a thick gray this morning. I'm happy to be done with the shopping and back home."

Maude rushed to grab a bag of groceries before it toppled onto the floor. "Shall we get the other bags out of the truck?"

"No, Alo's bringing them after he puts the frozen items away in the storage-room freezer. Let's just take care of these. We'll have plenty to eat no matter what, and plenty of coffee. Speaking of which, I need a cup. What about you?"

"No, thanks. There's coffee in the pot, but I've had my limit. And don't offer any more to Silas, please."

Maude started toward the pantry with several cans and two bags of rice but was stopped by Lita, who had bolted between her and the pantry door. "Why don't you pour my cup of coffee and let me put these away?" her friend suggested.

"I know, I know. You just don't want me messing things up in there." Maude smiled and released the canned goods and rice into Lita's arms.

Lita laughed. "For certain you do a better job of pouring coffee than you do of putting away groceries. You and that artistic brain of yours think it's better to just open the door, toss them in, and see where they might land. Only thing is I'll be the one sweeping rice and trying to find the canned artichoke hearts while I'm preparing meals for our guests." She continued into the pantry. "Did you get the guest list yet?" she called over her shoulder.

"Lily sent it this morning." Maude poured Lita's cup of coffee and added cream, handing it to Lita when she returned.

Lita took it with a grateful smile. "Did the number change?"

"No, still only ten. She also sent a rooming list and a brief description of our guests. Looks like an interesting-bordering-on-eccentric group headed our way." Maude grabbed the list and shared the details. "A retired military officer, an aging ballerina, a religion professor with his wife and a son who's recuperating from war injuries, a pharmacist and his music-teaching wife, a grieving widow who's a psycho-therapist, her daughter ... Need I go on? Oh, and then there's Lily."

Lita took a sip of her coffee, then began steady trips to the pantry and back. "Well, sounds like they have it all covered. We'll have music and dance, religion and politics. Oh, and with a grieving psycho-therapist who has a single daughter, we're bound to see tears. And, as you say, there's Lily. She always brings the drama with her latest man-grabbing stories."

Alo came through the kitchen door with more grocery bags hanging from his arms, shoulders, and hands. He grunted as he kicked the door shut. "We could have left the frozen goods outside. Feels like they wouldn't be thawing 'til June. How many guests are we expecting? You have enough groceries here to feed a hungry tribe."

"Maude, would you pour him a cup of coffee? Might help his grumps." Lita took some of the bags from Alo and headed toward the pantry again. "Maude just went over the guest list of ten. But we have more than one tribe to feed. I didn't want to leave the mountain again unless I had to, so I bought food for when Catori and Doli and the grandchildren arrive for Christmas."

Silas got up from his chair and patted the ten-pound bag of beans. "Looks like we can feed them beans until after the New Year." He fixed a look on Lita. "Did you get plenty of eggs and cream for the eggnog?"

"I did, and it would have been cheaper to buy a cow and a couple of chickens."

Maude's eyes widened. "Don't give him any ideas. I finally got him retired from doctoring and taking care of folks. We don't need anything else around here to feed or take care of. We just need to get through the next couple of days, and then we're off."

"Oh, sure. You're off to the warm waters of the Caribbean, spending Christmas with strangers under palm trees." Lita shook her head. "Wish you'd just stay here with us. Our casita looks like I've been spending too much time in the Christmas store in Santa Fe, and Catori and Doli would love to see you. Would you just think about it, Maude?"

"And I'd love to see them and all your new decorations. But our cruise is already paid for, and my achy joints are ready for some tropical sunshine. And I'm finally putting my toes into the water off Curaçao. Another check on my checklist." Maude grinned in anticipation.

Alo removed his jacket. "Tell me again: how many different countries have you visited on your Christmas excursions?"

"Curaçao will make seventeen countries in the last twenty-two years," Silas answered.

Lita rolled her eyes. "There's just something wrong about Christmas in Curaçao. No snow, no pine trees, no fireplaces. And 'Silent Night' samba style?"

Maude raised her eyebrows. "Just think, though, Lita—it's all about interesting cultures. You started this. I never saw your venison rump roast with a cactus pear Christmas salad on a Christmas dinner table in West Texas. Oh, or your Hopi Cold Christmas Cake."

"Yes, but all of that is *our* tradition," Lita retaliated.

"True, and *our* Christmas tradition is to see how many culturally different Christmas dinners we can have before we're too old to travel. Then it'll be your venison rump roast again."

All four adults in the kitchen went silent. Escaping Christmas had become Maude and Silas's tradition, and even after twenty-two years, remembering still brought pain.

Lita broke the silence. "And what if I'm too old to cook it?" she asked.

Alo put his hand on Lita's shoulder. "See, I've been telling you to teach your daughters how to cook in our tradition."

"I did teach them, and they'll do a fine job when it's their turn. But for now, it's still my turn. And right now, it's my turn to get the rest of these groceries put away and the beef bones boiling to make beef stock." Lita pointed to the door. "Alo, could you take the rest of the boxes down to our casita? And Silas, could you check the cabinet to make certain you have enough nog for all the cream and eggs I bought? And Maude, maybe you could get a pad and pencil and we could finalize the menus while I get the water boiling."

Maude rummaged for writing supplies, then sat on the barstool, ready to make notes. "Hmm, the butcher must adore you, paying money for all those beef bones that he'd have to throw away."

"I'm not certain we'd want to know what they do with these beef bones if I didn't buy them, but I can't make good soup and chili without good stock." Lita added salt and pepper to the pot.

"I guess that means we can work soup and chili into our menu, right? Maybe for tomorrow's lunch?"

"They're arriving for lunch tomorrow? And they'll be back for tomorrow night's dinner?"

"Yes on the lunch, no on the dinner. They'll eat in town tomorrow night. You might go easy on the heat in the green chili, though. Lily says these folks have Midwest palates, and I'm not certain they can handle New Mexico green chili."

"Well, let's tingle those delicate palates and give them a true Sangre de Cristo Mountains experience," Lita said. She grinned impishly and added more black pepper to the pot. "And Lily's not bringing a man with her this trip?"

"No, I couldn't believe it. Such a rare occasion. But I think that's why she put this trip together."

"Why? Because she's manless right now?"

"Maybe." Maude shrugged. "Or maybe she's got her eye on the single military guy."

"Which one? The old retired guy or the young soldier?" Lita dumped a bowl of beef bones into the stock pot of boiling water and secured the lid on top.

"Now, Lita, Lily has her ways, but I don't think ..." She trailed off. Lita was already shaking her head.

"Uh-huh. I still don't understand how you two became such friends. She never married and changes men more often than we change the light bulbs around here, and you've been a one-woman man all your life." Lita washed her hands and dried them on the dish towel, then reached for a basket of fresh peppers.

"I don't think our friendship had much of anything to do with our mating instincts. I think it had to do more with our mutual curiosity. When we met, she was Manhattan in a sack dress and a fur-trimmed jacket. I must have looked like Annie Oakley to her—my third day in Chicago and standing on the corner of Madison and Wabash trying to find my way to the main building on Michigan Avenue. She took pity on me and walked me to the front door a few blocks away."

"Somehow I can't picture Lily being kind to a stranger."

"Like I said, I think she was just curious. We were so different. It's a lot more than eighteen hundred miles separating Lubbock from New York City. We had much to learn from each other. And of course, we shared a passion for art," Maude finished with a smile.

"But that was so many years ago, and you're still friends."

"That we are. I guess those long walks on Lake Shore Drive stretched more than our legs. And then there were the late nights in the studios trying to finish a project. And all the days and evenings we spent in museums together while I was filling up time and missing Silas."

"Was she man crazy then?"

"You might say that she liked *variety*, and she was a bit—" Maude paused. "Ahead of her time. At least, ahead of my time."

Lita laughed out loud. "Guess she taught a young, small-town, yes-ma'aming, church-going, skinny thing like you a few new tricks."

"Well, friendship with Lily exposed me to a bit more than art. But that was—is—Lily. Underneath all that flamboyance is a good soul who loves life and sees the world differently than most of us."

"She's still raising eyebrows with her flamboyance. Last time she was here for a retreat, I heard a young artist ask her where she grew up, and she shook that flaming red mane of hers and said, '*Grow up? I didn't grow up. Who wants to grow up?*'" Lita mimicked the way Lily shook her long, curly locks. "Left that poor young thing speechless."

"Avant-garde. That's what she was and still is."

"Avant-garde or not, I'll be on *my* guard and prepared for most anything with her around. At least they'll be out touring Santa Fe most of the time."

"Yes, they will. And while they're out, I'll be packing my red crepe pants and kimono for Christmas Eve in Curaçao," Maude said with satisfaction.

Chapter Two

Tuesday, December 20

*M*aude sat on the brown leather sofa, sorting room keys and papers and eyeing her college friend, whose curly hair was still pumpkin red after nearly five decades.

Backed up to the blazing, mammoth fireplace in the gathering room, Lily had pulled her green plaid poncho up above her buttocks. She stood, humming for a moment, then smoothed the poncho back down over her green wool pants. "Almost nothing warms my backside like a roaring fire. Mind you, I did say 'almost.'" She gave Maude a look that Maude knew too well.

The rest of the visiting entourage sauntered in from the dining room, where Lita had just served them coffee and *buñuelos*—her version of dense donut holes rolled in cinnamon and sugar.

Lily leaned over to put her mug on the pine coffee table and whispered, "Pardon me, Maude, but a couple of these folks cannot hear, and the rest of them don't bother to listen." That said, she stood, lifted the sterling-silver whistle from the chain around her neck, and blew into it as though she was trying to blow out the fire behind her.

Maude shrieked and covered her ears, and Lita nearly broadjumped over the sofa.

Maude should have known better. This was how it was with Lily—one unexpected surprise after another.

When Lily's nine had huddled around her, she announced, "This is our host, Maude McClane Thornhill. She and I have history going back to our college days at the School of the Art Institute in Chicago."

She gestured around the room. "Some of you would say Maude

and Silas own this place. But what on earth does that mean? How can anyone own a piece of the earth, especially when the people who owned this part of the world from the beginning are all dead and they never got a penny for it? I own no property, but apparently Maude and Silas do."

She paused with a flourish, and Lita snuck an eye roll at Maude.

"Now, Lily, we know who really owns this property, so let's just say we are in possession of the deed to the property for a while. And we do try to be good stewards of it while we enjoy the peace and serenity we have found here."

Lily acknowledged Maude's explanation with a nod of her head before turning back to her charges. "All that said, Grey Sage is their home, and we are their guests. As Maude noted, they are the earnest caretakers of this land and this inn, and I assure you we will be treated royally. Maude is an artist and teacher of sorts, so she aptly named each of the inn's suites after an artist. And when you enter your suite, you'll understand why. You'll find stellar art and sculpture and mind-expanding reading material. As I told you on the drive out, Maude's artists' retreats here are heralded across America."

Maude felt her cheeks turning red not from the roaring fire, but from Lily's extravagant comments.

Lily held fast to her clipboard with one hand, trying to tame her spongy red curls with the other, and continued her formal introductions of Silas, Alo, and Lita. Once finished, she announced, "People, as I call your names, you may pick up your key, and Alo or Silas will escort you down the hallway of this wing to your suites." Lily pointed to her right. "You have about twenty minutes to freshen up and meet me back here at eleven for departure to downtown Santa Fe. We have things to see. By all means, dress warmly." She gave the group a stern look. "If you're here on time, there'll be no need to blow the whistle."

Maude glanced over at Lita. She had a hunch that during the morning's room cleaning, Lily's whistle might accidentally find its way under the bed, only to be found Thursday afternoon right around the time of Lily's departure.

Lily positioned her glasses, easily mistaken for large red teething rings, on the end of her nose and looked down at her rooming list. "Greg." She motioned for Maude to hand him his key. "You and Iris are in the Renoir Suite at the very end of the hall. I think you'll find it most impressionable."

As Greg and Iris walked away, Lily leaned in and whispered to Maude, "You think he got it? Remember, he's a theologian, so I'm not asking him any serious questions, because I don't want to sit and listen for the next half century."

She returned to her list and sized up the Martins' son. "And, Kent. You're in the Wyeth Suite, first door to the right as far away from your parents as I could house you." His left arm in a sling, Kent took the key with his right hand, politely thanked Maude, and winked at Lily.

"Beatrice ... my dearest Beatrice. I think you'll find the Degas Suite absolutely stunning, just like you, my darling. Degas must have been obsessed with dance. He splashed ballet dancers over many a canvas. Silas, could you help Beatrice, please?"

Silas extended his arm to Beatrice to make certain she found her suite and conversed with her as they walked away. Lily leaned in to Maude again. "She's a bit eccentric and pirouettes around the room periodically to music that only she hears. But if she remembers to come to dinner, I don't think she'll show up in her tutu."

Maude still marveled at Lily's boldness. "Shush, Lily. Beatrice could hear you and be offended."

"Perhaps, but she'd forget all about it in less than ninety seconds." Lily looked back at the clipboard. "Dr. Sutton, you and Laura will be in the Monet Suite. I'm hoping what you see there might inspire you to delight us with a little Debussy after dinner this evening, Laura. I'm certain you didn't miss the Steinway in the corner over there." Lily nodded toward the piano and wiggled her fingers on her right hand as though playing a keyboard. "Don't forget your gloves for our trip downtown," she told the woman. "Must keep those delicate fingers warm."

Maude handed Ted Sutton the key and caught the grimace on Laura's face. "Or maybe you'd prefer playing some Christmas music for us. After all, what is this season without its glorious music?"

Laura worked at a smile, said nothing, and followed her husband to the hallway entrance.

Lily took another key from Maude and turned to the two handsomely dressed women on her left, the older one in gray and the younger one in navy pants and a red sweater, both in pearls with leather tote bags on their arms. Obviously mother and daughter, they stood next to the wing chair. "Reba, you and Emily will share the Picasso Suite—twin beds and a panoramic view of all of North America." She made a dramatic, wide sweep with her free arm.

Emily slipped the key from Lily's hand. "Thank you, Lily. I know we'll enjoy the view." They followed Alo down the hallway.

Lily leaned toward Maude. "Translated, that means 'My mother is in serious need of therapy, and I'm trying to make the best of it.' I'm thinking of removing that tortoise-shell clamp from Reba's hair to see if that might loosen her up. Meantime, she's the therapist, and I assume she'll enjoy trying to read something into Picasso's techniques."

Maude chortled. "Lily, you're still as wicked as ever. Maybe more."

"And finally, Colonel Walton, because you are the classic gentleman, you'll be staying in the Rembrandt Suite, right next to mine. I hope you will find everything to your taste."

Maude handed him the last key. The colonel took Maude's hand and kissed it before taking the key. "I'm most certain that it will be impeccable. And if not, I'll park myself in that wing chair next to that blazing fire." He walked away, but just before entering the hallway turned back to Lily. "And did I miss the name of your suite, Lily?"

"I'm right next to you in the Pollock Suite. You know how eclectic and colorful I can be. Don't you think it appropriate?" She lowered her chin and her eyelids ever so slightly and then tossed her hair like a sassy fourteen-year-old.

Once he was a few steps down the hall, Lily put her clipboard on the rustic coffee table in the center of the room. "Don't you think he's charming? He's ninety-plus but doesn't look a day over seventy."

Maude, still amazed with Lily's flirtatious, seventy-two old girlishness, replied, "He is every bit of charming, and he's traveling alone. Is the colonel the reason you planned this trip?"

"Maude, when do you call 'babysitting a declining ballerina' traveling alone? Beatrice's third husband was Henry's friend, and Henry made one of those deathbed promises that he'd look after Beatrice. Some women—excluding me, of course—need to be taken care of, and Henry's too much of a soldier and a gentleman not to make good on his promise. Oh, but he's a divine dancer, smooth and certain."

"Ah, do I detect that rapid heartbeat you get when you find a man attractive?"

Lily rolled her eyes. "Only slightly accelerated."

"Got a minute to sit with me?" Maude patted the brown leather cushion next to her, and Lily sat down. "When you called, you only told me you had a group of people who needed rooms in the inn at Christmas."

"Yes, and you promptly told me there was no room in the inn because it was closed for Christmas. I think I've heard that 'no room in the inn' Christmas story before. So I asked you again because I couldn't bear to put these gallant gentlemen and refined ladies in a barn. I *begged*."

"As I recall, you did. You begged, and I said yes."

Lily removed her red glasses. "Thank God. What would I ever do without you, Maude?"

"I know you've always been like the Pied Piper with a gaggle of followers, but even you would admit this crew is a bit—well, more than a bit—interesting. What I'd really like to know is why they would want to travel at Christmas?"

Lily stared back at Maude. "I can't believe you, of all people, are asking me that question. Why do you and Silas travel at Christmas?"

Maude bit her lip and swallowed the words she did not want to say. "I don't need to explain that. You know why we travel at Christmas."

"I do. And is it too much for you to imagine that others might find the holidays a bit difficult as well, and they don't want to be alone in their murky miseries when they're supposed to be making merry?"

"I certainly can. But a road trip from Chicago to Denver with an out-of-the-way side trip to Santa Fe? Why not New York or London or—"

"And why not Christmas at the Broadmoor in Colorado Springs?" Lily interjected. "It's an elegant five-star hotel. What could be more perfect in December? Snow. Mountains in the distance. There'll be divine musical performances, and we get to glitter and shine two evenings for formal dinners. The food is world class, along with the spa. So many colors to paint over our miseries." Lily flittered her hands in the air like a bird flying away.

Maude recognized the mannerism from decades ago—Lily's way of signaling her desire to escape reality. "Sounds lovely, and if we hadn't booked a cruise, perhaps Silas and I would have joined you. But ... this group. How did *this* peculiar party ever come together?"

"That's quite a long story, but the short of it is three of them were in my pottery class back in the early fall—Beatrice, Reba, and Iris. When someone mentioned my summer study tour in class one evening, Beatrice—whose mind connects dots quite differently than most, as I told you—immediately told us she was spending Christmas at the Broadmoor. She was planning to meet her grown children there, but she was looking for transportation and someone to accompany her."

"Couldn't she just fly?"

"I suppose so, but after she mentioned the Broadmoor, I checked it out. Why couldn't I—the single, childless woman that I am—get Beatrice to Colorado Springs for Christmas? I volunteered to accompany her, and then Henry said he'd go too. Then came Reba. Her husband died a few months ago, and she and her daughter didn't want to spend Christmas at home. Then Iris said she had always wanted to spend Christmas in a mountain chalet, and she thought it would be good to get Kent out of the city, since his physical therapy had been so grueling. He's recovering from injuries in Iraq. One conversation led to another, and so here we are—a most unlikely Christmas party. And that's what I told them we were: an Unlikely Christmas Party on Wheels."

"But, what about the Suttons? Didn't I see on the register they're from Ann Arbor?"

"Yes. Both are professors at the University of Michigan. He's in pharmacy and she teaches music theory. I've known them from other study tours they've done with me. They're quiet and easy, so on a whim, I called them to see if they might be interested. Ted may have hesitated long enough to clear this throat. They never had children and have spent their free time traveling and collecting."

"Collecting? What?"

"Art. He comes from old—no, ancient—money."

"Oh, lovely. You have the most interesting friends, Lily. They sound safe, so I have no need to watch the silver, right?" Maude hugged Lily, thankful that her friend always brought life and fun and unexpected pleasures that made for good stories ten years later.

As Lily shuffled her papers, Maude pondered the situation. *I do wonder what stories will come out of this visit. Far too many interesting characters for there not to be a tale or two.*

"Won't you come with us into town, Maude? We're walking the Plaza and going by the Loretto Chapel late in the afternoon before we come back to Grey Sage for dinner. I was hoping they'd have a vespers service in the chapel."

"You should have done your homework, Lily. The Loretto is a museum now—no more masses or services, only elegant weddings."

"Well, then, we'll be back early for dinner. But won't you come? Please."

Maude knew Lita had already prepared lunch, which could now

become dinner since Lily had changed the schedule. So Lita wouldn't need her help. "Of course, I'll come with you. Don't know about Silas, though. He may use this quiet time to continue working on an article he's writing."

"That's even better, my friend. Not that I don't dearly love Silas, but this way I'll have you all to myself." Lily stood up and walked over to the fireplace. "By the way, can you suggest a hotel in town for Gordy?"

"You mean your van driver? And what kind of name is Gordy?"

"I don't know, but the name suits him. I had a near disastrous time finding a driver for the holidays." Lily pulled up her poncho to warm her backside again.

"Why don't you have him stay here? We have room." Maude shuffled the papers she'd put on the coffee table.

"Because he's charging us twice as much as he should, and I'm having to fly him back to Chicago from Colorado Springs to be with his impossible mother on Christmas Eve and Christmas Day, and then back to Denver to drive us home after New Year's. He can find his own hotel," she huffed. "Besides he's no fun, and I mean *no* fun. He finds gauges more interesting than people—the gas gauge, the tire gauge ..." Lily looked at her watch.

Maude heard Silas and the colonel chatting as they entered the gathering room and turned to Lily. "Yes, I'll go with you. And I'll find a room for Gordy in town, even though I still think it's easier if he just stays here." She stood up. "Let me speak with Lita and get my coat and gloves."

She started out, then paused and pointed her finger at Lily. "I'm warning you: if you blow that whistle, I'll be getting you an adjoining room next to Gordy in town."

Lily picked up the whistle and dropped it safely underneath her poncho, hidden from sight.

With a grin, Maude left the room and met Lita in the kitchen. Lita stood at the pantry door and motioned for Maude to join her. When Maude put her papers down and walked toward the pantry, Lita took

Maude's arm and practically dragged her inside before shutting the door.

"Maude, you've known me for a long time. You know that I'm a kind, generous, and jolly person, right?"

"I do. But could you let go of my arm and turn on the light? You're pinching me."

Lita let go of Maude's arm. "We don't need the light on for me to tell you that Lily's only been here an hour and she's already stretching my nerve endings. At Grey Sage, we serve breakfast and only occasional dinners for special events. Three days ago, Lily requested lunch on Tuesday, and we agreed. So I shopped yesterday and rose early this morning to prepare lunch for their arrival around eleven. Then she shows up two hours before she's supposed to, after lunch prep is well underway, and cancels lunch and orders dinner instead."

"I know, I know. But it will be fine, Lita. Could we turn on the light to have this conversation?"

Lita kept talking. "Now I must prepare dinner and put lunch in the refrigerator."

"Weren't you having chili and salad and pudding for lunch? Why not serve that for dinner?"

"I'll not have these fine folks returning to Chicago telling their friends that we don't know how to serve a proper dinner. But I can tell you this: I know it's Christmas, and the Christmas spirit is supposed to bring out the best in us. But if I prepare a proper dinner and Lily Mayfield cancels at the last minute, well ... well ..." Lita took a slow, deep breath. "Well, I'm planning to set her red hair on fire."

Without another word, Lita opened the pantry door and walked out.

Maude followed, trying not to laugh. "I guess this means you're finished with this conversation."

"Yes, I am completely finished with this conversation. But don't say I didn't warn you about her hair."

"Got it. I was planning to go in to Santa Fe with them, but if you need me here, I'll be glad to stay and help you."

"No, thank you. The best thing you can do is to make sure this Christmas party is back and seated at the dinner table at six thirty, or we'll be smelling flaming red hair right next to the uneaten roasted pork loin."

"Understood." Maude headed for the mudroom to get her coat and boots. When she returned to the gathering room suited up for the cold weather, the party had assembled for Lily's announcements about their plans for the day.

Colonel Walton spoke up. "Sounds like quite an excursion you have planned for us, Lily. I'm certain you'll be keeping your eyes and ears on the weather."

Before Lily could respond, Beatrice stepped out of the group and stood front and center. "I'd really like to know where the Christmas decorations are around here. I've seen absolutely nothing that looks like Christmas." She twirled around, extending her arms to point out the entire room. "My daughter sent me pictures and said this place would be spectacular with Christmas trees and life-sized nutcrackers. So where are they?"

Lily cleared her throat. "Beatrice, I think your daughter was describing the Broadmoor Hotel in Colorado Springs."

"Yes, she was."

"Well, this is the Grey Sage Inn just outside Santa Fe."

"Oh. I see. This isn't the hotel where we'll spend Christmas?"

Colonel Walton joined Beatrice and put his arm around her narrow shoulders. "No, but we'll be here for a couple of days, and then we'll head to the Broadmoor, Bea. And your daughter will meet you there, and there'll be Christmas trees and nutcrackers and maybe even a sugarplum fairy."

"I've had my fill of sugarplum fairies in my day, and I can't wait to see my daughter and my grandchildren. But this is an inn, and I expected a bit of Christmas. My room is just fine, and Degas's painting of me is quite lovely." Beatrice perked up and turned her head like a prima donna waiting to be photographed. "Although I don't remember being quite that heavy. Anyway, without a Christmas tree anywhere in this place, how are we supposed to know it's even Christmas?"

Lily looked at Maude and rescued her before Maude had to speak. "Now, Beatrice, remember Maude is my friend, and she only opened Grey Sage to us because I asked her to host us. Normally, Grey Sage is closed during this season because she and Silas always take a Christmas trip. I told her there would be no need for decorations if she would just allow us to stay here."

Beatrice stood resolute in first position as she often did out of her habit from decades as a ballerina. "Well, I'm just not certain you should have agreed to that. I can only imagine this place would be quite lovely if decorated for Christmas."

Lily responded, "You're right, Beatrice, but it's also lovely like it is. And our rolling Christmas party of folks is all the decoration this place needs. Wouldn't you agree, friends?"

The group applauded.

Maude felt a bit of relief in this awkward moment, but she also felt the sting of embarrassment and regret for not having even put up a Christmas tree or one of the nativity scenes in her collection.

She surveyed the room, remembering other Christmases at Grey Sage when handmade stockings for the five Thornhill cousins had hung from the mantle. A tall fresh pine, cut from the property and dressed in an assortment of hand-blown glass bulbs and other ornaments made by local artists, filled the corner between the fireplace and the window right next to the grand piano. Red velvet draped the table behind the sofa. On it was displayed Maude's favorite nativity scene—the one Silas had bought for her in Italy.

In her memories, fresh pine boughs secured with red ribbons swagged every doorway in and out of this room. And red candles— only red candles—of all sizes were scattered about, some inside crystal globes and votives and others held by rustic candlesticks Elan had made for her from limbs of hardwoods trees they cut down for firewood. An Advent wreath and an assortment of books from her Christmas book collection covered the rough-hewn pine coffee table in the middle of the room. Christmas pillows and knitted throws covered the leather chairs and sofas.

But the dining room was something else. Decorated in white and silver, it could have been mistaken for a showroom of silver mercury glass—shimmering silver trees of varying sizes on the mantle and a classy display of silver candlesticks with white candles—only white candles—on the sideboard. The massive table in the dining room, never covered in a cloth, was set with white damask placemats and white napkins. Additional silver and crystal candlesticks with white candles meandered down the center of the table like a cascade of watery light through a bed of pine and cedar. Fresh greenery in a variety of small crystal containers identified each place setting.

More rooms—some rustic, some with bold color, and others seemingly sprinkled with Christmas fairy dust—had become Maude's palette for the Christmas season years ago. Those scenes scrolled through her memory like an old movie reel. A bit of sorrow tugged at her—sorrow that the rooms seemed bare and sorrow that her guests would not leave with memories of Grey Sage at Christmas.

Beatrice might have been surprised to find there was a ten-by-fourteen-foot storage room down the east hall that housed nothing but Christmas decorations—and that its door had been locked for twenty-two years. Beatrice and the other guests would never know that once upon a time, this gathering room had overflowed with Christmas in every way ... that there was a time when both Christmas and Maude's life were quite enchanting.

But those days were no longer.

Citing the need for a hat, Maude excused herself from the room.

Chapter Three

The snow had stopped, but the air was fiercely cold, and the sky was thick and gray. Maude was the last one in the van, tugging at her knitted wool hat and still getting the I'm-warning-you-if-Lily-cancels-dinner eye from Lita. She waved goodbye to Lita and Silas and took the front aisle seat next to Lily, across from Colonel Walton and Beatrice.

Gordy had driven no more than a hundred yards down the lane when Lily got up and crawled over Maude to get into the aisle. Maude knew the ride down the lane to Bishops Lodge Road was bumpy, bordering on treacherous with all the snow and ice. She warned Lily. "You might want to grab hold of that post behind the driver's seat. This is not Chicago, you know."

Lily took an uncertain step toward the driver, reached for the microphone on the dashboard, and nearly fell. Gordy grinned and handed it to her as she clung to the metal pole behind him.

Lily forced a smile to hide her disdain for Gordy and held her gloved finger to the microphone's button. "We should thank Gordy for keeping our van so toasty warm on such a frigid day."

The travelers responded with a chorus of thank yous.

"For today, or for what is left of it, I've made a change in plans to accommodate the weather. I'm aware that it's cold, but tomorrow may be worse, so we need to do our outside walking today. Gordy will drop us off at the historic Palace of the Governors right downtown, where perhaps there'll be some local Native American artists with their wares. You'll be on your own to walk the Plaza before we gather for lunch. After lunch, we'll have the afternoon to walk Canyon Road and visit the galleries and shops. Then more free time to look around at your own pace. Be kind to the local economy, people. I've been a starving artist. So show some Christmas spirit."

Beatrice, whose voice was heavier and huskier than her diminutive frame, spoke up. "I intend to buy some Christmas spirit and take it back to Grey Sage. I'll get that place looking like Christmas. Laura told me earlier there's a famous Christmas shop right downtown, and it will be my first stop." She looped her arm in the colonel's and looked up at him. "And Carl has agreed to carry all my packages."

Lily lowered the microphone to her side and whispered to Maude, "Don't mind her, Maude. She sometimes thinks Henry's her husband, Carl, and she's lost all lines of discretion. Should have asked you earlier, but would you mind being the guide down Canyon Road this afternoon?"

Maude smiled and shook her head. "Of course not. It would be my pleasure."

Lily straightened and nodded to Beatrice. "Thank you for your announcement, Beatrice. Next time, I'll hand you the microphone. Now, all of you will be pleased to know that Maude has agreed to lead a walking tour through the galleries and shops on Canyon Road for those who would like to walk with her this afternoon. She is an art patron and a friend to all the gallery owners and has so much knowledge to share about the local culture and art scene. That's a treat you didn't pay for."

There was a sudden buzz down the aisle of the van. All of the travelers with the exception of Ted and Laura Sutton planned to follow Maude. Ted explained they had been here several times and had particular galleries they wished to visit, so they would strike out on their own.

Lily continued. "Tomorrow, we will have more inside activities since the forecast is for increased precipitation. Wednesday's tours will include El Museo Cultural de Santa Fe in the Railyard Arts District, then lunch and the Georgia O'Keefe Museum, and our last stops will be the St. Francis Cathedral and the Loretto Chapel, where we'll see the mysterious staircase said to have been built by Saint Joseph himself. Christmas seems a most appropriate time of year to see the work of this famous carpenter."

The van jarred through a pothole in the lane, and Lily clutched the pole with both hands. "I think I'll sit down while I can still do it of my own accord. Enjoy the scenery through the mountains on this drive. One last thing: I'll stay in touch with Gregarious Gordy here so that he can pick us up after lunch. He'll be spending his day looking for accommodations and trying to stay warm."

Lily handed Gordy the microphone and crawled back over Maude to the seat by the window.

Twenty minutes later, they were in town. When the van was safely stopped, Lily announced, "It's eleven thirty. We'll meet at one o'clock right here and walk the short distance down Lincoln Avenue for lunch at the historic and famous Plaza Café. Their menu includes something for everyone, but Maude says to skip the pork because that's what we're having for dinner."

Beatrice was standing by then, and she began to move slowly into the aisle. She had finally stopped her incessant humming of the "Dance of the Sugar Plum Fairy" from *The Nutcracker Suite.* "When did we get to New York? I adore the Plaza, especially High Tea at The Palm Court there. Oh my, their clotted cream is like this heavenly cloud of buttery goodness, just like I was served in London." She paused. "But Lily, you need to check your plans. They don't even serve lunch at The Palm Court. Why are you taking me there?"

Lily responded with forced politeness. "Beatrice, we're having lunch at the Plaza Café in Santa Fe. We'll go to New York the next time, if that would please you."

Lily moved so that Beatrice and the colonel could make their way down the steps. She whispered to Maude, "I told you how she connects the dots. But thank goodness, she's deliriously happy and easily diverted."

When all of the travelers were off the van, Lily dismissed Gordy and instructed him to keep his cell phone near. Then she and Maude went straightaway to the Plaza Café to see if it was possible to set up a table for eleven for lunch. Maude thought it best to have them all at one table where she could give them a bit of information about Canyon Road.

When all was confirmed, Maude and Lily walked arm in arm across Lincoln Avenue, where Maude had insisted Lily visit the New Mexico Museum of Art to see their latest acquisitions. An hour later, they awaited their party just inside the door of the Plaza Café. Beatrice and Henry were the first to arrive. They were so laden with shopping bags and boxes that Lily summoned Gordy to the restaurant to pick up the bags and instructed him to hang around to drive them to Canyon Road after lunch.

In a matter of fifteen minutes, the group had gathered and found their seats around the large table that had been set for them. A caramel-skinned young woman, short in stature with a round face, high cheekbones, and shiny sable braids down her back, promoted the dishes that had made the Plaza famous and then took their orders. Even with her spicy suggestions, most of this Unlikely Christmas Party settled for a bowl of steaming tortilla soup. Kent, the young soldier, ventured out for the Green Chili Meatloaf stuffed with corn, sautéed greens, green chili, and cheese. The Suttons wanted a repeat of an earlier trip to Santa Fe and shared the Indian Taco with shredded chicken, squash, beans, cheese, green chili, lettuce, and tomatoes served on Indian fry bread. With bellies warmed and full, they asked for one more cup of coffee to prepare them for the biting cold wind just outside the door.

Maude sipped her last bit of hot tea and stood at the end of the table. "While you're enjoying your coffee, Lily has asked me to acquaint you with a bit of history and what you might expect this afternoon. I must first tell you this: I've traveled the world to see great art but find myself still walking Canyon Road with great anticipation and continual appreciation." Maude went on to tell them that this half-mile strip in the historic district bordering the Santa Fe

River was shaded by 150-year-old chestnut trees and lined with over a hundred art galleries, studios, ethnic restaurants, and boutiques.

"These adobe structures house some of the finest paintings and sculpture anywhere in the Southwest. I think you will be surprised at the international artists represented here. You will also see exquisite glass, handmade one-of-a-kind pieces of jewelry, clothing, and home furnishings. In fact, many of the pieces of pottery and glass you will see at Grey Sage were purchased right here in the galleries you're about to visit. I know it's cold, but as you meander around, look for a hidden courtyard or a unique fountain. They're around. I invite you to return in the spring when you would enjoy the smell of lilacs and the mists from the many fountains. And Beatrice, the hollyhocks will be taller than you and just as delicate."

Beatrice beamed, proud of her petite stature and erect posture at her age.

Maude continued, "I'm sorry they're bare now, but the chestnut trees lining the riverbank are spectacular during the autumn. Oh, and Christmas Eve? How I wish you could see it. Canyon Road will be darted with bonfires and strolling musicians, and many of the shops will be open and serving hot drinks to those last-minute shoppers. Each season comes with its own beauty and events on Canyon Road, but Christmas here is just as Christmas should be—no place quite like it."

Maude's voice wavered as her mind was suddenly catapulted back to their family traditions. She had tucked those memories away like family mementos in the attic—heirlooms having value and meaning to only a few. But now those memories spilled out unexpectedly.

She remembered as if it were last Christmas how she and Silas and young Elan had walked Canyon Road as was their Christmas custom—a custom Silas and Maude started their very first Christmas in Santa Fe. They came to purchase one unique gift for Grey Sage, as though their home was a cherished member of the family.

For Maude, it was. Grey Sage was alive and provided so much for them. It was only right to remember Grey Sage at gift-giving time.

Maude would instinctively gravitate toward the paintings, Silas the sculptures, and Elan the brightly colored glass. After Elan turned five, they always carried home a beautifully wrapped, hand-blown glass piece and put it under the tree. Then, after Christmas, they carried that piece all over the house to find just the place to display it—a place to maximize the ever-changing light coming through the windows at Grey Sage. Through the years, the colorful, yet fragile gifts selected for Grey Sage were the only pieces of Thornhill Christmases that were not locked away in the Christmas closet.

Drawing the curtain on her memories, Maude told more stories about Canyon Road's Native American and Spanish roots and how the area had evolved from an agrarian community in its earliest days to an art colony, and now to an extraordinary shopping experience. She then answered a few questions about specific galleries and where to look for particular items of interest.

"I think it's time you experience Christmas on Canyon Road," she wrapped up. "Shall we go?"

Ready for the afternoon's adventure, the party members eagerly pushed away from the table. Lily led them to the van and took hold of the microphone again as Gordy drove down Alameda. "Help the economy, people. Encourage an artist with your acquisition, and purchase at least one spectacularly beautiful item that will always be a remembrance of your December afternoon on Canyon Road. We'll have a show-and-tell at the dinner table this evening."

Lily looked at her watch. Nothing digital for her, she'd once told Maude. It had reportedly taken nearly the full price of one of her commissioned paintings to have her father's railroad watch mounted as a wristwatch with a heavy sterling-silver band. The watch face was the size of a silver dollar minted in 1900 and could be seen without her glasses. "It's two o'clock. So you have three hours to feast on the beautiful. Go and gorge yourselves, and meet me at five o'clock sharp at the same spot where Gordy drops us off. You will have walked a mile, and you'll be ready for the scrumptious dinner Lita is preparing for us. Maude will lead us." She pointed her finger at the Suttons.

"Ted, I know you and Laura will be taking off on your own. Enjoy yourselves. Just remember, five o'clock sharp. Okay, people. Let's go."

They departed the van, and Lily gathered the group around Maude for more logistics before starting their walk.

As she spoke, Maude's eyes surveyed the group. *Glad they dressed warmly—and in Christmas colors, no less. Hope no one mistakes us for a group of carolers about to stroll down the street.*

She motioned for them to follow and kept a constant eye on them, observing them as they moved from gallery to gallery. The group was quite the study in humanity.

Beatrice naturally takes the colonel's arm, which always seems to be extended to her. I'm glad they found each other. We all need an arm every now and then.

Greg and Iris huddle together most of the time. They really seem to like one another. Kent follows closely behind, not too interested in art. I can only imagine what his eyes have seen.

Reba gravitates toward the jewelry, but Emily doesn't seem to be too interested in things. She's tense. Emily's being pulled back and forth in a tug-of-war between her role as a dutiful daughter attending to her grieving mother when she really wants to respond to Kent's interest in her.

And Lily. Lily's still finding everything either stunning or startlingly awful, always moving through the galleries like a gust of opinionated wind, rarely using discretion in announcing her uninvited evaluation.

When Maude wasn't studying her fellow shoppers, her eye always seemed to be looking for an exquisite piece of glasswork. She picked up several small finds to see how they reflected the light, inquired about a few larger bowls, and ultimately was drawn to a shallow bowl created by a Brazilian artist. She studied it with her trained artist's eye.

This could be a table centerpiece. Or it's shallow enough I could suspend it in front of the window by the piano. The way it would play with the light from the window or even firelight would probably be mesmerizing. The red and gold spiral design looks like the lollipops Elan loved— the special ones from the candy shop on San Francisco Street. Maybe that's why I like this bowl so much.

She decided against purchasing it and returned her attention to the others. It made her happy that all of them were true Christmas revelers, enjoying themselves as they looked for just the perfect purchase.

Lily excused herself and said she'd catch up with them a bit later. When she returned, she clutched a rather large package and refused to give even Maude a hint about what was inside.

After hours of walking and removing hats and gloves with every gallery entrance only to put them back on again when exiting, Lily's weary, bag-laden Christmas party gathered at the pickup spot. The sound of "Deck the Halls" played by a brass choir jolted them as Gordy opened the van door with his cheerful greeting. "More snow in the mountains. Need to get going."

Lily replied, "Could you please turn the volume down on the radio? We're already in a fa-la-la-la-la mood, but it might be better if the van stopped pulsating."

The passengers situated themselves, and Lily walked down the aisle and back, admiring a multitude of bags tied with Christmas-colored ribbons. "We're all here except the Suttons. I'm certain they'll be along promptly. They're never late, and we're a few minutes early." When she reached her seat, she asked, "Did you find a satisfactory hotel, Gordy?"

Gordy was in no hurry to answer. "Yes, ma'am."

Maude looked out the van window. "Here they come." She strained to see through the late-afternoon gray. "Oh, my, they're dragging something with them. Can't tell what it is, but it's large. Is there an extra seat back there?"

Kent responded quickly. "There's an extra seat beside me and a couple behind me."

Lily stood up. "Good, it may take two. If this is any indication, perhaps we'll have a most interesting show-and-tell this evening."

Ted and Laura Sutton approached the van as Gordy opened the door. Ted sent Laura in first as he wrestled to get a tin structure through the narrow doorway. He pushed and she pulled and together they finally made it through the entrance and up the steps. Next came the sharp left turn into the aisle.

Kent rose and invited Laura to take her seat. He walked to the front and, with his good arm, helped Ted hoist the contraption above their heads and down the aisle to the empty seats in the back.

As they passed the colonel and Beatrice, she gasped. "Heavenly days, would you look at that thing! Who in their right minds would buy a six-foot whirligig? Haven't seen one of those in quite awhile, and I don't think I ever saw one that big. They don't have children, so who'll be playing with that?"

Ted smiled. "I'll explain later, but I knew we had room, and I didn't want to ship this prize home."

Gordy zipped through the city streets, but drove more slowly when he reached Bishops Lodge Road as it began to snake through the foothills. The sky was almost dark, but the snow coming down was still just flurries. The van crawled through the mountains for over half an hour before turning down the lane for Grey Sage.

Maude had taken the window seat, having learned from their ride into town that Lily would be up and down like a jack-in-the-box. But she'd been wrong; Lily was quiet and still the bulk of the drive. Maude leaned over and whispered to her, "You really should reconsider having Gordy stay out here. We have vacant rooms, and he wouldn't be chancing the drive to town and then back out in the morning."

"Good grief, Maude! You're always trying to take care of someone. Fine. He has a room, but I'll ask him anyway." Lily walked the few steps to the driver's seat, all the while holding tightly to the metal pole to keep her balance in the growing darkness. She and Gordy had a brief conversation, and she returned to her seat. "He wants to stay in town. Think about it, Maude. He's forty-plus. Who knows? Maybe fifty. He's a single man who lives with his mother. Give him a break, and let him have a couple of nights on the town without his mother or a group like us. After all, it's Christmas."

"Fine. Let him have his fling in Santa Fe. He can't say we didn't offer."

Maude looked back out the window, straining to see through the darkening sky as they approached the inn.

Lovely, that last bit of daylight against the snow on the peaks. Gives an eerie outline to the range. The wind's settled, but that's no accurate indication the weather's getting better or worse. Alo will know.

Chapter Four

Silas and Alo met them at the front entrance—two solid wooden doors that had seen a rabble of folks going and coming over the years. The wind gusts practically blew the group in, packages and all. With Alo's help, the guests made it inside the doors with their loot and started to their suites to freshen up for dinner. Before they were out of the gathering room to the hallway, Lily blew the whistle.

"Sorry to have to do that, but it works every time." Lily tucked the chain and whistle under her poncho. "Listen up, people. Dinner is at six thirty, and be prepared to tell us about your afternoon's acquisitions and why you made the choice. I can hardly wait after seeing all these packages. It will be like my university art students explaining their latest creation." Lily picked up her bag and headed to her suite.

Fortunately, Maude was already heading away and had escaped the main blast of the whistle blowing. She slowed when she passed the dining room, noting something unexpected. She stood for a moment, looking at the table, and smiled with satisfaction.

When she entered the kitchen, she found Lita in a bright-red apron in front of the oven. "Thank you, Lita, for the fine surprise. The dining table's quite festive, and I'm so glad Alo built a fire. I know our guests will enjoy it, and so will I. I'm chilled to the bone and back. You seem to know what we all need exactly when we need it."

Lita breathed a sigh of relief. She had hoped Maude wouldn't mind the decorations, but she hadn't been sure. For that reason she'd kept it simple and had chosen not to surprise Maude by using the silver, crystal, and white that had dressed the table in Christmases past. Instead she'd used a rustic look with forest-green placemats, red and green plaid napkins, cedar branches speckled with pine cones, and a few red candles dotted around.

"You're welcome. I didn't want the prima donna ballerina to be disappointed in the way we do Christmas around here. It didn't take much effort. Besides, I had to put something on the table. Might as well look a little like Christmas."

As Lita took the last of the bread loaves from the oven, Maude tossed her coat in the mudroom and returned to the kitchen, smoothing the gray tendrils that had been tucked under her wool hat all afternoon. She leaned over to smell the warm bread still in the loaf pans. "We're here. We're on time. And the aroma of this fresh-baked bread is considerably better than burning red hair." She pinched off a tiny crumb and then joined Lita as she was putting the salad onto the plates. Together they made final preparations for the meal.

At six thirty, the Unlikely Christmas Party gathered in the dining room, lining the wall underneath the window with their parcels and bags at Lita's direction. She invited them to find their seats at the table, where she had made place cards and glued them to small pine cones. She knew Maude, and she knew how Maude would want the guests seated. And she had seen the eye-darting between Kent and Emily and wanted them to be seated to their best advantage.

When they were all comfortably around the table and Silas had served the wine, Lita and Maude started the parade of plates. The first was of fresh field greens, slivered almonds, crumbled blue cheese, dried cranberries, and slices of fresh pears with a splash of vinaigrette. The bread basket was passed around the table, and herb-seasoned butter followed.

While the rest of the dinner guests took their first bites, Greg took Iris's hand. They both bowed their heads as he whispered a prayer. Kent, although seated across the table and next to Emily, immediately put down his fork and joined his parents in silence.

Conversation stopped but quickly started again when Greg whispered "Amen" and raised his head. The clinking of silver forks against the handmade pottery plates was music to Lita's ears. Their visitors were eating.

Lita never rushed their dinner guests, especially when the room was warm with firelight and pleasant conversation. So she waited until the plates were good and empty before she served the second course of lean pork loin slathered in a mustard sauce with rice and her *calabacitas.*

Emily, obviously realizing Kent would have a difficult time slicing the pork with one arm in a sling, offered to help. Kent graciously accepted and smiled gently at her—not embarrassed at all, just more aware of her.

He handed his fork and knife to her. "Guess you don't want to take the chance of wearing that mustard sauce on your fine red sweater. And frankly, I don't want it on mine either. So thank you, lovely lady. You're very kind."

"You're very welcome, and you're right: I never looked good in mustard." She looked up at him and grinned. "You'll not think I'm so kind when I expect you to spoon-feed me dessert." She finished her job and handed him his knife and fork.

Kent liked imagining that and decided to eat rather than continue the conversation. After he had taken one bite of the calabacitas, though, he wiped his mouth and called out to Lita. Lita all but ran from the kitchen into the dining room.

"Miss Lita," he declared, "I have no idea what this is that just passed my lips except it's about the best thing I ever tasted. Would you be kind enough to tell me what it is?"

Lita grinned with relief. "That, sir, is my calabacitas."

Kent grinned. "Calaba-what?"

"Calabacitas. That's the Spanish word for 'squash,'" and around here, it's also basically any squash dish with whatever else the cook wants to add to it. Every cook in New Mexico has her own calabacita recipe. Tonight, you're having my Christmas version with squash, zucchini, sweet corn, red onion, garlic, and cheese." She paused. "And my secret ingredient."

Kent swallowed another bite. "Do you share the recipe? I'd really like to be able to prepare this when I get back home to Chicago."

"Oh, I'd be most happy to share it."

"Even the secret ingredient?" Kent grinned at her and raised his eyebrows.

Lita took one step back toward the kitchen. "We'll have to see about that. I've never given that to anyone except my daughters."

Dinner continued, and when the last bite of pumpkin praline pie was eaten, Maude watched as Lily rose from her chair and left the room. She returned with Lita. "We just would like an opportunity to tell you how very much we enjoyed this meal and this setting, Lita. You cannot find this kind of food and hospitality in Chicago." Everyone around the table applauded. "Since we're so comfortable around the table with the fire burning over there, why don't we just stay here for our show-and-tell? But before we get started with that, Laura, Reba, Emily, and Iris, will you help me clear the table? Let's be gracious and give Lita a hand. Then perhaps we could have another cup of coffee while we visit."

The ladies cleared the table quickly and helped Lita stack the dishes. Within minutes they were back in their seats, and Lita and Maude served the after-dinner cup of *dulce de leche* coffee, topped with whipped cream and sprinkled lightly with cinnamon. Lily relaxed back in her chair, holding the cup under her nose. "Lita, would you just adopt me and take care of me and make me coffee like this every evening?"

Everyone except the Suttons laughed and held up their hands as though they wanted to be the next ones adopted.

Maude watched. *Lily's playing Lita like a fine violin, and Lita's resonating. No, she's softening. Maybe Lily's hair is out of danger.*

Lily turned to Silas. "Silas, this is your home and you're the consummate host, so maybe you'd like to moderate our show-and-tell this evening."

Silas, always the gentleman even when he didn't want to be, agreed to Lily's request. "Please forgive me if I cannot recall your name." He patted his thick, white, wavy hair. "The same thing that leeched the color out of this hair has leeched my brain cells, especially the ones having to do with names." He paused and looked around the table. "Why don't we begin with my lovely wife? I do remember her name, and I do know that it's not possible for her to visit Canyon Road during Christmas without a purchase." He wrinkled his brow. "Although, I'm not certain I saw her come home with anything."

I wish I had purchased the red glass bowl that caught my eye in that second gallery. It would have been a return to our tradition. But maybe we don't need to turn back.

Maude sat up straight in her chair. "Oh, you know me well, dearest, and I did make a purchase. Unfortunately, they didn't come home with me."

Silas chuckled. "See, I told you, and I think 'they' means more than one."

"Actually, they were sold as a pair—a pair of very old, heavy wooden shutters from one of the old adobe homes torn down to make room for a new restaurant downtown. And I plan to hang one on each side of those giant double doors out front." Maude looked to her right where Lily was seated. "Now the reason I made this purchase is that I was drawn to them and couldn't bear to leave them sitting out in the cold courtyard. The panels are worn with age and the patina on the wood is shiny and dark, and I know they will accent the front door."

Maude paused. "And from now on, they will be a remembrance that this Unlikely Christmas Party came through our doors during the Christmas of 2005."

Reba dabbed her eyes with her monogrammed linen handkerchief. "That's quite lovely, Maude. We must return to see them."

Silas continued. "And ma'am, since you spoke up, why don't you tell us what your newest treasure is?"

Reba carefully moved the small, deep-purple bag from her lap to the table. She reached inside for the box it contained and opened it. "This caught my eye, and like you, Maude, I couldn't leave Canyon Road without it. This delicate ring, a turquoise dragonfly set in sterling silver, was made by a local Hopi Indian. The shopkeeper told me the dragonfly is a Hopi symbol of resurrection, of life again after hardship."

Reba dabbed her eyes again, and her chin quivered slightly. "As a therapist, I know what to do after losing my husband. However, making myself do it has been quite another issue. But I'm beginning to, and I'm beginning to realize that I truly have no other option except to move forward. My choice is to learn to do life differently." Reba paused and wiped her eyes again. "I will remember this Christmas season, the first without my Charles, and how I spent it with new and old friends and my daughter Emily in such a mystical and beautiful place." Reba put the ring on her finger, held it out in front of herself to admire it, and smiled.

Silas allowed the silence to linger before he spoke. "And Emily, did you purchase something as meaningful and beautiful as your mother did?"

Emily's cheeks reddened. "Unfortunately, my sensitive, deep-thinking mother gave birth to a very practical daughter." She stood up and bent over to pull a rather large box from underneath her chair, opening the lid to remove the contents. She held up a mailbox painted teal blue and drenched in hand-painted sunflowers. "I bought this because it made me smile when I first saw it and because I hope it will make my mailman and passersby smile too. Don't you just love it?"

She held it up, but as she turned it for everyone to see, she almost dropped it. Kent reacted instantly and was out of his chair to assist her before the mailbox could hit the table and crash the coffee cups. When they were both balanced, his arm at her back, she looked up at him. "Thank you, Kent. I'm so sorry. I fear that I'm almost as clumsy as I am practical."

Kent took his seat, and Emily looked around the table. "I'll especially remember this afternoon on Canyon Road when I receive correspondence from you, my new friends." She returned the mailbox to its box and sat down with it in her lap, clutching it. Then, almost shyly, she said, "And besides, I needed a new mailbox."

The guests laughed. Silas continued. "Let's see. I do remember you, Greg, and your lovely wife, Iris. Did you buy jewelry for your bride?"

Greg looked at Iris. "Hardly." He carefully pulled a foot-tall tin sculpture of a prickly pear cactus from his bag, not so much because it was fragile, but because the piece could inflict pain if handled without caution. The tin was painted cactus green and dotted with yellow curled-tin cactus blossoms.

"I bought this for my desk. I think it will remind me that we are resilient. Ponder it: a cactus can practically grow out of rock and can survive with the least bit of water, and yet, even with its prickly spines, it is still a thing of beauty. I also learned today that the prickly pear cactus provides nourishment. Its pads and flower blossoms can be eaten. But—" He lowered his head and looked over his reading glasses with a grin. "—I'd suggest preparing them with great care first. I'm told the spines are very sharp. And these fine, almost hair-like spines they call glochids are difficult to see but cause so much pain. They're hard to remove. Sort of like us, I suppose. I know I get prickly, and I can inflict pain without meaning to. And often it's hardest to see spines that inflict the most pain on others."

He caught himself. "There I go, preaching again. Oh, but then comes the sweet part. Jelly can be made from the prickly pears themselves. Such unexpected sweetness. I think this sculpture will be the source of a few sermons for me." He paused and cleared his throat. "As I have gotten to know my fellow travelers on this trip, I realize that we all chose this journey because we've been pricked. We have experienced some pain and just needed a different kind of Christmas this year. This little tin beauty will remind me that even during our struggles, we can survive, and perhaps we can help nourish someone else's soul in the process."

Lily piped up. "I really like that, Greg. That's what art should do: make us think and feel beyond what we're seeing."

Greg nodded and turned to his wife. "Iris is practical like you, Emily. She bought a small wreath of red peppers to hang in our kitchen back home, but then ... Show them, Iris."

Iris slid something flat and apparently fragile from her bag and held it up—a piece of stained glass about a foot square. "Yes, I must admit vanity got the best of me today. When I saw this iris hanging in the window with its many shades of purple, it just had my name on it."

The guests laughed, and Maude responded, "Well, I guess it literally did. How lovely, just like you, Iris."

Kent stood up and adjusted his sling, but had no package. "I know exactly where Mom will put that—in her sunny kitchen window. I suppose I'm the last of the Martins, so I'll take my turn." He turned to Reba. "Mrs. Parker, I seem to have fallen into the same trap as you when it comes to Hopi Indian jewelry. So I bought this belt buckle."

He reached down and adjusted the belt buckle to reflect the light. "It might have even been the same shopkeeper who told me this design is called 'Man in the Maze.' I'm not sure if you can see it, but it's there—a circular maze of seven paths representing the journey of life and symbolizing the journey is not always easy. Seems that's nothing new to any of us, as my dad said. Anyway, it reminds me of my journey, which has taken me to some hard places—places I didn't expect, like the war in Iraq and now my recovery." He nodded at his dad. "I'm learning that the journey is not always about the destination, but sometimes it's about the surprises along the way, just like being with all of you." He looked down at Emily beside him, smiled, and took his seat.

Maude recognized that smile and the pat on his arm that Emily gave him. "Kent, you are so wise, young man. You must be such a joy to your parents."

Kent's face relaxed. "I hope to be, ma'am."

Silas turned to the colonel. "Well, Henry, what about you and Beatrice?"

"Now, Dr. Thornhill, what does an old fellow like me need with anything? My kids'll just have to dispose of it before long." Henry slid a small object from a burlap bag tied with red-checkered ribbon. "But I did like this little wooden angel. Quite a lot actually—especially her face. Reminded me of my sweet daughter when she was small. And it'll be a reminder that God has sent his angels to protect me on three continents. And I must tell you I've kept them quite busy. I can just imagine they'd like a rest after ninety-two years of hovering around me." Before anyone could respond, he nudged Beatrice. "Show them what you bought, Bea. They're going to love it."

Beatrice removed a glass paperweight from a velvet bag. "Look, it's exquisite, and I met the artist, who told me all about how she made this. These tiny glass ballerinas are each hand-blown separately, and then she melts them into the glass she's blowing. She said the figures expand as she blows the glass, sort of like blowing up a balloon with writing on it. A crystal ball filled with ballerinas—most appropriate, don't you think? Would you like to see it up close?" She passed the paperweight to Iris, and it went around the table.

Silas waited until it reached him. "You're so right, Beatrice, it is most appropriate." He faced the Suttons, and Maude was surprised to find that he remembered their names. "I believe that leaves you, Ted. What did you and Laura purchase today?"

Ted went to the window and stood next to his acquisition. "Well, we've collected art from all over the world, but we have nothing like this piece of kinetic art, and we think it would be quite catching in our moss garden next to the creek. It's made of tin and is a wind sculpture, always moving and reflecting the light, sort of like a whirl-igig—like you said, Beatrice." He gave the structure a twirl, and it reflected the firelight, casting colorful rays around the room. "Should be tall enough we can see it from the back deck and our bedroom window. And we're driving all the way, so we didn't have to ship it. Would you like to say anything about it, Laura?"

Laura shook her head in silence.

Ted and Laura aren't really a part of the group, Maude noted. They're just travelers along for the ride. He made no reference to what he would remember about the afternoon or being with this Christmas Party. Maybe they have an ache around Christmastime, like I do. At least I have story-book Christmases to remember.

Maude spoke up. "You'll enjoy that, Ted."

Silas looked at Lily. "Okay, Lil, what unusual, indescribable work of art did you find this trip?"

Lily rose. "Okay, people, close your eyes and don't open them until I tell you." She reached under the table, rummaged as they listened, and thirty seconds later, told them to look. Everyone expected some exquisite work of art, but what they saw was Lily, arms akimbo, dressed in a black, shaggy, furry vest that reached her knees. After the *oohs* and *aahs* had faded, Lily announced, "This is Mongolian lamb fur—dyed black, of course. It's extravagant, but it's warm. And every time I wear it, I'll remember how cold I was walking down Canyon Road on Tuesday afternoon, December 20, 2005." She assumed a model's gait and sleekly strutted around the table.

Silas chuckled. "Why, Lily, you look like the long-haired, dwarf Nigerian goat we had once. Of course, she didn't have red hair."

Everyone laughed. Even Laura Sutton managed a grin.

Lily pulled the vest up around her neck with both her hands. "Laugh if you like, but you'll be seeing this for the rest of the trip, and don't bother asking to borrow it."

Maude rose at the end of the table. "Where in all the world could we have purchased such a diversity of creative gifts except on

Canyon Road? It seems we've all bought ourselves a unique treasure for Christmas."

"Yes, we did," Beatrice retorted. "And I bought several other gifts, and I can't even put them under a Christmas tree because there's not one to be found in this place."

Henry patted her hand and whispered something to her.

Beatrice looked up. "Carl says it's fine because we'll have Christmas trees in Colorado."

Lily rolled her eyes and made a face at Maude. Then she turned to Laura. "Laura, what would you think about playing the piano for us this evening? Maybe some Debussy or some Christmas carols? Or a song about a whirligig? We don't care."

Laura, never changing expressions, glanced at her husband and then to Lily. "I think not, Lily. I'm rather exhausted, and if you'd all excuse me, I'd really prefer to retire to my room."

Lily attempted to recover from the awkwardness. "Of course. Maybe we should follow you. After all, we have a long and exciting day planned for tomorrow."

Everyone agreed.

Lily stood. "Breakfast at eight o'clock, people, and don't make me use the whistle. Good night and pleasant dreaming."

Maude and Silas headed to the kitchen with the last of the coffee cups. Lita and Alo had gone home and left the last of the dishes for them. It only took a few minutes to have the kitchen just like Lita liked it when she arrived to prepare breakfast. Silas checked the fireplace in the kitchen while Maude put away the last of the cups and saucers.

"I'm done. Let's go to bed." Maude knew Silas would have the fire ready to start in their bedroom.

When they passed through the gathering room to turn out the lights, they saw that Kent and Emily had become quite comfortable in the wing chairs flanking the fireplace. The embers were only slightly glowing, but enough to light Emily's peachy cheeks.

Maude said good night and walked arm in arm with Silas down

the hallway to their bedroom. "Isn't young love something, Silas?" she whispered.

"I'd say so."

"I mean, look at those two. They have most of their lives ahead of them, and they look at each other like there's no one else in the room."

"Yes, Maude, but they just met a few days ago."

"So what does that mean? I met you when I was ten, but I knew. And here we are sixty years later. And besides, don't you think Grey Sage is a perfect place for a young couple to fall in love? Especially at Christmas?"

"I'd say so, Maude."

Chapter Five

Wednesday, December 21

*S*unrays usually streamed through the kitchen windows by this time during the winter, but not so this morning. Maude had designed the house for the light. The kitchen faced east for sunrises and that slanting light of early morning, and her studio faced northeast, washing the room with the indirect light that she preferred for painting. But there was not much light of any kind from any direction this morning. Skies were still thick gray, and the pine limbs were lightly dusted with fresh snow. The wind was curiously still. Grey Sage was quiet at seven o'clock, except in the kitchen.

Silas filled the coffee urn with Guatemalan coffee and distilled water. Alo was loading up the fireplaces in the dining room and gathering room. By their nature, adobe structures were cool in the summer and warm in the winter, but nothing warmed them as quickly as a crackling fire.

Lita took the last sausage patty out of the iron skillet and began to gather the ingredients for blue-corn piñon pancakes while Maude measured steel-cut oats to be cooked in apple juice for those who liked a lighter fare. The zucchini bread with pumpkin seeds Lita had made yesterday was ready for her to slice and butter for toast. "Are you planning to surprise the preacher with your homemade prickly-pear syrup for his pancakes this morning?"

Lita snorted. "Not unless we raise the nightly fee at least five dollars per guest. Prickly-pear syrup doesn't go easily into a jar. You do remember Silas removing those hairy spines from the palms of my hands last summer, don't you?"

"I do, but surely after all Greg said about his cactus last night, you'd be generous enough to allow him at least one spoonful to taste."

"We only have a couple of good jars left unless you count the batch of jelly I made that never set up." Lita poured buttermilk into a bowl. "But it is Christmas, and if I must, I'll put a small—no, I mean a very small—pitcher of syrup next to his plate. We'll see how generous he is and if he practices what he preaches. And then for the others, I'll have the maple syrup from the pantry."

I'll head that way, Maude predicted, *but Lita won't let me near the pantry, and she'll come back with maple syrup in one hand and prickly-pear syrup in the other.* She started toward the pantry door.

"Two gallons in tins on the bottom shelf on the left in the corner." Lita knew every inch of that pantry, which could have been mistaken for a small, neighborhood grocery. Maude, on the other hand, had a way of never putting things back in their right places. Lita wiped her hands. "Not to bother, Maude. I'll get it."

Maude smiled.

Alo entered through the mudroom with an armload of wood and passed the butler's pantry on his way to the gathering room. "Hey, Silas, that coffee ready yet? I'm in need of something warm."

"I'm working on it, friend. But I have a better idea. Maybe we should make a small pot just for us in the kitchen. It'll be faster. And besides, we prefer it a bit stronger."

"Sounds good. I'll join you when I get the fire started."

By the time Alo had both fireplaces glowing, Silas was pouring stout coffee into their mugs, and the weather report was blaring on the small television in the kitchen. He handed Alo his coffee. "Looks like more snowfall headed our way."

Alo rubbed his hand over his leathery chin. "Don't need the meteorologist to tell me we have snow coming. There was a halo around the moon last night. We've had snow the last three week-ends. Remember when I told you the Gambel oaks were putting on more acorns than usual and the rock squirrels were gathering them like there would be no spring? And the cornhusks were thicker than normal? All signs of a harsh winter. Good that I made preparations with so much firewood."

"I'm not so concerned about the winter as I am the next few days," Silas replied. "Lots of folks in this inn have travel plans, and your daughters and their families are trying to get home too. Weather's not looking so good."

"When are the guests leaving?"

Maude joined the conversation. "They're doing their last tours of Santa Fe today, and they're headed to Taos early in the morning, and then on to Colorado Springs on Friday."

Alo's face may be as expressionless as the wooden Indian at the general store down in the village, but he can't hide he's worried, she decided. *If he's worried, then we'd better get ready.*

"Are you saying it's going to get worse?" she said aloud.

"Maybe. But it doesn't matter what I say, the halo around the moon says snow." Alo set his mug on the counter and reached into his pocket for his gloves.

Silas glanced at him. "Where are you off to now?"

"Best to get more wood stacked closer to the house and under shelter before the wind sets in. It may be still now, but storm's coming. I don't want to have to dig through drifts for firewood."

Lita returned from the pantry with a gallon tin of maple syrup and a small jar. She set them on the counter and nudged Maude with her elbow. "What are you planning today? Going back with the group to Santa Fe?"

"If I know Lily, she'll ask me to go, and if I know myself, I'll feel guilty if I don't. So the answer to your question is probably, but only if you can handle dinner preparation without me."

"I can handle dinner, but I was thinking of heading into town right behind you. I know my husband, and he knows bad weather's coming, and I want a full larder just in case."

"Well, with any luck you won't need the extra food. But I trust your judgment like you trust his." Maude buttered the last slice of zucchini bread.

When she heard voices in the gathering room, Maude joined them after putting two pitchers of warm maple syrup on the dining table. "Good morning, Henry and Beatrice. I do hope you rested well."

Beatrice replied, "Who couldn't sleep floating on such a mattress and then covered in warm goose down?"

"I'm hoping that means yes?"

Beatrice smiled and nodded.

"What about you, Colonel?"

"I'm a man with a clean conscience, Maude. I sleep well every night."

"If you're interested in a glass of juice or a cup of coffee before breakfast, follow me to the butler's pantry."

Beatrice took Henry's arm. "Oh, they have a butler, Henry. I stayed with a family who had a butler in London once. They lived in a castle. It was so cold and damp there."

Within a few moments, all the guests were gathered and holding mugs of coffee while moving toward the dining table at Maude's invitation.

Interesting, she noted. *They're taking the same seats as dinner last evening, just like the artists do at retreats. People are so predictable in such unpredictable ways.*

When they were all comfortable and chattering, Lita entered the dining room holding a small brass bell. She rang it gently, and their voices quieted. "Good morning. I do hope you had a good rest and that you're hungry." She pulled slips of paper from her apron pocket and a fistful of small pencils. "We have a warm and hearty breakfast for you on this blustery morning—blue-corn piñon pancakes with eggs and sausage. And if you prefer, we have Irish oatmeal with cinnamon and raisins and toast made from zucchini bread with pumpkin seeds. Or we have a variety of cold cereal with fruit." She began passing out the slips of paper with pencils. "Please put your name at the top and check the boxes for your preference, and you'll be eating your breakfast in a few minutes. There is a basket of fresh-baked breads with honey butter on the table. That should keep you happy while you wait."

Maude watched in satisfaction as another meal around the dining table at Grey Sage was enjoyed by the Unlikely Christmas Party. Kent asked for more pancakes. Greg made over the prickly-pear syrup and wanted to know where he could buy some. Their plates were all but licked clean when everyone had finished.

Ted Sutton cleared his throat. "Without a television in our rooms, we haven't been able to hear the news and the weather report." He turned to Silas. "Can you update us?" he asked.

Silas wiped the last crumble of zucchini bread from his mouth. "Well, it's cold. Twenty-five degrees earlier, but it's predicted to get up to thirty-five later in the day."

"What about the snow?" Ted asked again.

"There's more snow predicted for later in the day. I think around mid-afternoon and into the evening. But you should be fine through your day in town."

Lily pulled her clipboard from the bag next to her chair. "Let's see. I planned for us to visit the Railyard District this morning and the Georgia O'Keefe Museum after lunch with our last stops at the St. Francis Cathedral to see the basilica and the magnificent sculptures of the Stations of the Cross in the Prayer Garden. And of course, the Loretto Chapel is to be our last stop. But the weather ... Well, maybe the snow will hold off until we've finished our tours."

Ted started the conversation. "Lily, your plans might be a bit much for today. We'll be outside of the time touring the Railyard District and the Basilica's Garden. And frankly, I don't think the snow knows or cares we're even here."

Almost before he finished, they'd all chimed in, giving Lily suggestions in line with their own personal preferences and talking on top of each other to make their voices heard. Lily, who lived life fully every day and rarely let circumstances like weather dictate her decisions, was quite perplexed at their responses.

"Look, people," she said in exasperation. "I've planned a

remarkable day of opportunities for you, but if you prefer to sit out here at Grey Sage and count snowflakes, we can do that."

Maude watched with intense curiosity.

No one responded. Finally, the colonel, accustomed to practicing diplomacy and planning logistics, spoke up in his most charming southern accent. "Now, Lily, no one is complaining about your beautiful day of opportunities. It's just that it's not a beautiful day, my dear, or did you not look out your window this morning? Perhaps we could modify your plans slightly and spend more time indoors this morning. The temperatures are below freezing and not all of us have that Mongolian rug you bought yesterday." Maude heard several snickers. "Would it be agreeable with you if maybe we chose two indoor activities? Say the Georgia O'Keefe Museum and the Loretto Chapel, and then we could be back here before the snow sets in. I think that fire in the gathering room will be calling my name by then. How does that sound to you?"

The guests mumbled around and finally decided on the Railyard District because much of it was indoors and offered a variety of interests. And then they wanted to see the chapel.

"Well, it's not everything I planned, but it is more than staring out the window counting snowflakes or pine cones."

The colonel stood. "So we're all in agreement then? The Railyard District it is, and then the chapel to see the work of Saint Joseph himself."

Everyone clapped and stood up from the table. Lily stuffed her clipboard back in her bag and stood up too.

Lita approached. "Here, Lily, try this little brass bell. I think it works very well." She handed her the bell and prissed away like she'd just won a door prize.

Lily rang the bell. "Listen up, people. Gordy will be here at nine fifteen to take us to Santa Fe. Please meet me in the gathering room." She looked at the big-faced watch on her arm. "You have about twenty minutes to do whatever it is you need to do before our departure. Need I tell you to dress warmly?"

As the guests left for their rooms, Maude approached Lily. *Lily will take all this discussion as harsh criticism. She doesn't take confrontation well. And the only kind of change she likes is when she decides to make it.*

"Wise decision, Lil," she told her friend. "I think what I heard is that everyone was so satisfied with the day you planned yesterday and their opportunities to see the art on Canyon Road that nothing could disappoint them about changing your plans today. They're very aware that as good as you are, you don't control the weather."

Lily didn't hide her "I've been rejected" look very well.

"Certainly. Would you go with us again today, Maude? I don't think these people like me anymore. At least you like me."

Maude put her arm around Lily. "Lily, these people like you. They love you. You're spending your Christmas helping them make some fantastic memories. Why wouldn't they love you?"

Ah-ha. Her facial muscles are tightening, and her saggy face is disappearing. She never lets her self-pity last too long.

"You're right, Maude. They should like me, and they do. But I'd still like you to go with us. Will you?"

"Certainly I'll go. If nothing else, just to spend some time with you, my friend. I'm assuming you'll eat dinner here tonight?" Lily nodded, and Maude headed off to the kitchen to speak with Lita.

The colonel was the first guest back in the gathering room, and he joined Silas in the wing chairs at the fireplace. "Well, Silas, you and Maude have made yourself quite a sanctuary here. Surely does have a peaceful presence about it."

Silas rubbed the palm of his hand on the worn arm of the leather chair. "Thank you, Henry. This is all Maude's doings. She seems to have the gift of creating beauty out of most anything."

The colonel looked around the room. "Yes, Maude's got that artist's eye—and a gift for not only making things beautiful, but comfortable."

"Well, thank you, Colonel. She was one determined woman when we bought this place. Insistent on designing and building a structure that, as she said, 'would rise from this earth and blend with the sky.'"

He paused a moment, remembering back to a time when all was new. "Actually, Alo built this house. About the time Maude finished the design and was ready to begin construction on Grey Sage, I met Alo and Lita when I delivered their second daughter. I found out that Alo was Hopi and that he was an expert in building adobe structures. But more important, he was looking for a job."

"It would appear Alo is every bit the artist Maude is, in his own way."

"Oh, yes. When I brought Alo to meet Maude, I remember exactly what Maude said. 'Grey Sage was meant to be. And you, Alo, will create walls and windows out of these visions in my head and scribbled on these plans.'

"That was the beginning of our lifelong friendship. Alo was on site, working every day to build the walls and rooms from Maude's sketches. He brought Lita and their two young daughters to the work site. Lita took care of our son and their girls and did the cooking while Alo constructed the place." He gestured. "Those walls are made of sand, clay, and straw."

The colonel rubbed his chin. "You don't say. Back where I'm from, building is a lot different."

"Oh, I know. And Grey Sage is not the typical design of a Santa Fe pueblo home. Every time Alo thought he was finished, Maude would show him new design ideas. The footprint of the house just kept growing with Maude-designed rooms connected by *portales*. She wanted a house built for the land, and she said the land called for a larger kitchen with a keeping room and huge fireplace, more bedrooms, open living spaces, four more smaller fireplaces—or *kivas* as they're known in these parts—and large windows.

"But the day finally came when the house was finished. And then we surprised Alo with one last project: the building of a *casita* in the pine break down by the stream that would be their house. Alo and Lita and those little girls of theirs became like family."

Silas fell silent, remembering. Henry picked up the conversation. "Being a soldier didn't allow for putting down too many roots, but I understand the 'friends becoming like family' part."

"Oh, they were family and business partners too. Maude and Alo developed quite a reputation around these parts for designing and restoring houses. In between, Maude started teaching art lessons to the children around here. She was living her dream back in those days—painting, designing, and making life magical for our son."

He noticed the look in Henry's eye. "What about you?"

"I had a wife like that. Her name was Joy. Always told her that her mother gave her the perfect name. She was a wee thing, like Bea. In fact, I called her Little Bit when I didn't call her Joy. She was quite a woman, no matter her size. Waited on me while I fought World War Two, and when I got home, we had two babies—a boy and a girl. It pained me to leave her and those babies when I headed off to Korea. But she was strong, taking care of those kids by herself and saying she never, ever doubted I'd come home."

"Not many women like that in the world."

"No, not like my sweet Joy. When I wasn't in combat, that little woman followed me to military stations all over this world, and she made a home out of every dump where we had to live. And, oh, how she made over holidays! American holidays and the holidays of every country where we were stationed. Sarah and George went to school on base, but it was Joy who really educated them. She was always reading to them and taking them places to see the local culture. And back then, transportation and communication weren't so easy. But the kids grew up and made some fine adults and gave me some grandkids."

Silas was almost afraid to ask. "Where are your kids now?"

"Well, Sarah's in heaven with her mother. She got breast cancer and died at thirty-seven. Grieved her mother so much. Then Joy died two years later with a heart attack. I think losing Sarah just broke her heart in too many pieces."

"I understand that broken heart. Maude's strong, but she's never been the same since ... since our son, Elan, died." He noted the understanding that broke across Henry's face. "Yes, seems like we have something in common, Henry." He cleared his throat. "But I'm glad you have some grandchildren. We didn't have that blessing."

"They *are* a blessing. My son, George, has two, and Sarah left two little girls behind when she died.

"Sorry you had to go through all that, Henry. I can imagine with your distinguished military career, death is no stranger to you."

Henry stared at the fire. "No, it's no stranger, but always an unwelcome one. Don't think you ever get over missing somebody you love."

"What about your son?"

"Oh, my son. George is my pride and joy. Still think of him as a freckle-faced little boy, but he's about to retire. He's been running a US mining operation in Indonesia for the last twenty years. His kids are grown now with children of their own, and they wanted to spend this last Christmas all together in Tembagapura since George and Vera will be coming home for good in March."

Silas was curious. "You didn't want to make the trip?"

"Oh, I would have enjoyed it. Been there several times. But I made this promise to my buddy Carl that I'd look after Bea. He'd done some favors for Joy and me through the years, so it was time I obliged."

"I see."

"And it's a long trip. Not as bad as those flying tin cans that used to transport me, but it's still a long trip for these aching bones of mine." He looked up from the fire into Silas's face. "What about you? Any other children you're going to see this Christmas?"

Silas hesitated. "Elan was our only child. He would have been forty, just in the prime of his life, but he died when he was almost seventeen."

"So sorry. Nothing quite like losing a child. What was his name? Elan?"

"We named him Elan Hamilton Thornhill. He was born about a year after we moved into Grey Sage. That was back when it was just the small cottage. I wanted to carry on the family tradition with the middle name *Hamilton*, but I told Maude to name him. She decided on Elan. It's an American Indian name. Means 'friend of all.'"

"Interesting. He must have been a great young fellow with you two as parents and growing up here at Grey Sage."

"He was, and his mother named him appropriately, just like Joy's mother named her. Elan never met a stranger, and he had this spirit about him, always wanting to take care of people and things. It was that spirit that took his life, though. He ... tried to rescue a rock climber. Saved the climber, but Elan ..." Silas stumbled. He still had trouble saying it after all these years. "Elan fell to his death."

Henry sat silent a moment, then sighed. "Not much consolation for trying to help someone, was it?"

"No, not so much. We miss him. And of course things changed after we lost him. Different focus, different choices. Maude hasn't been able to bring herself to be here for Christmas since he died. Maude's a lot like Joy. She made over the holidays, and Christmas was always her favorite. She lived to give our boy the best experience possible each year. But after ..."

"I can understand that. There's always that undeniable empty seat at the holiday table. Oh, somebody else may be sitting in it, but it's still empty." Henry paused and stared at the fire again. "Something plain wrong about burying a child. But then, as trite as the saying is, life goes on. Look at me—ninety-two years old and have spent many a Christmas in some mighty interesting places. This is just another one with this Unlikely Christmas Party on Wheels, as Lily calls us."

Maude stood outside the doorway, not really eavesdropping, but not wanting to interrupt because she had no words.

I haven't heard Silas talk about Elan and Christmas in ages.

She pondered that thought. *Is it because of me? Because he doesn't want to hurt me?* She took a breath. *And does it? Does it hurt to hear him speak of Elan?*

She leaned against the wall, hands spread to either side of her, waiting for the pain that always attended thoughts of Elan, especially around the holidays. But although she felt the ache that never faded—that had never faded in all these years—she was surprised to find it didn't overwhelm her as it had in the past. She closed her eyes and breathed, thinking of the colonel's words. *He's right—the thought of the empty seat at the Christmas table is why I can't bring myself to celebrate Christmas.* To hear that explanation voiced was ... freeing, in a way.

Seems we're not the only ones feeling our loss during the holidays. But Henry doesn't let it keep him from new experiences.

Maude wasn't sure how that made her feel.

Chapter Six

The road conditions made Gordy a few minutes late. Greg watched as Lily, in her new Mongolian lamb vest underneath her overcoat, fidgeted and paced back and forth in front of the windows by the piano. She searched for van lights and wondered aloud if it might have been better after all for Gordy to stay overnight at Grey Sage.

The guests welcomed Silas's second urn of coffee while they waited. The colonel sat in his now-favorite wing chair by the fireplace. Ted and Laura meandered around the gathering room, entrance hall, and Silas's study, admiring the paintings and sculptures. Emily and Kent sat on the sofa, unaware of anyone else in the room.

Seeing their son engage with Emily pleased Greg, and to make certain that conversation was not interrupted by Reba, Greg took her arm and led her away. "Come on, Reba. Let's see if Lita will allow us into the kitchen. I'd like to know more about this prickly-pear syrup and where to get it. This morning may be my last chance. Sorry you didn't get to taste it."

Iris understood and gave her husband the old I-know-what-you're-up-to smile as she followed him and Reba into the kitchen. Maude and Lita were sitting on the barstools at the counter going over a list. Lita saw them first.

Greg stepped into the doorway, stopped, and sheepishly asked, "I wasn't told if there are any off-limit places in the inn. Are we allowed in the kitchen?"

Maude motioned for them to enter. "Come right on in. We're going over lists for dinner plans. Could we get something for you?"

Iris walked through the kitchen into the keeping room. "Oh, I love this room, warm in every way. You even have a fireplace and a daybed built into that bay window. The colors—and so many places to relax and read right in here in this big open space." She turned around to where Maude and Lita were seated on stools at the counter. "And look at this magnificent kitchen. All the cupboards and work spaces, and the sink underneath window. Oh, and all the windows. If I lived here, I'd never come out of this room except to sleep, and I might even decide to do that in the daybed."

Maude smiled. "Well, you know what they say about the kitchen being the heart of the home," she said. "And this one certainly is. We call this our keeping room."

Reba gently spoke up. "Probably because it's so comforting, it just keeps you here."

"Well, something keeps us in here. The kitchen is not original to the house, but I designed it, and Alo built it. We upgraded a few years ago when Lita decided we should open Grey Sage as an inn."

Maude was describing how to construct adobe walls to Iris and Reba, and Greg was taking notes of Lita's suggestions for finding prickly-pear syrup in town, when the tinkling of a bell interrupted their conversations. Greg stashed his note card and pen into his shirt pocket. "Ladies, sounds like Lily is summoning us. Thank you for this information, Lita. Oh, and thank you for suggesting the use of the brass bell. I didn't want Lily to get choked on that whistle."

"Tell Lily I'll be right there as soon as I get my boots on and grab my coat," Maude requested.

Maude had traded in her dressy wool pants and cardigan for her silk long underwear and jeans and a fleece-lined suede vest over a red cashmere turtleneck—her regular attire for a winter day when Grey Sage had no guests. She grabbed her coat and met the others as Silas and Alo ushered them out to the waiting van. Lily was the last one.

She was out the door and halfway to the van when she turned around to Silas.

"Oh, Silas, would you ask Lita or whoever tidies up our rooms to please be on the lookout for my whistle? I seemed to have misplaced it."

Silas, hands in his pockets, nodded. "Of course, Lily. We'll find it and keep it in a safe place just for you."

He kissed Maude's cheek just before she walked out the door behind Lily. "You stay warm out there, Maude. I'll be right here to welcome you home. Don't miss me too much."

Maude waved before climbing into the van. She took the seat Lily had saved for her next to the window and removed her gloves and coat. The van was warm, almost too warm, and she cracked her window for a bit of air.

Everyone in their same seats again, she thought, looking around. *Wish Emily was bold enough to leave her mother and take that empty seat next to Kent in the back.* She noticed Lily digging through her purse. *Lily doesn't have her whistle. She's always had a problem keeping up with things. Or maybe Lita did decide to hold on to it for safekeeping.* She smirked. *More like safekeeping Lily's health if she continued to blow it.*

Gordy was playing his favorite Boston Pops Christmas music. The volume of multiple conversations buzzed over an instrumental version of "Winter Wonderland."

They were almost to town before Lily took the microphone. "People, people. We're almost there. I hope you've had a chance to look at the maps and the information I gave you about the Railyard District. Fifty acres of pure interesting, and I'm not certain you'll be able to cover it all in the three hours we have. So choose wisely, and you're on your own for lunch. That is, if you need lunch after that marvelous breakfast. Maude's agreed to say a few words about what you'll see this morning."

Lily whispered something to Gordy before she sat down.

Maude stood, faced the passengers, and took the microphone.

"Yes, as Lily said, the Railyard District is almost fifty acres of urban space that has been carefully planned for your pleasure. About thirteen of those acres are open spaces for a park and walking trails and a plaza, but I'd suggest not trying to see that today because of weather. Skipping those areas may afford you time to see the cultural museum, more galleries, and the live-in artist studios where you can watch the artists work and even take classes from them. But don't sign up for a class today. I don't want you to miss the farmers market—one of the best in the country. Remember, it is winter, so I'm not certain how many vendors will be there, but some will be selling craft items, Christmas baked goods, and jarred goodies. All kinds of interesting and delicious things."

Greg spoke up in his preacher voice. "I'm headed straight there. Any of you want cactus-pear syrup and jelly? Just follow me."

"Greg's been talking to Lita, and I'm certain he will find what he's looking for and more. Everything, and I do mean everything you buy at the market is grown or produced right here in Northern New Mexico. And the folks who grew it or made it will be the same ones selling it. Engage them in conversation. They love to talk about what they do."

Beatrice interrupted. "Who wants to have a conversation with acres of farmers? I certainly do not."

Maude graciously recovered. "Now, if you're not into the market, you really could spend all your time out of the weather in the cultural museum. It's a huge warehouse of things to experience and see. Oh, there's also quite a nice candy shop. I can imagine you'd enjoy that, Beatrice."

Beatrice clapped her hands and smiled.

"Lily and I will be wandering around. If you can find us, I'll be happy to answer your questions."

Maude motioned for Lily to stand up. Lily took the microphone, but before she could say anything, Beatrice announced. "If I can't be found, look for me at the candy shop." She turned to Henry. "I so hope you're feeling strong and able enough to carry my shopping bags this morning."

Henry smiled at her.

"Thank you for these bits of information, Beatrice. I'm certain we couldn't lose you if we tried, but we'll know where to look first," Lily trilled.

Reba leaned forward. "If you don't mind, Colonel, I think I'd like to walk around with you and Beatrice this morning. I've seen quite enough art, so that candy shop sounds like a perfect place, and I don't want to miss it."

The van slowed, signaling they were almost ready for the drop-off.

Ted adjusted the muffler around his neck. "Where and what time should we be back, Lily?"

"Gordy will pick us up at the same place he drops us off." She turned to Gordy as she announced, "Be ready to load the van at one thirty sharp, people."

Maude and Lily were the first off the van and stood at the door while the other guests passed. Ted and Laura took off in one direction with a map of the district in their gloved hands, headed most likely to the live-in studios. Greg folded his map and stuck it in his coat pocket, and he and Iris headed toward the farmers market. Emily and Reba had a quiet conversation before Reba left her daughter standing alone. Reba took the colonel's arm that Bea hadn't grasped, and off they went toward the shopping area.

Lily watched them all head off, then heaved a sigh and turned to Maude. "Shall we?"

"We shall," Maude answered with a smile. Arm in arm, she and her best friend headed toward the galleries.

There was an awkward silence as Kent and Emily were the only ones left standing beside the van. Kent approached Emily. "I think my parents are tired of me. Your mother abandon you too?"

Emily, a puzzled look on her face, seemed somewhat stunned. "I think that's what she did."

"What do you say we walk down to the park just to take a look?

Unless, there's something else you prefer. We can catch up with the others later."

Emily adjusted her gloves and stuck her hands in her pockets. "I think I'd really enjoy that."

Beatrice surprised Henry. "Why don't we go to the market first while we're still warm?" She looked up at him. "I know I said I didn't want to go, but I'd like to take a look. Not to worry about packages. I'm not buying zucchini and apples and red peppers. But after the tea shop, I can't promise what you might have to carry."

So the candy-loving trio followed several steps behind Greg and Iris.

Reba spoke to Beatrice. "I hope you two don't mind that I joined you this morning."

Beatrice didn't answer, but Henry replied, "You just bring added pleasure, Reba."

"I'm not sure what I bring anymore. I just needed to get away from Emily for a while." She adjusted the strap of her bag on her shoulder.

Henry chuckled. "You? You needed to get away from Emily?"

"Yes, she's hovering. It seems our roles have reversed since her father died. I love her dearly, and I couldn't be more grateful that she's so caring, but I'm almost to the point of suffocation from all her attention."

They came to a booth with baked goods. Beatrice stopped. "Oh, I've seen everything I care to see here. But I see a candy store. It's over there across the way."

Reba moved to Beatrice's side. "Bea, you've found every candy shop between here and Chicago. It's like you have candy radar or something."

"Well, if you had danced half your life and had to deny yourself anything that would push your weight over ninety-five pounds, you'd be looking for candy too, my dear."

It was comfortably warm inside the candy store, Henry decided. For once, his old bones weren't chilled. He waited as Beatrice stood at the counter and sorted through the bags of candy already packaged by the pound and handed five bags to the shopkeeper. She continued sorting through the bags of spiced nuts. "Reba, what's your favorite candy?"

"My favorite?" Reba eyed the chocolates. "I'd have to say I'm not quite the adventurous connoisseur you seem to be. My favorite would be just the plain old English toffee."

"Add a pound of English toffee to my order, please," Beatrice said to the young shopkeeper, who had obviously eaten too much chocolate. "No, make that two pounds. My daughter Dorothy loves toffee too."

Reba responded quickly. "Oh, Beatrice, you don't need to do that. I wasn't asking for toffee."

"I know you weren't asking, but it is my peace offering as a gift to accompany my apology to you."

"Your apology to me? For what?"

"For thinking that you're a whiny, demanding mother and that you are holding on much too tightly to that beautiful young daughter of yours. I was wrong. So I apologize." Beatrice gave her head a quick downward nod, noting the end of that conversation. "Besides, I like buying candy."

Henry hid his smile at Reba's bemused look.

The shopkeeper came to Bea's assistance. "Let's see, ma'am. You have two pounds of English toffee and a pound of Piñon Rolls with a center of fudge, dipped in caramel and rolled in piñon nuts. Good choice. And you have pound bags of the Chile Pistachio Bark, Red Chile Peanut Brittle, and the Rocky Road. I think you'll like the marshmallows inside the Rocky Road. We make them here, and we add pecans that are grown nearby. All these are excellent, excellent choices, ma'am."

Beatrice tapped on the glass. "And pray tell, what are those?"

The shopkeeper removed the tray and offered her one. "We call them Piñon Tortugas. *Tortuga* is Spanish for 'turtle.' Caramel and pecans dipped in milk chocolate."

"Well, why didn't you just call them turtles? Then I would have known." Beatrice devoured it in thirty seconds. "Good. I like it. Give me a pound, please."

The shopkeeper knew she had a live one. "But ma'am, you're missing something very special, especially at Christmas." She took another sample from behind the glass. "These are our famous *Bolitas*—our best chocolate fudge shaped in balls, dipped in dark chocolate, and rolled in ground almonds and powdered cocoa. Can't get much more chocolate than that." She handed the Bolita to Beatrice on a sheet of wax paper.

Beatrice took it, eyed it, and put the whole thing in her mouth. Seconds later: "The best yet."

"And even better, ma'am, we have a legend around here that the Bolitas will bring you great happiness."

"That's what Christmas is supposed to be—a whole lot of happy. And I'm going to buy everybody some happy." Beatrice looked around for Henry. He and Reba stood at the window watching the whole scene. "Henry, how many are in our Unlikely Christmas Party?"

Henry, amazed at the twists and turns in the gears of Bea's mind, studied for a moment. "Ten, including Lily."

"Young lady, I'd like ten pounds of those things that 'bring you happy,' but I'd like them in one-pound bags and tied with a Christmas ribbon, please."

She paused, thought a moment, then gasped. But the shopkeeper had disappeared to the back. She spun around on one foot. "But Henry, what about Maude?"

"What about her?"

Beatrice grew impatient. "How many live with Maude at Grey Sage?"

"Just Silas and Lita and Alo. So that makes four."

Beatrice tapped the bell on top of the counter. "I don't know your name, but I know you're back there somewhere and you have chocolate on your apron. I need four more pounds of happy, please."

Henry sensed that Beatrice was up to something that she might regret later. He approached her. "Bea, what are you doing?"

"It's Christmas, Henry. I'm buying everyone candy to make them happy."

"Ah. Of course." Sardonically, he added, "Well, by all means, don't forget Gordy."

"Oh, that's right. But he's such a sourpuss, and I really don't care for him very much." She pondered. "All the more reason to buy him candy." She tapped the bell. "One more bag of that happy candy, please, and that will be all."

A few minutes later, the shopkeeper returned with three giant shopping bags filled with one-pound bags of candy. "That'll be three-hundred seventy-four dollars and twenty cents."

Reba joined her. "Really, Beatrice? That's a lot of money for candy."

"Well, I had three husbands, and two of them were rich, so I have a lot of money, and what else can you do with money? I like candy. And besides I'm buying more than candy. I'm buying happy."

Henry stepped in again. "Beatrice, that's almost twenty-five pounds of candy. I can't carry that all day."

The shopkeeper interjected quickly before someone came to her senses. "Oh, we'll be most happy to keep it right here for you, and you can pick it up later. I'll put your name on it right now and put it in the back. I can even put those bags in lovely gift boxes."

"See, Henry, this gracious and smart young woman took care of your problem. She's been such a help. Now point me to the tea shop, please."

Defeated, Henry pulled his handkerchief from his back pocket and wiped the powdered cocoa from Beatrice's nose and the smear of chocolate from the corner of her mouth. Before extending his arms to his ladies, he waved to the smiling clerk. "Merry, merry Christmas. Thank you for spreading such happiness this morning."

While the Suttons visited with artists, and the Martins filled up burlap gift bags with local jellies and prickly-pear syrup, and Maude and Lily darted in and out of several galleries, Kent and Emily sat on a park bench unaware of the biting cold.

Kent fiddled with the button on his coat. The brace on his wrist and the sling made clothing challenging. "First Christmas without your dad, is it?"

"Yes, and I'm so glad Mother and I are here and not at home. I think we would have both been miserable, and I can't bear for Christmas to be miserable."

"Something not right about a miserable Christmas. Tell me about your dad." Kent angled his body toward Emily. He had interest in what she said, and he liked looking at her. Hers was a simple beauty.

"My father was the best. My mother is too. But with my dad, things … Things were just easier. Mother was always this dedicated professional and a bit of an overachiever. She was so disappointed when I told her I wanted to teach kindergarten."

"Why on earth would she be disappointed about that? Maybe frightened for you. Kindergarteners can be scary, you know. But disappointed?"

"She just thought I could do more. But honestly, I couldn't think of anything more that I wanted to do. Children completely fascinate me. Somehow, I thought if I could just get to them young enough, I could give them a healthy self-image and a wholesome way of look-ing at things, and then there'd be no need for so many doctors in my mother's profession."

Kent squirmed. If he had ever given therapy a thought, he'd thought of it as something other people did. But since he'd come home from Iraq two months ago, he'd spent many hours talking to a therapist. "That's a noble thought, but sometimes things happen, Emily—things you didn't count on—and they change you."

"I know, but it doesn't stop me from doing what I do. My dad understood I wanted a normal life—a cottage with a garden, regular work hours minus the midnight calls my parents received. I didn't want to live in the city—too busy and too noisy. I think I just wanted a simpler, quieter life, maybe the kind of life people had a few generations ago. So I finished graduate school, moved a hundred miles away to a small community, and bought myself a quaint cottage with a garden. No picket fence yet, though."

"Sounds like you have it all, and now you have a new sunflower mailbox to go with that simple, near-perfect life of yours."

He'd made her smile. "I do, don't I?"

"But is it all you thought it would be? Are you happy with your simple life?"

"I am. I wake up every morning so ready to get to work. I come home to quiet late afternoons. I enjoy my neighbors and the community. I'm trying my hand at writing and illustrating a children's book, and I have holidays and the summer to do that and to travel. What's not to like, unless you're my mother?"

Kent nodded. "My life started out that way. I mean, simple and good, growing up in the Chicago suburbs. My mom spent all her time taking care of Dad and me. And Dad? Oh, he worked at doing the normal dad things, didn't miss many ballgames, and taught me all about fishing. But now that I look back, he was much more interested in having deep theological and philosophical discussions with his son than he was in snagging that trout in the stream. Fishing gave us plenty of time for those conversations. I thought every dad talked to his son about life like my dad did. Sure learned differently when I went off to college."

"Sounds a bit like my childhood. Try growing up with a psychotherapist mother and a dentist father. One checking my brushing habits and the other always wanting to know how I was feeling. I thought that was normal too. But I always felt loved."

"So did I, and my childhood memories are good ones. But I've been to some hellish places, and I've seen way too much devastation of human life." Kent paused, not uncomfortable with the silence. "I'm trying to get back home. Really home." He slid closer to Emily and put his arm around her shoulder. It just seemed the natural thing to do.

Emily lowered her head. "I don't think I can even imagine those things."

"No, you can't. They'd be so foreign to you, so don't even try. One of the things I like about you is your goodness. Your life is pure, not tainted like mine. I want to get back to a life like yours, and I'm getting there."

"Maybe you'll forget those terrible things with a little passing of time."

"No, I don't think I want to forget, but I'm learning to deal with the memories in a healthy way. But for now, I want to make some new memories. Isn't that what we're all doing on this trip?"

She surprised him by taking the hand cradled comfortably in his sling and holding it in both of hers. "We are, aren't we? We put all those beautiful memories of Christmases past away and boarded a van traveling south. Sort of like perusing the family photo album and putting it back on the shelf. You return it to the shelf because you have other things to do. Things like living and taking more pictures."

He slid even closer to her to absorb her warmth for a moment, then sighed. "You know, I want your mother to take a liking to me," he admitted, "but I'm afraid she won't if I keep you out here much longer. She'll be worried. We'd better join the group."

They rose together, and he took her hand. They walked in silence through the grayness of a wintry morning. But for the first time in his recent memory, he felt something familiar returning: there was color and warmth inside him. He'd never been more aware of a woman's presence.

He squeezed her hand and broke the silence. "You know, Emily, about those photo albums with all our Christmases? They're always on the shelf when we need to look at them." Like she'd surprised him by taking his hand in hers while they sat, he surprised her and himself when he leaned down to gently kiss her cheek.

Chapter Seven

*W*ith more than enough candy, tins of tea, and jars of sweet goodies to fill many a Christmas stocking, the travelers boarded the van for the Loretto Chapel. Lily did a head count and asked Maude to take the microphone to tell them what they'd be seeing.

Maude instructed Gordy to circle back around the Plaza and take San Francisco for a drive-by of the St. Francis Cathedral. "We are coming up on the cathedral now, right in front of us. I know you chose not to visit it today because of weather, but perhaps you will return sometime to see the cathedral and the prayer garden, with original sculptures of the Stations of the Cross. The sculpture is worth your trip. You'll find no romanticized depictions there. In fact, some who visit find the sculpted pieces a bit disturbing and grotesque."

Beatrice had eaten too much chocolate, which had only erased whatever faint lines of discretion she had left. "Heavenly days, who'd want to spend time looking at something … did you say 'disturbing and grotesque,' Maude? It's Christmas, for God's sake. Maybe I didn't buy enough bags of happy."

"You do have a point, Beatrice. Artists sometimes have their own ways of depicting truth, but I suppose we all prefer beautiful things, especially at Christmas. And what you're about to see is beautiful." Maude continued with a brief history of the chapel and the legend of the mysterious staircase as Gordy circled the block again to find parking.

An hour later, the travelers boarded the van again for Grey Sage. The sky was growing thicker with heavy-bottomed, gray clouds, and the wind gusts whirled the snow across the road in front of them. Maude became aware that she was tightly gripping the armrest separating her and Lily.

Alo was right. The wind's picking up. Not snowing yet, though. I'd better check with him on the latest weather and talk to Lily about timing for tomorrow's travel plans.

Traffic had slowed such that it took them almost an hour to get back to the inn. Silas greeted them at the front door. "Come in, you weary and frozen travelers. Go put your coats and packages away. Alo has the fire blazing, and Lita has made some of her famous hot chocolate. *Auténtico*, as she says."

Emily put her purse and one package on the bed, removed her coat, and hung it on the coat rack. "Did Beatrice keep you entertained today?" She headed for the dresser.

Reba hung her coat and hat on the rack. "Indeed, she did. I know most of you think she's just senile, but she's fascinating to me. She's a wealth of stories, and she has such an interesting way of telling them. And yes, I quite enjoyed myself."

Emily brushed her hair, pulled it high on her head, and secured it with the cloisonné hair stick her father had given her for Christmas last year—a beautiful piece he'd purchased on their anniversary trip to Japan. She stepped aside and looked more closely at the Picasso next to the mirror. "Did you read about this painting last night, Mother?"

"I did. He called it *Girl Before a Mirror*. Full face, profile, young, old, and all that unexplainable in between. Ghastly. Not so pretty as you in the mirror."

Reba replaced Emily at the mirror, removed the clamp from her graying hair, brushed it, and pulled it severely to the nape of her neck before clamping it again. "Quite a brain Picasso had. He would have been a case study. I don't know why Maude had to put us in this room with these sharp-edged, anguished paintings."

"Oh, I think she meant nothing, Mother. I mean, look at the view. And the room does have twin beds. I'm certain it was just a matter of practicality."

"I'm certain you are correct, my practical daughter. But look at this one." Reba took Emily's arm and led her to the framed work in the corner above the wooden rocking chair. "Look at this. Nothing short of purely painful."

Reba's strong reactions to the paintings surprised Emily. "I agree. I don't think I'd want either of them hanging in my cottage. What do you know about this one?"

"*The Weeping Woman.*"

Emily looked at her mother, not sure she believed her. "You're not joking, are you?"

"No. Apparently Picasso thought the world needed one more image of universal suffering, and when I look at it, it feels like he's been inside my head the last few months."

Emily took her mother's hand.

Reba stared at the painting. "How thoughtful of him. Picasso called women 'suffering machines,' you know. Although, by nature, I suppose we are." She let go of her daughter's hand. "But I refuse to look like that on the outside or to feel like that on the inside. After all, it's Christmas, the season of hope, peace, joy, and love."

She pointed to the painting on the opposite wall, a monochromatic blue depiction with softer lines. "I'm assuming Picasso loved his mother. He entitled that one *Mother and Child*. Or perhaps it's the Mother Mary. Or maybe it's you and me, daughter. At least it makes me feel better."

"Me too."

"Speaking of feeling better, daughter of mine, at the risk of sounding as though I were spying—which I can assure you I was not—how are you feeling about holding a certain young man's hand this morning?"

Emily looked at her mother, turned, and walked toward the door. "Later, Mother."

Reba, feeling nothing like Picasso's *Weeping Woman*, watched Emily leave the room and smiled. "Later, daughter."

Iris stood at her window. "Greg, have you really looked at this view? I know it's in shades of gray now, but it's still magnificent. I'm so glad we decided to make this trip."

Greg joined his wife at the window, put his arms around her, and looked toward the Sangre de Cristo Mountains. "I can imagine it's even colder on those peaks. If I'm not totally turned around, I think Taos is through those passes, and we'll be headed there tomorrow."

"I can only imagine what this panorama would look like with the sun shining?"

"Maybe like this?" Greg pondered the painting next to the window. "Didn't Maude say something about the chestnut trees down on Canyon Road?"

"I think she did."

"I'd wager that's why she chose this Renoir, *Chestnut Tree in Bloom*."

"Oh, it's lovely. Makes me want to sit down by the water in its shade for a spell. You may be right about why Maude chose it. I've never known you to be a betting man, but I wouldn't bet against you."

"Ordinarily I'm not." He pointed to the painting on the wall next to the closet door. The subject was a well-dressed man reaching down to the take the hand of a young maiden. "See that. Not sure if they're in a garden or a park or on a path through the woods, but he's inviting her to go with him somewhere."

Iris approached the painting to read its title on the brass plate beneath it. "*La Promenade*. I think that's French for taking a walk, maybe a leisurely walk. And this lovely lady seems a bit coy and yet eager to take that walk."

"I'm hoping she is."

"Are we talking about Renoir's *La Promenade*, or are we talking about Emily and Kent?" Iris's face brightened with her wifely, motherly, knowing smile.

"You know who I'm talking about."

"I do, and I have a very good feeling about this."

"Frankly, I'm hoping. I can remember standing in the trout stream in Wyoming when Kent was fifteen, describing the kind of girl he should be dreaming about. And I tell you, I was describing Emily as if I already knew her. I know we haven't known her long, but my discernment is that she would be quite a catch."

Iris cautioned her husband. "Now, let's don't go and get our hopes up too high. They are both adults—adults with good judgment—and we should just leave them be. Kent's still mending. If Emily can spark his interest, then I'm all for it. But no meddling, understand?"

"Well stated, wife. No meddling. But since I'm in this wagering mood. I'll wager you a jar of prickly-pear syrup there'll be a smile on our boy's face for the next few days, like it was Christmas morning every day."

Iris batted her eyes playfully, took his hand, and led him to the door. "Let's go sample that hot chocolate and get to know Reba better. After all ..."

Christmas music seeped through the background of several conversations in the gathering room, making a blur of sound like the blur of color when watercolor paint touches water-washed paper. Silas and the colonel were deep in conversation again. The Suttons sat silently on the sofa. Greg and Iris joined Reba in front of the fire. Beatrice was absent.

Kent and Emily stood in the curve of the piano, sipping their hot chocolate and talking with Lita. Kent asked, "So there's another secret ingredient in the hot chocolate? I get the chocolate, and the cream and milk combined with a sprinkle of cinnamon." Kent licked his lips. "Is it vanilla I taste?"

Lita beamed. "Oh, yes, Mexican vanilla and Mexican cinnamon."

"You mean there's a difference? I never thought about where vanilla and cinnamon come from, but Mexico would not be my best guess."

"Oh, my friend. Vanilla originated in Mexico, so I only use Mexican vanilla. Something special about the alcohol content. But you're right about the cinnamon. But for it to be Mexican cinnamon, it must come from Sri Lanka. Only from there. It has the best taste."

"Mexican cinnamon from South Asia? Okay, if you say so." Kent took another swallow and closed his eyes. "And the secret ingredient?"

"Still my secret, my friend."

Lily entered the room in a flurry. She clapped her hands. "Sorry, Party people, but I still can't find my whistle. Dinner's in an hour, so just make yourselves comfortable until then. I don't think we'll have a show-and-tell this evening since I saw only bags of jelly and chocolate. So what do you say we talk about our impressions of the Loretto Chapel? And especially the part about Saint Joseph?" She pointed her finger at Greg. "As our resident theologian and philosopher, perhaps you could lead our discussion and offer us some sage wisdom."

Greg responded. "If I have any left after dinner, Lily, I'll be delighted to share it. But you might consider getting Alo in on this discussion. He's a builder and carpenter, and he knows things none of us know. He even knows about halos around the moon."

"Good idea. I'll ask him." Lily looked around the room. "Where's Beatrice? I thought I counted heads. Please tell me we didn't leave her in the tea shop."

Henry answered. "I think she's resting, coming down off her chocolate high."

"Fine. Just make sure she knows dinner's in an hour." With a swish of her shawl, Lily headed off to the kitchen.

Another of Lita's specialties was served for dinner, followed by her mincemeat pie.

"The only way to finish off mincemeat pie is with a cup of Silas's eggnog," she stated. "He's famous around here for it. Why don't you find a comfortable spot in the gathering room? Alo is looking forward to sharing the legend of the miraculous stairway at Loretto Chapel with you, and I'll be serving eggnog a little later. And just so you can look forward to it, I'll tell you now you've never had anything like it. Can't find this in any store, and you'll need a spoon—no sipping."

Lita returned to the kitchen to oversee the cleaning. *But I also need to serve the eggnog*, Lita thought to herself. The local girls who lived down the road could finish the cleaning—they needed the extra Christmas money. But she needed to serve the eggnog.

Maude and Silas gave their guests first choice of seating before sinking into one of the well-worn love seats off to the side. Maude took the afghan from the back of the seat, spread it over their legs, and scanned the room.

The colonel's in his favorite wing chair next to the fireplace, and Greg is opposite him. Hmm, Reba is between Iris and Beatrice on the sofa. Kent and Emily are cozying up on the other loveseat. But Ted and Laura took the chairs next to the window. You'd think they'd want to take advantage of the fireplace. I think I have an idea to fix that later.

Lily took Alo's arm and guided him to stand in front of the fireplace. "Alo has agreed to tell us the legend of the miraculous staircase we saw this afternoon. It seems a fitting thing to do since it's Christmas and the legend involves Joseph."

The fire backlit Alo's chiseled, leathery face and his shiny black hair worn in a ponytail. There were still a few of his ancestral ways that Alo refused to relinquish. His hair was one and his hunting bow the other.

"My friends," he began, "you have seen the Loretto Chapel today. No doubt you enjoyed the building itself, designed and built by the famous French architect Antoine Mouly and his son. He was also the architect and builder for the St. Francis Cathedral, which took over ten years to build.

"It is said the Sisters of Loretto who ran the school wanted a small chapel and appealed to the bishop when Mouly was nearing the completion of the cathedral. The bishop agreed to allow Mouly and his son to design their chapel in the style of the bishop's favorite small chapel in Paris. History tells us the sisters raised what monies they could and gave their inheritances to raise the thirty thousand dollars to build the chapel.

"If you visited the other chapels in the area, you would see they are built of adobe, but not the Loretto. It is built of stone that was quarried from around Santa Fe, and the sandstone for the walls and the volcanic stone for the ceiling had to be hauled for miles by wagon. The stained glass was made in Paris and had to sail across the Atlantic to New Orleans, where it was placed on a paddle boat to St. Louis and then brought by covered wagon over the Old Santa Fe Trail to the chapel. Quite a trip."

Beatrice interrupted. "Amazing. I've made that trip across the Atlantic. But heavenly days, I'd have never made it on a paddle boat and covered wagon. And that beautiful, fragile glass."

Alo assuaged her concern before continuing with the story. "So very true, ma'am. It took two years to build the chapel, and it was completed in 1878. Well, I should say it was almost completed. There was a choir loft over twenty feet above the floor without a way to get to it. But the sisters were determined to use that choir loft. They called in other carpenters, and all agreed that the chapel was so small that a staircase would take up too much room, so a ladder was their only answer.

"But as I said, the sisters were determined, and they couldn't see themselves climbing a ladder. So for nine days, they committed to special prayers to Saint Joseph, the patron saint of carpenters. Legend has it that on the ninth day of their prayers, a stranger on a donkey appeared at the chapel. He had a toolbox and was looking for work. Six months later, he had completed the staircase, and he left as he came, mysteriously and without pay. The sisters searched for the man. They ran an ad in the local paper. They contacted local merchants to see if they sold wood or supplies to the mysterious carpenter. No one knew who he was. The sisters considered him the answer to their prayers and concluded that he was Saint Joseph himself."

Beatrice waved her handkerchief. "You mean Joseph came from heaven just to build the staircase?"

"That's what the legend suggests, ma'am. Because I'm a carpenter of sorts, I can't quite imagine building that staircase with such primitive tools of that day. I find the design ahead of its time. There is no visible means of support in the staircase. It makes two complete circles with thirty-three steps. And there are no nails; it's entirely put together with wooden pegs. Legend says that the wood is not even native to the area, which adds to the mystery. I'm happy you were able to visit the chapel and see the staircase, especially during Christmas, the season of miracles."

Alo nodded to Lily, and Lily thanked him. "Alo, your father must have been a Hopi chief, and you got your storytelling talent from him."

He acknowledged her and stepped aside to stand by the window.

As if on cue, Lita and the two young girls entered the gathering room with trays of eggnog and butter cookies. When everyone had a cup, Lily thanked them and turned to Greg. "So, Greg, is it a miracle or not?"

"Well, Lily, since you didn't start with an easy question, maybe I should at least have a taste of this famous eggnog before I give my answer."

"When you're ready, Professor, your students will be ready to listen." Lily took the last cup on Lita's tray and sat down next to Beatrice.

Beatrice took a taste and stood straight up. "Why are you giving me a cup of whipped cream? Or is it ice cream? I don't know what this is. I thought I was getting eggnog."

Lily pulled on the back of Beatrice's pants leg. "Sit down, Bea. This *is* eggnog. It's the absolute most delicious eggnog you've ever tasted. None of the store-bought-carton stuff for you. You are so special, dear. Silas made this just for you." She looked at Silas. "Tell her, Silas, how you make it."

"Well, this recipe was one my grandmother used, and we only make eggnog at Christmas. Maybe that's another reason it's so special. We have to wait a whole year for it."

Silas described beating the egg yolks with sugar until creamy and then slowly adding the whiskey—or the nog, as he liked to call it. He explained how the alcohol made the raw egg safely edible. The egg whites were beaten separately with sugar and folded into the egg yolks. Then heavy cream was whipped with powdered sugar and a dash of vanilla and gently folded into the mixture. "After all that's done, into the freezer it goes for about half an hour. And now you have the Thornhill Christmas Eggnog, sprinkled with freshly ground nutmeg, of course."

Beatrice waved her spoon. "Heavenly days, this stuff was beaten and whipped and then frozen. I'd say that's horrible treatment, but it's delicious. But tell me again why we're having Christmas eggnog when it's not Christmas and we don't even have a Christmas tree."

Lily spoke quietly to Beatrice.

Greg finished the last spoonful of eggnog. "No question, the best eggnog I've ever tasted, Silas, and certainly the only eggnog I've ever eaten with a spoon. Thank you for sharing your home and your family recipe with us." He paused. "So, let's talk about the Miraculous Staircase. Was it a miracle? The answer, simply put, is I don't know."

A collective "What?" reverberated around the room.

"I know, you think we theologians have all the answers. And we do have answers to the most important questions. But we don't have them all. And frankly, some of those answers rely on an acceptance of the mystery of God. Maybe a good place to begin is to tell you how I define *miracle*. Regardless of your faith background, I think we can accept that a miracle is some incomprehensible event that can only be attributed to God himself. It's when he steps in and breaks the laws of nature that he designed and performs some action that is totally unexplainable outside of his doing. Can we all agree on that?"

They nodded without question.

"So, is the staircase a miracle? I'm not absolutely sure. I wasn't there, but it appears that this information we have comes from reliable sources. I believe that God answers the prayers of his people, and the sisters prayed. I believe that God can do whatever he chooses, and if he chose to answer their prayers by sending a carpenter who was Saint Joseph himself, or a Hopi Indian, then God could have done it. Interesting though that the design was ahead of its time and that the carpenter appeared and disappeared so mysteriously."

There was a warm quiet that settled upon the room. Greg continued. "This is the season of miracles, is it not? So I choose to think that God intervened and answered the prayers of the Sisters of Loretto and gave them a miracle."

"Me too," echoed through the room.

Maude glanced over at Alo, looking out the window, the moon lending just enough light to see. From where she was seated, Maude could see too—the wind gusting and the snow blowing sideways.

Alo's worried. Temperature must be in the teens by now. The next miracle might be getting these travelers on the road in the morning. Nothing we can do, though. No use worrying Lily or our guests tonight.

Chapter Eight

Thursday, December 22

aude rolled over to see the time. Almost five o'clock. The shadows through the window told her only that there were strong winds.

Wind's blowing from the northeast. Cold. Wonder if we got a dump of snow last night. I should get up and pack. The weather could affect Lily's departure this morning. Then I'll be rushed the rest of the day to get ready for our flight in the morning. I hate leaving everything for Lita and Alo to clean up and secure, but I may not have a choice.

She snuggled closer to Silas. "Are you awake, Silas?" She knew he was. They always woke together and lay quietly for a while.

In these early morning moments as of late, Maude had been thinking more of their younger years and the paths that had brought them to this place. She couldn't remember a time in her life when she hadn't loved Silas. As a ten-year-old girl growing up in West Texas, she'd been determined to marry him from the first time she saw him riding the fences on their neighboring ranch. From then on, be it school, church, the local library, riding the range, or cruising in his 1957 Chevy, they'd been inseparable—until high school graduation sent Silas to the university in Austin and exiled Maude to study art at the School of the Art Institute of Chicago. For her, they might as well have been on different planets. She didn't come out of her room in Chicago for the first three days, and she cried until her eyes were nothing but slits in her puffed red cheeks.

But for the next four years in Chicago, when she wasn't in class or studying, she visited every museum, gallery, and lecture offered.

It was her way of filling up the time and holding her breath until she and Silas were together again at home during holidays and summer breaks. It was then she could finally inhale and exhale. And then they parted and the crying started all over again.

Lily used to get so frustrated with me. Maude smiled at the remembrance of her fiery friend stomping around and telling Maude to "*stop being such a ninny.*"

Thankfully, the crying stopped when they set off for Boston together for Silas to attend Massachusetts General as a medical student and later a resident. Their parents had given their blessings and a wedding the likes of which had never been seen under a West Texas sky.

As a young bride and art teacher in an elementary school only a few blocks from their modest apartment near the hospital in downtown Boston, Maude made Silas's life as easy as it could be. She prepared meals at odd hours and never complained about his workload or schedule. When she found herself lonely, which was much of the time, she haunted the art museums and galleries, dreaming about having her own art studio and living in a place where the weather was warm and the sky was big and she didn't look out on brick buildings.

After nine winters in Boston, Silas hesitated all of two seconds before accepting Dr. Aaron Thomas's invitation to join his practice. "Maude, want to move to New Mexico? If you do, we'll be trading in this three-room apartment for a four-room casita only blocks from the Plaza in downtown Santa Fe. That's temporary, mind you, until you can find us a real home."

It took Maude even less time to say goodbye to concrete buildings and city noise and pack up the evidence of their lives in Boston.

Coming to Santa Fe was like coming home.

During that first summer, there was not one art gallery or museum or mission that Maude did not find and explore from the bottom up, studying not only their treasures but their architecture. All the gallery owners on Canyon Road knew her by name. The summer evenings found her and Silas enjoying night skies in the desert and the outdoor performances of the Santa Fe Opera. Again, Maude had a way of filling up time while she held her breath. This time she was holding her breath until she found them a real home.

The summer days and nights slowly turned to autumn, and Maude sensed a need to nest. While Silas built his medical practice and relationships with the locals, Maude began to look for property. Not a flat-roofed pueblo in town, but a place out in the mountains, with a small house that would be their intimate sanctuary and her studio and the nucleus of the sprawling home she intended to build. She had seen this home in her dreams. She had lived in it in her imagination.

Her first visit to these forty-seven acres was like the first time she had seen Silas. Maude knew. She knew *this* cottage on *this* mountain was it, the perfect spot of her dreams. She called Silas immediately and described in detail the corals and blues of the horizon and the deep greens of the pines in the woods and the silver sage and the running creek and the two-bedroom cottage.

On his next day off, she brought Silas to walk through the lush forest, and to picnic at sunset, and to sit on the hood of the car in the evening to see the expansive sky. "I think we should call the place Grey Sage, and someday I'd like to add a wing facing the east for a few more bedrooms. Who wouldn't want to wake up to the sunrise? And then I'd like a studio with massive windows facing slightly southeast, and porches—lots of porches and breezeways. We have to build for the land, Silas."

Maude had only to describe her vision of what Grey Sage would look like in five years to convince Silas no other property would do. He could not deny her the place when she had already given it a name.

Maude thought she had always belonged to Grey Sage and to Silas.

How different this season of our lives would have been if Elan had lived.

But he hadn't.

She spoke softly again. "Talk to me, Silas. Are you awake?

He rolled toward her. "One eye open."

"I'm thinking we'd best get both eyes open and rise and pack. Weather may delay getting our guests off this morning, and we're not ready for our trip. We'll have at least an hour before I need to get to the kitchen to help Lita. I think we can get most of our packing done."

Silas cleared his throat. "You're right. Just seems odd to be packing shirts with palm trees on them and sandals when the wind is howling outside." He lay quiet with his eyes closed. "If you remember, Maude, I wasn't sure we should have Lily's party here so near Christmas. But I must say I've enjoyed it."

"Umm-huh. Me too. Rather interesting group. Of course, Lily always surrounds herself with unusual people." She searched under the covers for Silas's hand.

"True. I like the colonel, and I've enjoyed Greg and his wife. They seem like 'salt of the earth' kind of people. Can't quite get the Suttons figured out yet, though. And Beatrice … Well, she's entertaining."

"I can't decide if she's just unaware or uninhibited."

"She's probably always been somewhat uninhibited, and you mix that with a touch of dementia? Makes for entertaining. Then there's Lily. She's just getting Lilier."

"But, Silas. You love Lily."

"Didn't say I didn't love her. Just don't have a word for her other than 'Lily.'"

"And a budding romance right here at Grey Sage. I've watched those two around here and when we're out and about. I tell you, Silas, they're smitten, plain smitten. Just like we were."

Silas pulled Maude to him and kissed her cheek. "What do you mean *were*? I'm still smitten, aren't you?"

She hugged him. "Up. Will you get the suitcases? I stashed them in the closet. I'll get the packing list, and let's get this done."

Silas turned on the bedside lamp and got out of bed. They pulled up the covers and adjusted the pillows. "Think I'll put on some warm clothes first." He looked out the window on the way to the bathroom. "Might be an interesting day, Maude."

Six thirty. Maude and Silas made their way toward the kitchen. Silas stopped in the butler's pantry to make the coffee—his morning duty when they had guests. Alo already had fires blazing and sat warming himself in front of the fire in the keeping room.

Maude joined Lita at the kitchen island and gave her a morning hug. "We've been up awhile to get our packing done. Didn't know what the day might hold." Maude saw the oven light on. "I smell something good. What's for breakfast?"

"Baked oatmeal with maple-cured bacon, scrambled eggs, and almond scones. Should be hearty enough to send our travelers on their way."

"What's my assignment?"

"Would you fry the bacon while I make the scones?"

"Done. Let me get my apron." Maude headed to the mudroom. "Alo, what's the latest on the weather?"

"Not as bad as they predicted. Seems the storm is delayed."

"That's good news for getting our guests on their way this morning."

"Best to get them on their way early. Storm's coming through the mountains." Alo stoked the fire. "Not out of the woods yet. If it blows in like I think it will, we're in for some big changes. Just don't know exactly when yet. Aren't they headed to Taos?"

She tied her apron strings and opened a package of bacon. "Today in Taos, and then on to Colorado Springs tomorrow."

"Lily may want to change her plans."

Lita rolled out the dough for the scones. "Well, good luck on that one, Alo. *You* change her mind. Our job's to get them fed so they can be on their way to somewhere."

Maude agreed. "The inn ritual after we feed them, and then we'll say Merry Christmas and send them on their way."

The Unlikely Christmas Party gathered for breakfast, their luggage already lined up in the front hall according to Lily's last-night instructions. There was no sign of Gordy yet.

After breakfast was served, Maude rose from the table. "It has been our delight to have you as our guests at Grey Sage. I hope your stay has been pleasurable enough that you will want to return. We've done all we could to make it that way. Unfortunately, we have no control over the weather."

The guests chimed in their positive responses, some expressing their desire to return in the spring.

"And to you, Beatrice: I'm sorry we had no Christmas tree for you. It's just that closing Grey Sage is our custom at Christmas. I know you'll find more than enough decorated trees, wreaths, and nutcrackers at the Broadmoor. And while you're enjoying the sights and sounds of a true Rocky Mountain Christmas, Silas and I will be setting sail on the warm waters of the Caribbean."

"I accept your apology, Maude, and I have something for you because I think you need some Christmas." Beatrice pulled out four small gift bags and handed them to Maude. "Here is some chocolate—the kind the shopkeeper said was certain to bring happiness. Merry Christmas to you, to your husband, to your cook, and to your Indian."

Maude took the bags and rolled her eyes as she handed one to Silas. "Why, thank you, Beatrice. This is very kind of you, and I'll make certain to give Lita and Alo their gifts."

Lily joined Maude. "Well, there's one thing left for us to do—something required of all guests at Grey Sage." She turned to Maude. "Would you like to lead them, friend?"

Beatrice interrupted, "We're not joining hands and singing something, are we?"

Maude chuckled. "Not unless you'd like to lead us."

Beatrice shook her head.

"Usually my guests are here for an artist or writers' retreat. They stay longer, they have more time to enjoy the property, and we have longer to get to know them. But regardless of your stay, we have the same ritual. Most inns have a guest book for their guests to sign and write a few words. I have something else that I prefer. Would you follow me?"

All the guests rose from the table and followed Maude to the gathering room and through double doors into another hallway. This hallway was quite different—adobe walls replaced with glass doors.

Maude said, "This leads to my studio, which you have not seen. When the weather is nice, which is much of the year here, these glass doors are open on both sides, making this more like a breezeway. If you were here during an artists' retreat, this area would be lined with artists at their easels painting the local scenery."

The group continued the walk down the hall and into Maude's studio, a huge open room with twenty-foot ceilings. The northeastern and southwestern walls were floor-to-ceiling glass, also with large glass doors.

Maude added, "Seems the magnificent views are veiled in gray this morning, and I regret that you can't enjoy them. One of the delights of my days. Now, the reason I brought you here is that wall." Maude pointed to the adjacent wall covered in different-colored handprints—some large, some small, some almost on top of each other. "So, roll up your shirtsleeves or your sweater, and Lily and I will paint the palm of your hand. And then I'd like you to stamp it somewhere on that wall. I'll give you a pen to sign and date your handprint."

A murmur broke across the group. Reba spoke first. "I love, love, love this. Look at it. It's a work of art as it is. May I take a picture?"

"Certainly," Maude responded. "And thank you, Reba. This wall is a symbol that your presence here has left your soulprint in our lives and in our home. So let's get going."

Fifteen minutes later, the party emerged from the studio with clean hands. Lita met them in the gathering room with a small red paper bag for each guest. "Here is our Merry Christmas treat for your journey today. These are Feast Day cookies, similar to butter cookies, with some special spices and piñon nuts and a secret—"

Kent interrupted her. "Another secret ingredient? I'm leaving here in minutes, and I don't know the secret ingredient for your cal-abacitas or your hot chocolate or the cookies? Now I'll never know."

Lita had a knowing twinkle in her eye. "Come back here for your honeymoon, and I'll not only tell you what the secret ingredient is, I'll give you a whole jar full."

Alo and Gordy huddled in the corner. Gordy whined. "I didn't have that much trouble getting here from town, but now we have to turn around and go back. Surely US 285 will be clear, but what do you think about State Road 68?"

Alo shook his head. "Not sure. You really should forget Taos and head straight to Colorado Springs. Lot less chance of having trouble on I-25 with the weather coming from the northeast.

"No way. The boss is heels-in-the-dirt determined to get to Taos."

"Then forget the High Road. You need to take the Low Road today—the road along the Rio Grande. It's more direct, only about seventy miles, and you're not driving through the mountains until you're almost to Taos."

"Man, I talked to Ms. Mayfield about taking that road. She wouldn't hear of it. She wants the scenic route—someplace special she wants to stop."

"Not advisable. Even on a good day, it could take two to three hours if you drive the High Road, but it could take you all day with this weather—if it's even open."

"Could you talk to her? She's not listening to me."

Alo agreed to try and joined Lily and the Thornhills in the gathering room. He laid out his suggestions, but Lily was determined to get to Taos. The most she agreed to was to take the Low Road.

Alo hoped it would be enough to keep the group safe.

He and Gordy loaded the luggage as the Unlikely Christmas Party said their goodbyes and took their seats in the van. He stood with Maude and Silas at the front door as they shivered and waved. Gordy started the vehicle and put it into gear.

It was then that Silas suddenly patted his pocket, then walked briskly to the van, waving his arms, trying to get Gordy's attention. Gordy opened the door, and Silas climbed the first step.

"Lily. I almost forgot. We found it." Reaching into his pocket, he pulled out a silver chain and dangled it in front of her. It was her whistle. "Safe travels, friend."

Through the window Alo watched as Lily gave Silas the eye. She took the whistle, put it around her neck, and blew it hard. Even at the door to the house, Maude and Alo winced. Alo shook his head.

"That is one unusual woman."

A silent tension replaced the normal chatter on the van. The colonel and Beatrice sat in the front seats behind Gordy. Lily, in her Mongolian lamb vest, sat alone in the front seat across the aisle. The colonel asked, "Gordy, what route are we taking to Taos?"

"Sir, we're taking the Low Road along the Rio Grande. There's limited access to Taos even on good days—only a few passes, and they could be closed this morning. We should be fine, though. This is a more direct route."

Lily requested, "I'd like us to stop at Truchas. Some art studios there I'd like us to see."

Gordy wondered if this woman had looked at a map or even looked out the window this morning. "We're taking the Low Road, ma'am. Truchas is up in the mountains on the High Road."

Lily was snippy. "I don't like this. We'll need to stop somewhere along the way."

Gordy replied, "This route is only about seventy miles, and I'll be taking it slow. I suggest we stop in Española if we need to."

"Fine. We'll stop there."

More silence. Lily thumbed through the New Mexico guidebook for tourists. Beatrice, leaning against the colonel, slept. Ted and Laura both had books in their hands. Greg napped, and Iris slipped into the empty seat next to Reba and began a conversation.

Kent and Emily sat near the rear of the van, he in the aisle seat.

Emily looked out the window. "I never knew there were so many shades of white and gray. We have snow and blizzards in Illinois, but I don't recall these colors. Or maybe I never really looked."

"Gray, all right, but no whiteout conditions yet. I'm thinking we should have skipped Taos and gone straight to the Broadmoor. Started to say something to Lily, but I've noticed she doesn't like to be questioned."

"We should be fine. Gordy doesn't seem to be much of a risk-taker. Surely he checked things out before we got on the road this morning."

"You're right. I've been in sandstorms worse than this. And if we can't get out of Taos tomorrow, at least we'll be in a beautiful place."

Emily turned to face him. "You've been there before?"

"Once. My parents brought me when I was a teenager. That's another reason we took this Christmas trip—to see Santa Fe and Taos again. My mom likes returning to places she's been before."

"So do I. I like the familiar, like going home again."

"I suppose." Kent looked at his watch. "With some luck, we should be there in another couple of hours or so." He pointed out the window. "There. See the river? There through the trees. That's the Rio Grande. We made this drive in the summer before. It was amazing, but not like the drive through the mountains."

"Maybe that's a reason for me to return next summer. I think I'd like to visit Grey Sage again. Maybe attend one of Maude's writers' retreats."

Kent rested his hand on top of Emily's and gave it a squeeze. "Sounds like a plan. I could be your driver and guide."

"Sounds like another plan, and I'd really like to see these mountains in shades of green."

"Oh, the only green you'll be seeing today is the money you spend. Taos is at about nine thousand feet, so we'll be doing some climbing the closer we get. Mountain peaks around here still have snow on them in June, so more than likely all these mountains will be blanketed today."

The van remained silent except for the low hum of instrumental Christmas music playing. Until, with no warning, chaos entered their quiet peace. With a muffled cry, Gordy suddenly turned hard right and left the road. The loaded van careened off the highway, skidding through snow and into a leafless grove of trees between the road and the river. The vehicle buckled as Gordy turned the wheel sharply to the left. Without seatbelts to secure them, Kent and the rest of the jarred passengers instinctively grabbed the railings on the seats in front of them and held on tightly. Luggage and the Suttons' whirligig slid down the aisle. Purses and books flew through the air. Their surprised screams drowned out the music and the road noise.

Spinning out of control, the rear of the van on the driver's side slammed against a tree broadside. The van came to an abrupt stop, but the motor was still running.

When Kent looked up, he saw Gordy draped over the steering wheel. He looked around and took a quick assessment. "Emily, you okay?" He took her chin in his good hand and looked into her eyes. "Are you hurt?"

Startled, she replied, "No. I'm okay. I don't think I'm hurt anywhere, just rattled."

He kissed her forehead. "Good. Sit tight. I need to check on the others."

Kent took command as he had done with his unit in Iraq when the worst of the firefight was over. He climbed over the bags in the aisle and quickly checked the passengers one by one as he made his way to Gordy. No one reported injuries.

About the time Kent approached, Gordy raised himself up. "How bad are you hurt?" Kent asked.

Gordy wiped his nose on his shirtsleeve. "Just a nosebleed, I think." He moved his legs and arms. "Nothing broken."

Kent said, "Secure the vehicle. I'll check the passengers."

Gordy checked the gear shift and turned off the motor. He looked out the side mirrors and turned in his seat to face the door. By that time, Lily was screaming and waving one arm.

Kent caught her arm in midair. "Calm down, Lily. Are you hurting anywhere? Are you bleeding?"

"My arm. My elbow really hurts."

"You'll be just fine. You probably bruised it pretty good bouncing around." He stepped closer. "Let me see." No unusual protrusions or hanging in an odd fashion to indicate a break. "Can you move it?"

"I think so." Lily lifted her arm, moved it up and down, and to the side, and bent her elbow. She winced. "What happened?"

"Don't know yet, but no serious injuries. That's the good news."

Beatrice raised her head and whimpered. "Am I dead?"

Henry put his arm around her. "No, Bea. You're fine, just fine. We've had a little accident, but we'll be on our way soon." He looked up at Kent for reassurance.

Kent saw blood. "Colonel, looks like a nasty bump on the side of your head. I'll find something to take care of that."

"Not to worry, it's nothing. My head hit the glass, so you'd better check the window." The colonel winked at the young soldier.

Everyone else was shaken but secure. The action had seemed to move in slow motion during those few split seconds when the van swerved through the trees, but now time seemed suspended as the passengers realized what had happened.

"Emily, toss me my coat, and see if you can find my duffle bag in the mess back there. I'll be back in a minute."

Kent put on his jacket and followed Gordy outside. The wind blew sideways, lifting snow from the ground and from the limbs of the trees and whirled around them. "Man, what happened?" They trudged through powdery snow to check the damages.

"A car—a small red one—came around that curve right in the middle of the highway. It was either head on with it or take to the shoulder. I knew not to brake in case of ice, but I wasn't thinking about all these trees, just trying not to hit that car. Guess this powdery snow slowed us down, but the van was spinning so much coming off the highway. I can't believe we missed all these trees and just hit one." He wiped his nose with his handkerchief.

"You sure you're okay?"

"Yeah, just bumped my nose on the steering wheel."

Kent shielded his face and looked out into the distance. "Did you see what happened to the red car?"

"Man, it happened so fast I don't remember anything but trying to get the van off the road."

"Don't see any signs of another vehicle anywhere," Kent said, "but it's hard to see out there."

Gordy shook his head. "I had a bad feeling about this. I never should have taken this job, and I never should have let Ms. Mayfield call the shots this morning. That woman uses her head for wearing those funny hats of hers instead of logical thinking. This is all my fault."

"Placing blame's a waste of time. Things happen. You want to be a hero now? Let's fix the problem." Kent checked the passenger side of the van. No damage. He looked down the driver's side. The back third of the van cradled a tree trunk. "Well, we can't fix this, which means we're not driving out of here. We need a backup plan. What we need to fix is getting these folks to safety out of this cold. Your company has a policy about things like this?"

"You mean like canning the driver?" Gordy wiped his nose again. "In eighteen years, I've never so much as scratched a vehicle."

"Look, friend. You got witnesses. This wasn't your fault. It was your expertise that kept this vehicle from flipping and seriously hurting some folks. Or maybe we had one of those miracles Dad talked about last night. Not to worry. We'll go to bat for you. Let's get out of this wind. Can you call somebody?"

Kent and Gordy returned to the van, Gordy to the phone and Kent to let the folks know the latest. "The rear end is damaged, so we won't be driving this vehicle. But we can thank Gordy that we're not all either seriously injured or worse. He avoided a head-on collision and kept this van from turning over. He's on the phone now to get help."

Kent walked down the aisle to Emily. "Did you find my duffle bag?"

"Right here." She pointed to the seat behind her. "Why do you need your duffle bag?"

"First-aid kit. The colonel needs bandaging."

"You carry a first-aid kit?"

"Combat habit. I always carry supplies. They've come in handy more than once." He removed a small plastic box from his bag and carried it with him to the front. "Mom, the colonel needs a bit of patching up. As I recall, you're pretty good at that." He handed her the plastic box. "Thanks." He turned. "Dad, can you and Ted help me get the bags and luggage out of the aisles?"

They quickly followed Kent's orders.

When the aisle was clear, Kent said, "Mrs. Parker, you might want to move back and sit with Emily. She's not hurt, just a bit stunned."

Reba took her coat and purse and moved to the back next to Emily.

"Folks, your bags are back in place. We may be here awhile, so if you have jackets or something else warm, you may want to retrieve them."

He stepped to the front to talk to Gordy. "So what's the plan?"

"Supervisor's working on it and will call me back. Just heard on the radio the roads in and out of Taos are closed. Too bad because we're only about twenty miles out. But no help coming from that direction. Supervisor's calling Santa Fe to secure a transport vehicle. May not be so easy because of the weather and the holiday."

"Keep trying, and keep your passengers informed while I'm gone."

He turned to Lily. "Lily, you're good with that whistle. I need you to lower your window, and I need you to blow it loud and long every sixty seconds. Time it. Every sixty seconds. Do you understand?"

Lily rubbed her sore shoulder. "For God's sake, why?"

Kent was unaccustomed to someone questioning his command. "Because I said so, ma'am. You got it?" He used the lever to open the van door and took two steps down.

"Where are you going?"

Kent didn't bother to answer and slammed the door hard. As he turned away he saw Lily scrambling to get her window down and blow the whistle the first time. She blew again and again—multiple times—as he made his way back through the trees and up to the road. He made a careful survey of the area in both directions before returning to the van. By the time he stepped back in, his hair and eyebrows were covered in ice and snow.

"No sign of the red car. Just kept going, and my guess is the driver didn't phone to send help." Kent put his cold hand next to the vent where warm air was blowing. "Gordy, how long can you keep running the engine?"

"I don't know, but I'm running it until it stops or until the gas runs out. It's safe."

"It's so cold I can't even guess what the temperature might be."

Gordy looked out to the side-view mirror to see the outside temperature on the gauge there. "Eleven degrees."

Kent turned to Lily. "You can raise your window now, and put the whistle away." He looked at the colonel. "I see my mom got you fixed up, colonel. I gave her plenty of practice when I was growing up. She would have made a fantastic nurse. You feeling all right?"

"You bet. In great shape. Haven't had this kind of adventure in years."

Kent spoke to the group. "Any new injuries or reports?"

No one spoke up.

"That's good news. Seems the vehicle that caused our accident

went on his merry way and left us here to take care of ourselves."
Kent looked at his watch. "It's close to noon, and it may be a few
hours before the transport vehicle gets here. Roads in and out of
Taos are closed, so help is coming from Santa Fe. Gordy will keep the
motor running as long as he can so we'll have heat. I'd suggest you
get comfortable, find yourself some snacks or something to read, and
just enjoy yourself. We'll keep you posted."

Beatrice spoke up. "I have candy, lots of candy, and it's supposed
to make you happy."

Kent smiled at her. "Well, we may just need an extra bag or two
of happy. So glad you thought about bringing it, Miss Beatrice." He
walked to the back of the van and took a seat. It was only a matter of
seconds before Reba stood and offered him the seat next to Emily.

"Thanks, Mrs. Parker."

"No need to thank me. We should all be thanking you. I've never
seen anyone take charge so quickly and make us all feel safe. And
thank you for taking care of Emily."

He smiled. "My pleasure, ma'am." He sat down, put his arm
around Emily, and pulled her closer to him.

A quiet calm settled in the van. The wind blew relentlessly. Gordy
made periodic announcements, mostly to say help was on the way
without any details about time. Little to no traffic passed by, but three
drivers stopped. One offered help, the other two were just curious.

The passengers were amazingly content. Kent imagined they
were all silently grateful to be alive, to be out of the weather, and to
be together, much like his troops in Iraq after a skirmish.

Time passed. The gray turned almost black. The motor finally
stopped running, and the cold settled in. Kent, calm and comfortable and sure that help was on the way, didn't mind the passing of
time. Emily was near him, and he heard a familiar voice—his mother's bell-like soprano voice, the voice that had sung him lullabies.
She started the carol "Silent Night," and before long they were all
singing. Melody. Harmony. Even Lily's craggy voice with no sense of

either. It didn't matter, they were all joining in, finishing with a heart-felt, "Sleep in heavenly peace. Sleep in heavenly peace."

Only Gordy breathed a sigh of relief when he noticed the flashing red lights approaching.

Chapter Nine

Silas, comfortably seated in his favorite chair in front of the fire in the keeping room, read the daily newspaper. The pendulum clock on the mantel struck two.

Maude sat on the bar stool at the kitchen counter. She hung up the phone and scribbled something on her notepad before swiveling around to Silas. "Well, my dear, sounds like we may not be boarding our plane in the morning, which means we won't be boarding the ship either."

Silas barely moved. "And what's so bad about that?"

She joined him, sitting on the stone hearth right in front of him. "I suppose nothing, except there'll be no holiday in Curaçao. Of course, the weather could break. The travel agent said that if we miss embarkation, we could fly to one of the ports and catch the ship to finish the cruise."

He lowered the paper slightly and looked at Maude. "And why would we want to do that?"

"At least we'd have a holiday, and I could check Curaçao off my list."

He folded the paper and put it on the foot-high stack of reading material on the floor beside his chair before picking up his cup. "And would it disappoint you too much if we checked that off your list on another holiday?"

Sensing his reluctance, she confronted him. "Silas, did you not want to make this trip? You seem not the least bit disappointed."

He took a sip of coffee. "Not so much."

"What do you mean, 'not so much'? You didn't want so much to take the trip from the beginning? Or you're not so much disappointed now?"

"Means about the same thing in the end, doesn't it?" Silas put down his cup and slid to the edge of his chair, closer to Maude. "Now, look, Maude. You may find this a bit surprising, but I don't mind 'so much' being here at Christmas this year. Oh, I'd still take the cruise if we can get out tomorrow, but our recent guests brought a little Christmas back to Grey Sage, and to be honest, I rather enjoyed it."

Maude took both his hands. "Really, Silas? I mean, really, you enjoyed it?"

"I did. Reminded me of some mighty sweet times. And it was good."

Maude felt relief. "You don't know how happy that makes me. That's how I felt too, but I didn't want to say it. And when we were packing this morning, I found myself feeling dread about our leaving for this trip. Leaving this beautiful snow for sand and the pine branches for palm trees and the fireplace for some beachside bonfire."

Silas grinned. "So, would I be correct in assuming that neither of us is disappointed about being marooned here at Grey Sage at Christmas instead of on some tropical island?"

They both stood and hugged. The moment was both exciting and bittersweet.

With a pat and a smile, she motioned to Silas. "Let's go unpack our bags, and help me think of something to scramble up for dinner later."

Silas, checking Maude's decision one more time, asked, "But what if the travel agent calls and has the details worked out for us to join the cruise? We'll have to pack again."

"Oh, she won't be calling."

"How do you know? That's her job—to work out the details and iron out the wrinkles."

"I know because I'm calling her first to cancel this trip so she won't waste her time. We have trip insurance just for times like this."

Maude's calm sigh was one of purest satisfaction.

Maude stopped to make the call before unpacking. It was surprisingly easy to cancel everything. "Thank you so much," she finished up. "We'll be calling again soon to schedule another voyage, but for now, Merry Christmas."

She was hanging up the phone when Lita stormed through the door, tears streaming down her face. "Lita, my goodness, what on earth is wrong?"

Lita sniveled. "They're not coming."

"What? Who's not coming?"

"My little bluebird and her family. Their flight is canceled, and they can't get here."

"Oh, I'm so sorry. I know how much you wanted to see Doli and her family and to see her face when she opened the gift you made for her. What about driving?"

"Not possible—not enough time off work to make the long trip. That's why they chose to fly in the first place. I told them just to stay home, and we'll have a big family Christmas later." Lita wiped her eyes.

"What about Catori's family?"

"I haven't spoken with her. More than likely it means they won't be able to make it either. I think she's delaying her call to me. She knows how disappointed I'll be." Lita sobbed. "This Christmas will be a quiet one, just Alo and me, and that howling wolf that's been keeping me up at night."

Maude put her arm around Lita. "You won't be quite that lonely. Silas and I will be here too. Doli and Catori can't get in, and we can't get out."

Lita quickly turned to look at Maude. "Your trip? You're not going?"

"No, we're not going. Our flight's canceled, and no way to get there in time to embark and set sail."

Lita wiped her eyes and her facial muscles relaxed. "But you're not planning to drive somewhere else or visit family in Texas?"

"No, we just decided to stay home. We thought we'd spend Christmas with you and Alo and your girls." She smiled and shrugged. "So, now it's just the four of us. It'll certainly be a different kind of Christmas this year." She paused. "Did you come up here just to tell me that or was there something else?"

"I came because I needed your shoulder, my friend, but I'm done crying now. What would you say to a cup of hot chocolate, and we can talk about our Christmas plans? Where's Silas?"

"He's unpacking his bags, but count him in for the hot chocolate. I'll go and get him. We can unpack later." On her way out of the kitchen, she called over her shoulder, "What about Alo?"

"In the barn checking on the animals. I'll call him to come on up."

Alo was there before Lita finished grating the Mexican chocolate, and the four sat at the pine table in the corner with their steaming cups of cocoa. Silas got up without saying a word, left the room, and came back with a bottle of Kahlúa. "What about a splash of this? After all, it's Christmas." They all lifted their cups.

Without asking, Maude unfolded the Scrabble board, and play ensued. Old friends. Old habits. Old traditions. Another quiet afternoon around a familiar table. Talk of missing the girls and of Lily and her Unlikely Christmas Party trickled in and out of their conversation.

Alo glanced out the window. "Nearly dark out there, and it's only four o'clock." He rearranged his Scrabble tiles and studied the board. "It's your turn, Lita."

Lita placed five tiles on the board. "Look at that. *P-L-U-C-K*, and thirteen points. Write it down, Maude, and that puts me ahead of you, Silas."

Silas's lip curled into an impish grin. He added one letter to Lita's word. "As she said, write it down, Maude. That'll be seventeen points for me."

Lita knew Simon wasn't above making up words. "That's not a word."

"Of course it is."

"*Plucky*? I don't believe it. I've never heard that word. Have you?" Lita looked at Maude.

"Don't look at me. I'm not Mr. Webster." She reached for the paperback dictionary on the shelf. "You want to risk it? Double challenge rule, remember?"

"Yes, I don't believe it's a word. If it's a word, then what does it mean, Silas?"

He leaned back in his chair. "It means bold or fearless."

"*Plucky*?" Lita retorted. "Just listen to the way it sounds. No way that's a word. And if it is, it cannot mean bold or fearless." She looked at Maude. "One of us is about to lose a turn. Look it up!"

Maude thumbed through the dictionary, found it, and shook her head. "Looks like you're the one losing your turn, Lita. The old bird is right. He pulled another one on you."

Play continued until Silas had another victory and only darkness poured through the kitchen windows. They ate bowls of leftover soup at the same table, then Maude and Lita shared kitchen cleanup while Alo and Silas settled in front of the fire.

"The two girls I hired have Grey Sage and our casita all clean and ready for Christmas," Lita commented. "They did such a good job. Nothing left for us to do except to enjoy the holiday." She paused, unsure about how Maude would respond. "Why don't we have Christmas Eve and Christmas dinners down at our casita? We have a tree and some wreaths on the windows, and of course all my Christmas angels are out."

Maude surprised her with a quick and positive answer. "Sounds lovely. I'll help with the meals."

In the kitchen, Maude and Lita talked through plans for the next few days and how they'd spend this unusual Christmas that hadn't turn out as either had planned. Alo and Silas discussed the pros and cons of the new wind farm ideas and how much wood they'd burn before the storm let up. When the mantel clock struck seven, Alo got up out of his chair.

"We need to get out of here. Come along, Lita."

Silas followed them to the mudroom. "You shouldn't be walking in that cold. I'll drive you home."

"Thanks, but my truck's out back."

As Alo helped Lita with her jacket, the phone rang. Maude answered.

"Hi, Lily. Is your room in Taos as lovely as your suite here?" She paused. "What?" She listened some more. "Hang on, Lily." She put her hand over the receiver. "Don't leave yet. I have news."

Lita, Alo, and Silas waited at the counter, trying to make sense of Maude's side of the conversation. After a few moments of back and forth, she appeared to be finishing up.

"No, it will be fine. We're not leaving tomorrow, and your rooms will be ready for your arrival. See you in a while." Maude hung up the phone. "Seems we're not the only ones with a change of plans this evening. Lily and her party will be back here in an hour or so."

"What?" Lita asked, voicing the surprise on all their faces. "What happened?"

"They had an accident on the way to Taos and spent most of the day on the side of the road, waiting for a vehicle to pick them up and return them to Santa Fe. They couldn't get into Taos."

Silas, always the doctor, asked, "Anyone injured?"

"Nothing serious. Lily said the colonel had a nasty bump on his head and she has a bruised arm. That's all."

Alo took off his jacket and hung it on the barstool. "Where are they now?"

"Just outside Santa Fe. Lily called to ask for a hotel recommendation in town. She assumed we were still leaving tomorrow. I couldn't send this party to a hotel, so I told them to return to Grey Sage."

Lita immediately headed toward the pantry. "We'll stay and help get them fed and settled."

"Thank you. But no need to cook. Maybe some more hot chocolate. They'll have dinner in town before coming out here."

With a nod of understanding, Lita busied herself at the stove, wondering how weary their Unlikely Christmas Party must be. She could only imagine.

"How long will they be staying this time, Maude?" Silas asked.

"Not sure. Taos is off their itinerary, so the plan is to leave here and go directly to Colorado Springs."

"But when?"

She looked at Alo. "Maybe the halo around the moon would give a better answer."

Alo shrugged his shoulders. "Too cloudy to see the moon tonight."

"Lily's keeping their reservations for tomorrow night at the Broadmoor. Just depends on the weather as to when they can get away." She turned to Lita. "Are we good for breakfast and maybe lunch tomorrow?"

"We most certainly are. Have you seen the freezer and the pantry? We're good for the whole tribe through the New Year."

In spite of the situation, Lita grinned. She was always happier with a hungry crowd to feed. "We may be having a real Christmas around here after all."

The members of the Unlikely Christmas Party piled through the front door at Grey Sage, each guest loaded with bags and a story to tell. Gordy and the new driver helped with luggage and, after a brief conversation with Lily, departed for their return to Santa Fe.

Feeling a bit of déjà vu, Silas, along with Alo, returned their guests to the rooms they'd had before, while Maude put out a tray of cookies on the pine coffee table and Lita returned to the kitchen to make certain the pot of milk didn't scorch. Only a few minutes passed before the party reassembled in the gathering room, each one anxious to tell his or her version of what happened.

Lita entered with the first tray of steaming mugs of hot chocolate. "You sound like a gaggle of geese in here. I thought you might enjoy something to soothe your spirits and make you sleep like Baby Jesus tonight." She looked toward Silas. "Silas, anymore of those secret spirits of yours you care to share?"

Silas slipped away to the butler's pantry and returned with the bottle of Kahlúa. "This just makes it extra special—just like you, our Christmas guests."

No one refused. The colonel was the last to raise his cup. "So glad to be here, Silas. Wasn't sure I'd see you again on this side of heaven."

"Well, you did, didn't you?" Silas glanced at the bandage on Henry's forehead. "When you finish your hot chocolate, what do you say we slip down the hall to my office and let me take a look at that bump on your head and dress it with a clean bandage?"

Henry nodded and lifted his mug as though offering a toast. "I'm used to giving orders, but I always obey the doctor's orders."

"Don't do much doctoring anymore, but I haven't forgotten how."

Silas made the same offer to all the guests in case anyone had an injury, even a slight one that needed to be checked. Henry and Lily were the only takers who followed him down the hall.

Silas first cleaned up the cut and put a fresh dressing on Henry's head. "Didn't need stitches, and there's nothing to worry about, except maybe a slight scar." He went to the cabinet and retrieved a bottle of pills. "Here, take one of these before you retire. This and that cup of warm milk should take care of your discomfort. You should sleep well. I'll check on you again in the morning."

He turned to Lily. "Okay, what's ailing you, Lily?"

"Oh, Silas. It was dreadful. The van spun around like a top on an ice rink and slammed into a tree. It's true what they say about seeing your life pass before your eyes. I saw it, saw it all—my parents, my brother, all dead people except Maude and my students, all the paintings I've done, all the places I've visited."

"Sounds like you had a quick trip through a long life. So, tell me, where do you hurt?" He led her to a stool.

"You're still incorrigible, Silas. I'm dead serious. It was the most awful experience of my entire life."

"I'm sure it was, and you lived to tell about it. So, tell me, where do you hurt?"

"It's my right arm, mostly my elbow, right here." She pulled up her sweater sleeve. "I think in all the spinning and sliding, which seemed like an eternity, I hit my elbow really hard against the metal window frame. And trust me, I didn't laugh."

Silas saw the swelling and bruising immediately. "Okay, let me take a look." He held her arm gently and poked around a bit before manipulating the joint. "Um-huh. Sore?"

"Oh, yes. Very."

"Not so funny hitting your funny bone like that." Silas continued squeezing and examining her arm.

"Oh, no. Just one level funnier than you. Ouch!"

"You have the ulnar nerve that runs along the inside of your arm right about here," Silas explained. "When you bumped your arm, that nerve bumped the humerus."

"Don't get sassy with me, Silas Thornhill. Nothing humorous about this."

Silas chuckled. "No, Lily. The humerus is this long bone that runs through your upper arm to your shoulder. You've bruised this area. I don't think it's cracked or broken." He reached for the same bottle of pills. "Here, take a couple of these when you go to bed, and I'll get you an ice pack. We always keep a couple in the freezer. Twenty minutes with the ice pack tonight, and I'll check it tomorrow morning."

Lily softened. "Thanks, Silas. Thanks for checking me, but mostly thanks for allowing us to return to Grey Sage tonight. After today, we all needed a bit of comforting, and Grey Sage does provide warmth and comfort. And where else can you get real hot chocolate with a decadent dash of Kahlúa?"

She paused and pulled down her sweater sleeve. "Maude told me about your cruise plans. I'm sorry. Seems we've all had a drastic change in plans today, but I promise to get this party out of your house as soon as the weather lets up."

"Glad you're here, Lily, and your rolling Christmas party too. Tomorrow will be a better day."

They returned to the gathering room.

Most of the guests, Maude noted, were seated in the same seats they'd claimed upon their arrival Tuesday evening. Beatrice stood in front of the fireplace as though she were in her tutu at center stage in St. Petersburg. Her rendition of the day's events was dramatic.

"I'm so glad I wasn't dead. I was asleep, but then, it started—the spinning and the spinning—like a pirouette without enough rosin on my pointe shoes to keep me from sliding and no time or place for spotting to keep from getting dizzy. Oh, it was all so horrendous. I really thought I was dead, but Henry saved me. Then there was a loud thud, and we stopped."

When Beatrice breathed, Lily jumped in. "Oh, but you were safe, and now you'll have such an incredible story to tell your daughter. If the weather lifts, you'll be joining her tomorrow evening at the Broadmoor."

Beatrice perked her head. "Yes, and when we get to the Broadmoor, Dorothy will listen until I have finished my whole story. She will listen without interruption, Lily. She has more polite manners than you. What made you think that was the end of my story? It wasn't."

A soft murmur of laughter went around the room. No one else dared to speak to Lily like that.

Lily rolled her whistle between her fingers. "Oh, pardon me, Beatrice. You were nearly breathless, and when you finally inhaled, I thought you were done."

Beatrice looked at Lily. "Well, I wasn't." She tottered on her little bird legs and turned to the others. "When the van stopped spinning, Kevin there ..." She pointed to Kent.

To avoid any rebuke resembling the one Lily had gotten, no one bothered to correct her. At least she'd remembered the first two letters of his name.

"Kevin stood straight up and took charge. No one questioned him except Lily one time. But he told her and shut her up. He was just like a hero in a movie, like a general leading his troops. Why he was just the pluckiest young man I've ever seen! We should give Kevin a huge round of applause."

The guests obliged and cheered for Kent. Lily sat down on the sofa next to Reba.

Lita was seated next to Maude. At the sound of the word *pluckiest*, she squeezed Maude's hand and muffled her laugh, then leaned over and whispered, "Plucky, again? Never heard the word, and now twice in the same day. Suppose it means something?"

"Yes, it means you learned a new word, and that Silas and Bea have been working the same crossword puzzles."

Lily stood up. "Are you finished, Beatrice?"

"For now."

"With your permission, then ... We'll have breakfast at eight in the morning, people. We'll leave as soon as Gordy gets us another vehicle and we get some sense of clearance on the weather. Please have your bags packed. Could be on a moment's notice. I will stay in touch with Gordy about our departure." She turned to where Maude was seated. "Thank you again for opening the doors of Grey Sage to us and for making this Unlikely Christmas Party—on broken wheels, I might add—feel welcome again."

Maude nodded and smiled and tried not to think of what the weather might have to say about tomorrow's plans.

Chapter Ten

*M*aude woke, not because the fire had gone out in the kiva or because of the howling wolf outside or the hooting owl that had recently taken up residence in the pine tree next to the window, but because she had something on her mind. It was three twenty. She eased out of bed, put on her fleece robe, and grabbed her flashlight from next to the bedside table. She then walked through the halls to Lily's room and tapped on the door.

No answer.

She tapped again. Still no answer.

She used her master key and turned the lock and opened the door.

"Lily," she whispered. "It's me, Maude." No answer and no indication of movement. She stepped closer to the bed and touched Lily's arm. "Lily, wake up."

Lily's red corkscrew curls spilled out from the cord of her sleep mask and over her pillow like extra-long fringe on a wool horse blanket. She tried to sit up. "Ouch." She grabbed her arm and lay back down. "Oh my, that smarts. Maude, is that you?"

"Of course it's me." Maude sat on the edge of the bed.

Lily removed her sleep mask, smoothed her hair away from her eyes, and pushed up and propped herself on the pillows. "What in the world of all that makes absolutely no sense do you want? It's the middle of the night."

"Well, I—"

"Don't tell me. You still have that habit you had when we were in college. You get this bright idea for your art project in the middle of the night and you turn on every light in the apartment and start to work as if the whole world is awake and just waiting to see your creation."

"Something like that."

"Well, thank you for not turning on the light, but would you turn off the flashlight? We never needed a light to talk before. What's your bright idea?"

Maude obliged and turned off the light. "I was thinking. You and your group are already here. The weather's not looking good for the next couple of days. And even if it stops snowing, there's always the threat of warming and refreezing and ice on the roads. So, why don't you just make the decision right now to stay? We can all have Christmas here together."

"Right now, in the middle of the night, I have to make a decision? It couldn't wait until morning?"

"I guess it could, but why wait? Then I'll sleep better because I have some plans in mind."

"But we have plans too, Maude. We have reservations at the Broadmoor."

"They'll understand about the weather. Besides, aren't you staying there all next week? This way, you can have Christmas here and then again when you get to the Broadmoor. You won't lose any money even if you have to pay them. We'll charge you nothing for your nights at Grey Sage."

"Sounds inviting." Lily paused to think. "And I'd rather be here at Grey Sage with you and Silas than anywhere else for Christmas. But Maude, these people are expecting me to get them to Colorado Springs tomorrow, especially Bea."

"Only Beatrice is depending on that. The rest of them are with you because they wanted a Christmas to remember. And they can have a lovely Christmas right here with us. And besides, you probably can't get her there anyway. And if we go ahead and make a decision now, then I'll make plans for a Christmas they won't forget."

"A decision to stay? Right now?"

"Yes, right now. This way it's settled. No more up in the air about

Christmas. You can relax, and you'll have no problems. I promise to make it all right with Beatrice."

Silence.

"Lily, did you go back to sleep?"

"No, I'm thinking."

"Well, think in a hurry. I'd like to get back to bed and get some sleep. Big day tomorrow." Maude turned on the flashlight and pointed it toward the door.

"Okay, okay. We'll stay, but you promise to help me make it agreeable with everyone."

"Yes, right after I make it agreeable with Silas. Go back to sleep."

Maude slipped quietly back into bed with Silas, and slept peacefully for a while. When she woke again, it was almost too early to even be called morning. The embers in the corner kiva had gone cold through the night. Silas's muffled snoring sounded like a purring cat, but Maude was wide awake now, shrouded in flannel sheets and a down comforter and imagining her day.

I never have been one for surprises, but the surprise early storm dumping a foot of snow wasn't so bad. And the surprise of the inn filled with an Unlikely Christmas Party makes it better. And then the total surprise of Christmas at Grey Sage again? That's the best.

Maude had lived here for almost fifty years, and she had never seen weather like this. She had only to listen to the howling winds and to look through the undraped transom windows at the snow still blowing sideways to know that Lily's middle-of-the-night decision was a good one. She lay still, trying not to bother Silas, and thought of her guests, assessing how much food was in the larder and imagining how she might make a memorable time for these disappointed folks whose holiday plans had not included being stranded in an undecorated mountain inn during a snowstorm. If Christmas found the inn with filled with guests, then Maude determined the inn would be filled with Christmas, and everything that meant.

Maude pushed the covers away and sat straight up. "Silas ... Silas, wake up, we have work to do."

Silas turned over and rubbed his eyes. "Yesterday, you pushed me out of bed to pack. So what is it this morning?"

By this time, Maude was on her feet. "We have work to do. It's almost Christmas. We still have ten guests, and we don't even have a Christmas tree."

"But they're leaving this morning. We don't need a tree. We're having Christmas at the casita with Alo and Lita, and they already have a tree."

Maude shook the covers. "We *were* having Christmas with Alo and Lita, but plans have changed. I had a talk with Lily earlier, and they have agreed to stay."

Silas stretched and raised himself up on his elbows. "Earlier? My stars, Maude, it's ten 'til five now. When did you have this conversation with Lily?" Then he came to his senses. "Oh, one of those middle-of-the-night flashes of inspiration?"

"Yes. She's agreed to stay, and we need to get this place looking like Christmas."

Silas lumbered out of bed and grabbed his robe on the chair. "From the sound of your voice, I'm supposing that we'll have a Christmas tree up before the day's over."

Maude pulled up the sheets and comforter and straightened the bed. "Right again. We'll have a tree—no, two. One big one in the great room and a smaller one in the dining room. And fresh garlands on the mantle and candles in the windows. We'll get out the ornaments and my collection of manger scenes, and—"

Silas stopped in his tracks and rubbed his head. "Wait a minute, Maude. We're supposed to cut trees and garlands in this weather? And isn't all that other stuff you mentioned still packed away?"

"Yes, and I know exactly where. It's in the storage closet at the end of the east hallway."

Silas shrugged his shoulders. "I guess the way my bones are feeling this morning, I should be grateful we don't have an attic. Alo and I are getting too old for this, especially tree cutting when there's a foot of snow on the ground."

Silas was grumpier than usual and headed for the bathroom to get dressed. "You know, Maude, if you hadn't allowed Lily to bring her entourage back here last night, we wouldn't have all this work to do. We'd be having a quiet Christmas at home."

Maude followed him into their walk-in closet, which was almost as large as their bedroom. "Well, they're here. And Silas, those people are not Lily's entourage. They're folks like you and me: folks who are running from Christmas because life hurts sometimes, and Christmas is too tender a time to be alone." Maude reached for a heavy sweater. "And Lily was good enough to make Christmas travel plans for them so they wouldn't have to suffer through a miserable Christmas. And besides, if they weren't here, you and I'd be spending this Christmas here alone with Alo and Lita and that howling wolf. As it is, we'll have some interesting guests around our Christmas table."

"Pardon me, but as interesting as these folks may be, they're really strangers, all of them, except for Lily. And Henry. I like him."

Maude adjusted her shirt collar underneath her sweater. She picked up her hairbrush and brushed her long white hair, twisting it around her finger into a tight bun on the top of her head. "Silas, you said yesterday you were glad they came and that you enjoyed having them. Was that the truth?"

He reached for his pants. "It was the truth. I did enjoy them, but I didn't know I would be spending Christmas with them. They're strangers, Maude—well, except for Lily."

"It's Christmas, and they're here. Perhaps you should look at the rest of these strangers as friends you haven't made yet."

Silas grumbled some more. "So, what do you know about these interesting strangers who are about to become our friends?"

"Well, Lily's not a stranger since I met her about fifty years ago. And let's see, Ted and Laura Sutton are retired professors from back East. Ted's in pharmacology and Laura in music theory, I believe. Lily met them at some academic conference years ago, and they've been going on study tours with her. He seems interesting enough, but she ..."

Silas rolled his eyes. "She is cold. A very strange stranger."

"Oh, but there's Beatrice, the lovely, shriveling ballerina. You said she was entertaining." Maude couldn't hide her chuckle.

"Okay, what about the others?"

"Silas, I already told you about these folks before they arrived the first time."

"I know, but I wasn't paying much attention before. I didn't know they were moving in."

"You seem to like the Martins already. And then there's Reba and Emily."

"Hmm, so we have Lily the retired-art-professor-turned-travel-agent, a pharmacist, a pianist who won't play the piano, a wrinkled-up ballerina, two veterans of wars sixty years apart, a minister with a sweet wife, and a psychotherapist with a beautiful young daughter who's more put together than her mother. Sounds like the only thing they have in common is they all had a bright idea to take a Christmas trip." Silas just shook his head.

Maude walked over and hugged him. "So when did you get to be Scrooge?" She kissed his cheek. "Come on, Si, don't waste your time being so Scroogey. We have things to do, like making a memorable Christmas for all of us."

"You're right, Maude. I suppose if God could come to earth at Christmas and make us his children, we can at least try to make these strangers our friends."

Maude secretly smiled and headed to the kitchen. She could hear that Alo and Lita were already busy. The smell of brewed coffee warmed her soul as she passed through the dining room. She stopped in the butler's pantry long enough to pour herself a cup.

Maude knew Lita was making bread because she was humming. Lita always hummed a lullaby while she kneaded bread or biscuits. She declared it kept her from being too rough with the dough and kneading it too long.

"So, are you taking Silas's job this morning making the coffee?" She hugged Lita. "You're up earlier than usual."

"Couldn't sleep, so I figured I might as well get up and get busy. That howling wolf. Gives me the shivers and makes Alo pace. I only hear one, but he's convinced himself there are two and possibly three." She reached for more flour. "Brings out his hunter instinct. He wants to protect his animals."

"I'm with you about the shivers. I heard him again last night. He was doing a duet with the hoot owl in the pine tree right outside our window. Such is life in these mountains. What's for breakfast? I know it's bread. I heard you humming."

"Cinnamon scones, orange butter, chorizo-and-sweet-potato hash."

Maude leaned over the skillet where the chorizo and sweet potatoes were caramelizing. "Smells wonderful. Can you handle this by yourself for a few more minutes? I need to check some things in the storage room in the east hall."

"Certainly. The store room, huh? What do you need in the storage room?"

"Christmas decorations. Our guests are staying for Christmas."

"Since when was that decided? Alo hasn't even given you the latest weather report." Lita pulled the sticky dough from her hands.

"I talked to Lily earlier. It's the wisest thing to do, and it'll be fun." Maude put her mug on the counter to look for her keys.

"So after more than twenty years, we're celebrating Christmas at Grey Sage again?" Lita sounded surprised, if hopeful.

"That we are, Lita. I didn't think I'd ever spend another Christmas here, but ..." She paused, considering her words. "It's time we take these broken dreams and memories of past Christmases and make something good of them again."

Lita gave her a thoughtful look, then put a towel over the bread dough and moved to the sink to wash her hands. "I'm glad the inn is full. It makes me happy. I was feeling so sad that neither of the girls will be here. Catori called last night. This is the first Christmas we have ever been apart, Maude."

Maude had found the keys and started out. She turned around, came back, and hugged her friend. "I'm so sorry, Lita. But the girls will be here when the weather clears. And now, with the inn full and the girls coming later, we'll just keep having Christmas for a few days. And we're going to have a glorious Christmas for our guests. A snowstorm, an accident, and Christmas at Grey Sage weren't exactly in their plans either, you know?" She leaned over to kiss Lita's cheek, then headed out.

In the hallway, though, she stopped to take a breath. Everything was moving so quickly. Yes, it was mainly because of her own plans, which she felt were right and true. But still ... Some small part of herself questioned her decision to have Christmas again at Grey Sage.

For a moment, Maude relived those first few days of shock, disbelief, and agony following Elan's death. That season had been beyond anything they'd ever experienced before—or ever would. From the moment Silas had climbed down to the rock-filled crevice and cradled Elan's lifeless body, examined every limb, looked desperately for a pulse ... the world had changed. Elan's death became the hinge upon which time hung. On one side was the time they'd had with him, and on the other side was the time in which they had him no more. The house was cold and silent on that other side. But slowly, they'd learned how to do life without him. And in time, their faith, though shaken to its roots, sprouted again.

But Christmas was never the same.

Maude walked down the east hall with coffee in hand and jangled keys to find the one for the storage room. She stopped before opening the door and placed her palm against it.

I locked away Christmas in this room after Elan died. If it weren't for our Unlikely Christmas Party, I'm not certain I'd be standing here. She took a shaky but fortifying breath. *But ... it's time*, she told herself.

Inserting the key into the lock, she slowly turned it, then opened the door and walked in before she could change her mind. Her eyes perused the shelves and boxes like she was searching for Christmas again—her memories cloaking and squeezing her.

It's quieter than a tomb in here. And all the boxes ... These boxes are

covered in dust. Guess that's what happens when things are locked away
untouched for more than twenty years.

She chose one box, dusted off the lid, and placed it on the floor.
After a moment of staring at it, she knelt to open it. She was sorting
through the tree ornaments it contained when Silas walked in. He too
paused to take a look around the room, his eyes falling on the visual
reminders of Christmases past.

Finally, he cleared his throat. "Lita said I'd find you here. Need
any help?"

Maude got up off her knees and hugged him, hoping he wasn't
feeling the same pain she harbored. She tried to lighten the moment.
"So, Scrooge is gone, and my sweet Silas has returned?"

"Well, just the sound of that word *Scroogey* made me realize the
folly of my ways. And look—" He motioned as Alo came through
the door. "Alo's here with me, and we're waiting for our morning's
orders."

Knowing Silas processed things best when busy with hands-on
work, Maude pointed out the boxes and bins that needed to be carried to the gathering room. "And I'm looking for two Christmas tree
stands," she instructed. "They're around here somewhere. Once we
find them and haul these boxes into the gathering room, you gentleman will need to find us two Christmas trees and cut some fresh pine
for the garlands."

Silas reached for a box on the shelf above Maude's head. "Here's
one of the stands. I'm guessing it would have been too much for you
to have put them both together. And I was wondering about breakfast. I don't usually go to work until after I eat."

Maude stood with both hands on her hips. "Compromise?
Breakfast isn't for another hour anyway, so what about at least getting these boxes out of here before then? Then after breakfast,
maybe some of our guests will want to join you to find us a couple
of Christmas trees. And while you're out doing that, the ladies can
begin the decorating."

She carefully stepped back through the maze of boxes. "It's all yours, gentlemen. Start hauling. I'm headed to the kitchen to help Lita plate the hash and scones."

Grumbling, because that's what old men did at such chores, Alo and Silas moved boxes and wiped the dust away as they stacked them. That is, until Alo saw something he hadn't thought of in a very long time. He stopped, staring at the large black plastic bins on the top shelf next to the door, straining his eyes to read the faded words on the label. It was Maude's curly-cue handwriting.

Silas tried to hand him a box. "Here, Alo, take this."

But Alo didn't move, his eyes fixated on the shelf. Silas finally looked up, following Alo's gaze to the black plastic bins. Alo figured Silas knew all too well what filled those four bins.

Alo turned to look at him. "Elan's train. I forgot about Elan's train."

Silas moved toward Alo. They both stood shoulder to shoulder, staring at the bins. "I know. I packed those bins many years ago. I should have done something with that train set, but ... I never got around to it."

"Or my friend, maybe you decided it was Elan's, and you had no right to do anything with it."

They stood in silence for a few moments before returning to their work.

Maude kept herself busy helping get breakfast on the table. By the time it was ready and the chairs around the dining table were occupied by guests, the gathering room was filled with dusty boxes of tree ornaments and manger scenes and an array of luggage lined up in the front hallway.

Plates were served, and the coffee flowed. Amid conversation describing sore muscles and bruises that had appeared overnight, the colonel turned to Alo. "I heard some howling in the night. Didn't sound like a dog. Is that common around here?"

Henry's question brought a sudden silence followed by a round of comments from the other guests who had heard it too.

Alo spoke up in reply. "Wolves. Not so common, but they're moving back into these parts. Haven't seen one yet, only tracks."

Beatrice wiped the jelly from her lip. "Oh, I saw *Peter and the Wolf* last year in Chicago. The music was divine, and so was the dance. Made me want to get my ballet slippers out again. I do that sometime anyway. But honestly, I was a bit appalled with the wolf, especially after they strung him up." Beatrice, without even trying, totally perplexed the others.

Obviously attempting to rescue them all from Beatrice's rambling stories, Kent called for Lita. "Lita, most talented chef, could you describe what we're eating this morning?" He knew how to make her smile.

"The hash is made of sweet potatoes grown right down the road and chorizo, which is a spicy Spanish sausage, and scrambled eggs with a dash of secret ingredient." She winked at Kent. "And what goes better with cinnamon-and-raisin scones than orange butter?"

Kent waved his napkin in silent applause. "Delicious. We're all still waiting for you to adopt us."

When there was little left on their plates and the prickly-pear jelly bowl was empty, Maude stood at the head of the table to make her announcement. "Well, friends, Lily and I have talked, and the good news is that we are adopting you, at least for a couple of more days."

The guests glanced around at each other without saying a word.

"I know this Christmas isn't turning out exactly as any of you planned, and honestly, not as we planned either. The weather has made it impossible for all of us to travel. So we need to make new plans for us all since we'll be spending Christmas here together. Lita tells me we have plenty of food for the next few days. Now, it may not be a Christmas dinner like you would have in Chicago, but nonetheless, we'll have Christmas dinner Santa Fe style. Or maybe Lita-style."

Kent pushed back away from the table. "I'm not concerned about anything we eat at this table. I'll just have more time to discover Lita's secret ingredient."

Maude turned to Beatrice. "And since you'll be late meeting your daughter for Christmas, Beatrice, we have something special planned for you. We are decorating Grey Sage today, and we could use your help. The only thing that looks like Christmas around here is the snow on the cedar trees, but come lunchtime, I expect this place to look like Christmas exploded in here. Silas and Alo will go out to cut a couple of Christmas trees and some fresh greenery just for you. In fact, some of you gentlemen may want to go with them. And ladies, Beatrice could use your help adorning the trees and putting some garland and candles around."

Everyone clapped and smiled, and the chatter started. Maude was relieved. "And, I might add, as our Christmas present to you, there'll be no charge for your room and board for the next couple of nights. Please consider yourselves our guests for Christmas."

Maude saw Lita's wide grin from across the room.

Colonel Walton stood. "You mean we're going to have Christmas around here after all? Well, then, let's get started. I used to be fairly good at swinging an axe."

Lily rang the bell that Lita had placed next to her plate. "Okay, people, the first order of business is this: Get your luggage back to your rooms, and then get yourselves busy with making this place look like it's Christmas around here. Maude says when the decorating's done, then the real partying and games begin. Get to it, you Party people."

That handled, Lily went to Maude. "You did it. And I'm spending Christmas with my very best friend."

Maude hugged Lily. "See, I told you. They're happy, even Beatrice, and we're having Christmas at Grey Sage for the first time in many years."

Maude left Lily at the table and went straightaway to turn on the Christmas music. She stood at a distance in the doorway, imagining the hustle and bustle ensuing in every direction once the fun started this morning. The sound of Bing Crosby crooning "I'll Be Home for Christmas" coaxed her to tears. Happy tears.

I am home, and Christmas is returning to Grey Sage.

Chapter Eleven

*T*he return of Christmas at Grey Sage had been slow in coming, but the pace was picking up, and Maude was hoping for willing hands to assist her.

I'll put Lily in charge of the decorating the trees. Beatrice and Emily can help her. That way Beatrice is corralled and Emily and her mother are separated. Reba and Iris can handle the greenery and putting out the manger scenes. They need to get more acquainted. And Laura ... She sits around looking like someone licked all the red off her peppermint stick. I know how to fix that. That's the ladies taken care of. Now on to the gentlemen.

Maude turned to Henry. "Colonel, you seem to have a special knack for keeping that fire going. So, would you mind taking on that responsibility this morning? Oh, and if you'd please add the fireplace in the gathering room just off the kitchen, I know Lita would show you where the never-empty coffeepot is—the one with her special coffee concoction—if you'll keep her fire going."

The colonel bristled a bit. "But I told you I was mighty good at swinging an axe. I know you're just looking out for this old man, and I'll enjoy that special coffee, but in my day ..."

Alo responded. "We don't discount you, sir. But in this wind, I'm counting on my chainsaw to cut these trees down before the wind cuts me into."

Maude chimed in. "The keeper of the fire on a day like today, Colonel, is front-line work. And Alo, we need greenery, but we don't need the snow that comes with it, so give it a good shaking before you start bringing it in."

Before she could ask, Kent spoke up. "Ma'am, I only have one good arm, but it's a good one, so don't count me out with the tree cutting."

"Great. Why don't you and your dad go with Alo and Silas? It's biting cold out there, but if I know Alo, he's already chosen which trees to cut. He knows every inch of this property, and I've accused him of knowing the chipmunks by name. You boys will have this done in short order."

Kent saluted Maude. "Yes, ma'am, and these branches will have not one snowflake on them when we bring them through the door."

Maude moved closer to where the Suttons sat on the loveseat. "And Ted, would you help the colonel haul in the wood? You can follow Silas now, and he'll show you where it's stacked. Just leave your jacket hanging in the mudroom if you'd like."

Ted agreed. Laura sat silently beside him.

"Laura, I know Lita could use a bit of extra help in the kitchen. She's a great teacher if you're interested in a cooking lesson."

Laura appeared slightly alarmed, but Maude nodded encouragement. *Laura will come out of that kitchen with a different attitude after a couple of hours with Lita. Lita's a joy giver, and Laura needs an overstuffed gift bag of joy this morning.*

With a smile, Lita took Laura's arm and led her into the kitchen.

Maude continued passing out assignments. Her artists' and writers' retreats had sharpened her discernment about folks and honed her skill of pairing them together. "Now Lily, you and Bea and Emily are in charge of decorating the trees. You might want to start going through those boxes of decorations over there until the trees arrive. Hope you don't mind the dust."

Maude pointed Reba and Iris to the boxes with the nativity scenes. "Just choose three or four, and put them out where you think they should go. If you come across the one made of olive wood, maybe you could put that one on the hearth."

Maude remembered their trip to Israel one Christmas, and meticulously choosing this particular set for its delicate wood grain. But mostly she remembered why she'd always put it on the hearth: It was unbreakable. She turned to look at the stone hearth, and imagined a curly-haired little Elan assembling and reassembling every piece, telling the Christmas story over and over again.

The morning bustled with activity. The men traipsed off through the snow to cut trees and branches. The women brushed years of dust off boxes and brought the colors of Christmas back to Grey Sage. Christmas music poured through the speakers in every room, and Lita kept the coffee urn full and the teakettle whistling. Maude floated from the kitchen to the gathering room, directing and admiring their work, but mostly remembering how Christmas used to be at Grey Sage.

Lita opened a drawer, pulled out an apron, and offered it to Laura. "May I call you Laura since we'll be cooking together this morning?"

Laura reluctantly tied the apron around her neck and waist. "Yes, of course, please do. And I'll call you Lita."

Lita motioned for Laura to follow her to the pantry. "I'll hand you some things, and could you please put them on the kitchen island? Our mission this morning is to get a hot lunch prepared, and at the same time, start the baking. I've already done some baking because I was expecting our daughters and their families, but they can't get here because of the weather."

Lita organized a brigade of flour, cornmeal, sugar, a whole tray of bottled spices and seasonings, cans of tomato sauce, onions, and potatoes.

"Oh, my, this is an odd assortment." Laura looked around, lost.

Lita had grabbed a big stock pot. "Do you cook? Or do you like to cook?"

"I get by with simple meals, but if it goes beyond that, we call the caterer." That was nothing she wanted Lita to know, but it just slipped out. "Although, I do salads very well."

"Great. You will make the salad for lunch. But first you must make my famous Cold Christmas Cake, a family recipe passed down to me. Five generations of Hopi women in my family have been making this cake. It's important to get it made this morning. It has to stay in the fridge for two days before cutting."

"Oh, a cake?" She felt the doubt kick in. "I must tell you I've never made a cake before. Perhaps since it's such a family tradition and you have done it so often, maybe I could do something else while you do the cake."

"No, thank you. I trust you with the cake, but I trust no one to make my chili. This recipe will be a piece of cake for you." Lita laughed a hearty laugh that signaled how happy she was when rattling pots and pans. "You play piano, right?"

Laura nodded.

"My daughters play piano. I never got to learn, but I know playing piano means you can read music, words, and work your fingers. So that's all you need to make my Cold Christmas Cake." Lita patted Laura on the back and handed her a half pound of walnuts and a half pound of pecans. "See that cutting board over there? Get it and chop these nuts up coarsely, not too fine. Then I'll tell you what to do next."

Laura complied and slowly began chopping the nuts, checking to make certain they were the right consistency. As she worked, Lita told her about Doli and Catori growing up and taking piano lessons, and how the piano recitals always caused such a stir in their home. Surprised at herself, Laura rattled back about how it had caused the same stir when she was growing up, and how afraid she was to play in public, and that's why she'd decided to teach music theory.

"The nuts look great. Now put them in this big bowl." Lita handed her a large stainless-steel mixing bowl. "Next step—and we're cheating just a bit here, but cooks have secrets, and I hope you'll keep mine—we're using boxed vanilla wafers."

"Cookies in a cake?" Laura hadn't heard that one before.

Lita chuckled. "When you finish with these cookies, they won't look like cookies anymore." She handed her a rolling pin and a plastic bag. "Put the cookies in here. Roll them, pound them, I don't care. They just need to be fine, almost like flour when you finish. This is a good thing to do when your knickers are in a twist about something."

For the first time, Laura laughed. "That's funny. I don't think I've ever worn knickers."

"Maybe not, but I'd wager your apron strings have been in a knot about something or other."

Laura laughed again. "Yes, you'd be right about that." She pounded, rolled, then pounded some more, and listened to Lita's wild stories about growing up with a sister and a brother farther north in the Sangre de Cristo Mountains and all the wild animals they'd tried to make pets.

"That sounds like a perfect childhood," she offered at one point.

"I suppose it was. When you finish pounding and rolling, mix those crumbs with the nuts in the bowl. What about your childhood? Where did you grow up?"

"I grew up on the banks of the Huron River in Ann Arbor, Michigan. I was an only child, and quite frankly, I was born to parents who were too old and too set in their ways to have children. They were both professors at the university, so their idea of playing was a Saturday afternoon at the museum or some performance on the university campus." Laura rolled and pulverized the wafers like she was pounding away the crumbs of her childhood memories, trying to change them into something finer.

"But you said you grew up on the banks of the river? That must have been a great place to explore." Lita looked at the wafer crumbs and approved and pointed to the bowl.

Laura stopped the pummeling. "Oh, it would have been I suppose, but I wasn't allowed to do that. Too dangerous, my parents said, or I might have gotten too dirty. So I was only allowed to play in the garden—a very manicured garden thanks to my father and a hired gardener."

"Oh, what a shame! If you weren't allowed to explore outside, what on earth did you do with your time?"

"I read and practiced the piano. My mother insisted on violin lessons, but that never seemed to work. My grandmother taught me how to tat and embroider."

Lita wiped her eyes on sleeve, sniffed, and looked at Laura. "Not to worry, your story's not making me cry. It's the onions I just finished chopping. Although, your story is a sad one—tatting when you could have been tadpole hunting."

"I really shouldn't have complained to you, but—" She shrugged. "—you're so easy to talk to. My parents took good care of me and gave me a fine education so that I could support myself. But I fear they were fastidious and passed along those habits to me, and life-ingrained habits are difficult to break."

Lita laughed out loud. "I don't know what *fastidious* means, but it doesn't sound like much fun." She handed Laura a bag of shredded coconut and a box of raisins. "Another shortcut secret. My mother would have been cracking fresh coconuts and shredding it herself. This way is easier. Stir the coconut and the raisins in with the nuts and cookie crumbs."

Laura followed Lita's instructions, stirring gently and with a bit of hesitation.

Lita smiled. "Go ahead. Mix it up good. You're not going to injure it."

Laura tried, but just couldn't bring herself to stir all that vigorously.

"Now before the last step, you need to prepare this springform pan. Don't worry; there are no springs. The pan is made so we can unlock this clasp and remove the sides of the pan." Lita showed Laura the pan and handed her a stick of butter. "Grease the pan first."

Laura took the butter but didn't move. "Ah, do you have a secret easy way to do this?"

"Yes. Peel the paper off and rub the stick of butter all around the bottom and sides of the pan." She watched as Laura buttered the pan with the same careful hesitance as her stirring.

"Now comes the fun part." Lita opened a can of condensed milk and poured it over the contents of the bowl. "Now go to the sink and wash your hands with that soap in the bottle."

Laura did as she was told and returned. "What is that? That creamy stuff?" She was a head taller than Lita, she realized, as she stood and peered over her shoulder.

"Oh, sister, if you don't know what this is, then you've missed out on something you need to know about. It's sweetened condensed milk, extra thick and extra sweet. My ancestors would have used thick goat's milk with molasses, but we're fresh out of goats."

Laura backed away. "I guess I can be grateful for that."

"Here comes the fun part I told you about. Now put your hands in there and squish all that between your fingers and stir it and knead it until it's all mixed together. Might want to take your rings off."

Laura raised her eyebrows, then slowly pushed up her sweater sleeves and removed her rings. "My hands? In there? What about using the spoon?"

"Your hands are your very best kitchen tools. Get to work." Lita backed away to watch.

Laura started slowly until her hands disappeared into mush. "How strange this feels!" She pulled her hands out of the mixture and stared at them. Then she went back to work and slowly began to mix vigorously. Unable to help herself, she laughed out loud—not that apologetic chuckle from before, but a real, honest-to-God laugh. She held up her hands. "Look, Lita, my hands are dirty. And in case you're wondering, I'm not being at all fastidious, and my knickers are almost untwisted."

Lita joined her in her laughter. "When you get through playing there, dump that stuff into that springform pan and press it down real good. Then pat it softly like you would a baby's bottom. After that, it's ready for the fridge."

"That's all? You mean I've made a Cold Christmas Cake?"

"That's all unless you want to do it the way my ancestors did it. My grandmother told me her mother would wrap the cake in layers of leaves and bind it with vine. Then she'd take it down to the creek, where the water ran cold, and leave it there for the icy water to pour over it for a couple of days. On Christmas morning, they'd fetch the cake—if the bears hadn't already found it."

"Guess it kept the goat's milk from spoiling. But it just sounds like an adventure to me." For the first time in a long while, Laura felt a genuine smile come across her face.

Reba knelt on the floor next to a large green bin. She took the lid off a box, gently removed the tissue paper, and lifted the figure from the box. "Iris, look at the exquisite detail of this wise man."

Iris touched the robe. "That's a work of art. Feel the fabric and look at his face."

Maude had walked through the gathering room just in time to hear their conversation. "You're right, Reba, it is a work of art. And every box in that green bin holds another piece."

Iris took the figure from Reba. "More pieces like this?"

"The Holy Family, two more wise men, an angel, and two shepherds. I used to display these on the mantle, cradled in cedar branches. Sometimes I left them up for several weeks after Christmas just so I could enjoy their beauty."

Reba read the box lid. "Ferrigno?"

Maude knelt next to Reba and removed another box. "Yes, Silas and I bought these in Naples, Italy. And I was so fortunate to meet the artist who made them. Comes from over a hundred years of Ferrigno artists. We paid far more than we should have, but it was art, and very beautiful art." Maude got up. "Enjoy, ladies. Look closely. Just put the boxes back in the bin when you have all the pieces out."

Iris opened another box. "Oh, it's Mary, Mother of God. Look at her porcelain face and her eyes, sort of half closed and looking down."

Reba was engaged in putting the wise man's headpiece on and placing the gold box in his hands, extended and ready to offer his gift. Iris leaned over toward Reba to get her attention. "Look Reba, Mary looks just like Emily—that perfectly shaped face and those beautiful and gentle eyes."

Reba stopped to look. She put down the wise man and took the figure from Iris. "You're right. She does look like Emily, my beautiful daughter with a beautiful soul like Mary."

"And I think my beautiful son has taken quite a fancy to your beautiful daughter." Iris stood and began placing the unboxed figures on the table behind the sofa, giving them room to repack the empty boxes. "And I hope it's okay with you that I'm quite happy about that, Reba."

"I've observed the same, and I'm quite pleased myself. Even more, I think Emily's father would be pleased as well." She put the last empty box in the green bin. "What do you say we arrange these on the mantle for Maude? We can put the greenery around later."

"Oh, let's do. I think Maude would like that." She paused. "I don't mean to pry, but Kent has had so much disappointment in the past few months. He lost so many of his friends in Iraq, and then he's worked so hard to come back from his own injuries … I guess I am prying, but only to protect my son. Does Emily have someone in her life back home?"

"Yes, twenty-three of them in fact." She waited to see Iris's face. "Of course, they're all in kindergarten. They are the loves of her life right now." They both laughed.

Iris' expression showed her relief. "That makes her even more wonderful."

"Emily is capable of so many things, and I'll admit, I had to struggle to keep my mouth shut when she told us of her college and career plans. I fear I could have damaged our relationship had my husband not intervened. He encouraged me to keep quiet about my expectations, and he encouraged Emily to do what would make her happy and what she was passionate about."

"Sounds like a wise man and a loving father." Iris placed the last figure, the Christ Child, on the mantle and backed away to look.

"He truly was. I was always so driven, and I'm sorry to say I could be a real driver in someone else's life. I've had to fight that tendency as a therapist." She joined Iris to look at the nativity. "Why, I do believe that's the most elegant nativity set I've ever seen."

"I agree. It's so delicate and detailed." Iris smoothed the vintage fabric of Mary's shawl. "And such polished beauty. It's an interesting contrast to this one, don't you think? I'm certain Greg could say a lot about these two." Iris pointed to the olive-wood nativity set they had arranged on the hearth at Maude's suggestion. "This is one of a kind as well, hand carved out of roughness until it's smooth. Sort of rustic and earthy, don't you think? But beautiful in a different way."

"Certainly, and I do like your insight."

"Thank you, Reba. Although, I'm not certain if I'm comparing the nativity scenes or if I'm comparing our children."

Reba waited before responding. "As I said, you have great insight, Iris."

"Thank you, and what a kind thing to say, although I think that is more descriptive of my husband. But I do have my thoughts from time to time … like how these two works of art truly depict the real gift that Christmas is—our great God himself cradled in a crib, the world-maker as a vulnerable baby, with stars in his eyes and hay underneath him. That earthiness all around him—and at the same time, that indescribable thing that transcends."

Reba faced Iris and hugged her. "With a mother like you, I know Kent has a beautiful heart. You know that children get their concept of God from how they relate to their fathers, and they get their concept of how to relate to others from their mothers. I have no doubt that Kent relates in a healthy and beautiful way to Emily. And I know my Emily—she would choose no less."

They stood together and admired their work.

"All is well, Reba. All is well."

They had just finished with the last pine boughs on the mantle when the guys returned with cups of coffee and a need to sit in front of the fire. Reba reminded them there were stacks of bins in the hallway waiting to be moved.

Kent rose first. "Yes, ma'am. Consider it done."

Reba winked at Iris. "I like that young son of yours, Iris," she whispered. "And I see why my daughter does too."

By noon, a stately, well-dressed pine stood in the corner of the great room next to the fireplace. The mantle was draped in pine and cedar branches and secured with red velvet bows that had started out dustier than the barn floor. Iris and Reba had unboxed a half dozen manger scenes from Maude's collection and found just the right places for them. They saw to it that a pine bough and three red candles perched on every windowsill in the gathering room and in the dining room.

Grey Sage looked like Christmas, and the smell of coffee and chili and hot cornbread and a crackling fire floated through the halls.

Maude watched fondly as the Unlikely Christmas Party gathered around the dining table once again. Laura, in her spattered apron, helped Lita serve piping hot bowls of chili with the cornbread baked on top of each bowl. She proudly served her salad plates with croutons she'd made herself from Lita's leftover homemade bread.

Laura took her seat only after everyone was served and she and Lita could sit down together. Once there, she looked around the room and offered her first unsolicited comment in four days. "Oh, this is truly Christmas. Look how lovely, Ted. I've been so busy in the kitchen this morning I've not had time to see all that you ladies have done. It's ... it's spectacular!"

Lita announced to the group, "The salad is all Laura's creation. I opened the vegetable bin and told her to have at it, and she did. And that was after she made a special surprise that won't be revealed until Christmas dinner Sunday evening."

The group clapped and voiced their compliments. Ted looked surprised but said nothing.

"Thank you. It was really nothing." Laura paused. "And we're making cookies this afternoon."

Henry spoke up next. "Isn't it amazing what can get done when we all have jobs and we do them? Lita, you and Laura have provided us with the best lunch I've had all day."

Everyone chuckled.

Henry continued. "And, you ladies outdid yourselves making Grey Sage look like a magazine spread in the Christmas edition. And all Ted and I had to do was to keep the fire going and stay out of your way."

Beatrice turned to Henry. "Yes, and that staying out of our way must have been the hardest part for you. It would appear you have extra-special skills staying underfoot, Carl. But this place is as it should be now. And I have gifts to put under the tree. Thank you, gentlemen, for finding not one, but two perfect Christmas trees."

Greg added, "Yes, and we risked our lives doing it. We braved the fierce winds, and snow blowing in our faces, a chainsaw, and wolves, and then we had to drag the whole trees back to the house for miles uphill."

Kent's eyebrows nearly met his hairline. "Dad, let's leave the exaggeration for your pulpit and the classroom. I don't think we were in any danger and I think the mile uphill … well …"

"Okay, but we did see the wolf tracks, son."

The colonel leaned forward and put his elbows on the table. "So the howling was for real, Alo."

"Yes, sir. Like I thought, more than one. Saw their tracks in the packed snow down by the creek. But nothing for you to be concerned about."

Maude glanced at Silas and then back at the group. "What do you say we all take a little siesta and maybe assemble in the gathering room around two thirty when we're rested? We have some plans for the afternoon if you're interested. If not, *Mi casa, su casa*, and just make yourself at home to relax and or read or go out to the studio and get creative."

Laura spoke up quickly. "Oh, don't count on Lita and me. We'll be making cookies."

Maude smiled. *I knew Laura would get that bag of joy dumped on her when she put on Lita's apron.*

Chapter Twelve

*L*ita washed her hands at the kitchen sink. "Look, Maude, it's Christmas. An unexpected one. If these folks were home, my guess is they wouldn't change their bed linens every day. They'll be here three nights. Tomorrow's Christmas Eve, and the girls we hired to help earlier won't be available. So, the best we can do is keep them fed and provide them with fresh towels."

Maude sat on the bar stool at the counter and tapped her pencil on her pad. "You're right. I'm checking that off my worry list. And you're sure we have enough food?"

"Yes, and to make absolutely certain, we have more food coming in any moment."

"But you're here, and Alo just passed through the kitchen. So who's making the delivery?"

Lita reached for her recipe book and opened it. "Beth and Jedediah are in town getting their supplies. She had seen the inn lights were still on this morning and called to check on us. I gave her a list when she offered to bring any supplies we needed."

"Great to have good neighbors."

Laura entered the kitchen and Maude looked at the kitchen clock. "Did you rest at all, Laura?"

"Yes, thank you. I know Lita has so much to do, and I thought she might need my help this afternoon."

Lita knew Maude couldn't miss the grin on her face. "Well," said Maude. "I've learned over the years, if you hang out with Lita in the kitchen, you'll be up to your elbows in something, but that something is always good."

Lita slid the cookbook across the island for Laura to see. "Well, we've eaten our supply of Feast Day cookies, so it would be so helpful if you'd make us a fresh batch. If we double the recipe, then we'll have enough to last through Christmas. Only this time, we'll add a couple of ingredients not listed here. Grab yourself a clean apron from that drawer." Lita pointed to the drawer by the sink.

In a matter of minutes, Laura had her apron on and followed Lita from the pantry with an armload of flour, sugar, shortening, anise seeds, pine nuts, and other spices. Lita was getting out the mixer when the backdoor bell rang.

Maude got up from her stool at the counter. "I'll get it. Must be Beth and Jedediah."

Laura looked over the recipe. "More guests?"

"No, Beth and Jedediah live across the creek. They're actually our nearest neighbors, and they offered to bring in some grocery items from town."

"Will they be here to share Christmas dinner with us?"

Lita rolled off two sheets of wax paper and put them on the counter. "Oh, no, they both have parents and other family within driving distance, so they'll be getting together with them if they can get there. But they're always welcome at our table with that cute little fellow of theirs."

"You say they're your nearest neighbors? How far is that?"

Lita took Laura to the kitchen window. "By car, about two and a half miles up and down and around some sharp curves. As the crow flies, a little less than a half mile down that steep hill, back up and across the creek." She pointed to the west. "Grey Sage property extends to the other side of the creek, and Alo built a foot bridge at a narrow crossing. That way we don't have to get our feet wet to visit our neighbors. And our guests like to hike down there next to the creek.

"Okay. Time to get to work." Lita returned to the mixer and all the cookie ingredients. She instructed Laura on how to measure the dry ingredients and cream the butter and sugar. "The last step, not on the recipe, is the candied fruit we'll add just to make the cookies more festive and add another layer of sweetness." She chuckled. "That's just what Christmas does—adds on another layer of sweetness to everything and everyone."

Maude came through the kitchen with Jedediah, Beth, and their young son, Daniel, behind her. She introduced them to Laura and headed for the checkbook on her desk as they piled groceries on the far counter. Once that was done, Jedediah excused himself and headed to find Maude, receipts in hand.

"You going to your folks' for Christmas?" Lita asked Beth.

"We're going to Jed's parents' tomorrow for Christmas Eve dinner and then to my parents' for Christmas Day, weather permitting." Beth brushed her fingers through her son's hair. "Only about fifty miles, and hopefully we can make it. We must be home tomorrow night for a special visit from St. Nick. I'm so sorry Doli and Catori won't be home for Christmas."

"Don't start that if you don't want to see me cry. My first Christmas without my girls."

"No crying. You know they'll get here as soon as they can. No use losing sleep or getting your joy robbed over something you can't fix."

"It's that howling wolf causing me to lose sleep, not missing my girls."

"Daniel, why don't you help your dad and Maude?" Beth sent him out, then walked closer to Lita. "Oh, yes. That howling makes my skin crawl, and Daniel crept into our bed about one thirty this morning. It must make his skin crawl too. Jed puts all the animals in the barn at night, and Shep sleeps in the laundry room. I don't think the animals mind being in out of the cold."

"Good thinking. Alo spotted some tracks down by the creek this morning when he was cutting Christmas trees. Says there's more than one."

"Sounds like a pack, and that's usual, according to Jed. Just hope it's a small one. Since the barn cat went missing a few days ago, Daniel's been grieving that cat and frightened since he overheard Jed say it was probably the wolf."

Jed, Daniel, and Maude returned to the kitchen. Once the neighbors had said their goodbyes, Maude turned to Lita. "Really, Lita, eight gallons of milk? And six pounds of butter?"

"Can't make hot chocolate without milk, and you can't make anything without butter." She winked at Laura.

Maude looked at her watch. "Oh, it's two thirty. Best get to the gathering room to see who showed up. Careful, Laura. Lita will make a cook of you."

"Yes, I will. After the cookies, she's making another salad for dinner, and I'm teaching her to make Indian fry bread to go with our pasta this evening."

"Sounds delicious. And I'll be back to start brewing something warm to drink for our guests. Maybe some of the apple cider I just paid for."

Maude found her guests settling in the gathering room. The colonel, with his lit pipe in hand, was seated comfortably in the wing chair next to the fireplace. The chair had become his perch since his arrival. Alo sat on the hearth near him, conversing about weather predictions. The others trickled in and took their seats. Beatrice was the last, dragging two shopping bags as she walked.

Alo saw her and jumped to her rescue. "Let me help you. Where would you like these?"

"They will eventually go under the tree, but I have to write names on the name tags first. So please put them there in front of my seat on the sofa." She looked around the room. "Did anyone else bring gifts?"

No one answered, sitting with sheepish looks on their faces.

"Beatrice, you're always the thoughtful one," the colonel responded. "But you might recall none of us expected to be here for Christmas. While you do your gift tags, I want Alo to finish what he was telling me. Some of the rest of you might find it interesting how he predicts the weather."

Alo took his seat on the stone hearth again. "Sir, you give me far too much credit. I'm no meteorologist. These are the old ways my ancestors used, and they still work."

Henry removed his pipe and tapped it. "So you were saying that halos around the moon forecast snowfalls, and you were beginning to tell me how you predict an unusually cold winter."

"Yes, the halos have been telling us about the coming snow. And back during the harvest season, thicker than normal cornhusks told us to expect a cold winter. Then there was an unusual abundance of acorns this year, and that kept the squirrels busy for weeks. And the thick, bright bands on the raccoon tails. All signs of bitter cold coming. And then there was the whole army of mice that took up residence in the barn very early this year."

Beatrice interrupted. "Did you say an army of mice?"

"Yes, I did say that, but you're not to worry. You won't find a mouse anywhere around in Grey Sage. I took care of that."

"Remember, Bea," Lily added. "Alo has taken care of the mice. You have absolutely no need to give them a second thought."

"Of course I'm not worried. I once was Clara in *The Nutcracker*." The look on Beatrice's face let the others know that she had departed for a different time and place. "Yes, Grandfather Drosselmeyer gave me a nutcracker doll for Christmas, and that dreadful Fritz broke it, but Grandfather magically repaired it."

Beatrice rose from her seat and stepped in front of the hearth as though ballet slippers covered her bony feet. "And I fell asleep under the Christmas tree, holding that beautiful nutcracker." She, as though choreographed, shrank and folded herself up with fluid motion until she was curled up on the rug in front of the fireplace.

Eyes rolled as Beatrice drifted happily from one reality to another, but the telling of her story brought such joy to her, no one had the heart to interrupt her.

Beatrice jumped up spryly. "But in my dream the toys all came to life, and the room filled with a whole army of larger-than-life mice. And the Nutcracker, my Nutcracker, led the fight against the evil Mouse King and knocked him dead on his feet. Then the whole army of mice scampered away carrying that evil Mouse King with them."

With flawless and fluid motion, Beatrice lifted her arms until her fingers touched above her head. She extended her right leg with the same graceful motion and brought it slowly to the outside of her left knee and then out again. When her foot touched the floor, she began stepping and spinning to her right—and stumbled.

Her small audience was breathless, but Alo was there to catch her before she tumbled over the coffee table. Alo backed away when Henry stood and took her arm. "Bea, maybe you should sit down," Henry said.

She straightened her sweater, brushed her hair behind her ear, and pushed Henry away. "But you haven't heard the very best part." She assumed a perfect fourth position, with her angled right foot a step in front of her left, and continued her story. "My Nutcracker was suddenly transformed into a prince who took me to an enchanted forest and then to the Land of Sweets. I think that's why I like candy so much. And you're all getting candy from me for Christmas. That's the end of my story."

Beatrice waited for their applause and walked with grace and precision toward the sofa. Halfway there she stopped. "Except I must tell you, I hated that Sugar Plum Fairy. When she danced her *pas de deux* with that handsome cavalier, she was nothing so special."

Beatrice sat down. A stunned silence lingered for a moment. Maude stared at Silas, both in disbelief. An impromptu retelling of *The Nutcracker* from the ballerina hadn't been on Maude's list of entertaining things to do this afternoon, but no one would deny it was unforgettable.

Beatrice broke the silence. "I don't suppose I'll be seeing *The Nutcracker* this year. Although Alo, you were quite good in being my third leg, as any great partner is, so you and I just might perform a lovely pas de deux if we could get this infernal coffee table moved." She reached for another gift bag and her pen. "And tell me how to spell your name, please. I've never heard that name before."

Alo spelled his name.

Beatrice asked, "Is that American?"

"Yes. It's American Indian. My name means 'spirit guide.'"

Maude, realizing her guests' interests in Alo's culture, asked, "While we're all here, would you tell them about naming Catori? That's such a beautiful story, and it's sort of a Christmas story."

Alo stood again. "But Lita loves telling this story. Maybe we should wait and let her tell it."

"Oh, Lita's busy, so please tell it, and I'll go to the kitchen to check on something warm for us to drink."

Alo looked out at the group of expectant faces, collecting his thoughts. Then, taking a breath, he began.

"Forty-one years ago, Lita gave birth to our first daughter on the fifth day of December. Our family is Christian, but we have tried to stay true to some of our culture if it doesn't conflict with our faith. We have a Hopi custom about naming our children, and that custom was very important to our parents. When we brought our daughter home, Lita put her in her crib with an ear of dried corn. For the next twenty days, we only called the baby 'daughter,' and she slept night and day with this ear of corn."

He smiled, picturing his firstborn, remembering those days of early parenthood. They'd been so nervous, he and Lita.

"So, what is the significance of the ear of corn?" Greg asked.

"In our culture, corn represents Mother Earth. But our faith teaches us our God created Earth and everything else. So every night, we prayed to our Father God to bless our daughter. On the twentieth day after her birth, as was our custom, it was time to name her. And that made it Christmas Day."

"Ooh," several of his listeners responded, nodding in understanding.

He paused and rubbed his palms together. "This was the most memorable Christmas of my life. Before the rising of the sun on that cold Christmas morning, we drove to the top of the mountain from where we lived below. The baby's grandparents were with us. At the first sign of the rising sun, we stood in a clearing atop that mountain. We held our tiny baby up until the first ray of light touched her forehead, and then we named her. We named her Catori. Her name means 'spirit.'"

Maude and Lita entered the gathering room just in time to hear Alo finishing up his story. Lita joined Alo, drawing near him. "Yes, we did, and she has lived up to her name. I'm sorry that you won't have an opportunity to meet her," she told everyone, then looked at Alo. "She's a beautiful spirit, like her father."

You're both beautiful spirits, Maude thought fondly.

Maude spoke up. "Lita and Laura have the kitchen humming, and I'm told there is hot cider in the dining room, and then we can start the games—cards and Scrabble, and I have a Christmas trivia game for the whole group. What do you say we get something to drink and divide into teams?"

The Unlikely Christmas Party moved into the dining room and huddled in small groups, dividing themselves up and deciding how to spend the afternoon.

Emily approached Maude. "Maude, I'd really like to spend some time in your studio this afternoon, if you wouldn't mind. I will only use a few pieces of drawing paper and some colored pencils if you have them."

"Of course! Come with me, and I'll set you up at the drawing table. I'm out here most days painting, and I'm getting into sculpting again. I think you'll like being in the studio. Only, if it were a bright sunny day, you could see far into the mountains. It's my favorite place in the house."

Kent, a cup of cider in hand, followed them out of the dining room and down the hallway to the studio.

Maude turned and asked, "Kent, would you like to paint or draw?"

"No, ma'am, I think I'll be happy just to watch Emily."

Maude smiled and kept walking.

Emily sat at the drawing table facing the window and searched through the box of pencils, choosing colors and stashing them in her left hand. Kent walked around the studio, studying the works in progress, and revisited his handprint on the wall, and Emily's right beside it. He looked at his damaged arm and hand, still bandaged down to his fingers, and wondered how long it would be before he could use it again, if ever.

He walked to the end of the drawing table. "Guess I should have asked your permission to hang around in the studio with you this afternoon?"

Emily stopped searching for the Golden Yellow pencil. "Oh, I'm glad you did."

"Never was good at Scrabble." He looked at his hand again. "And card playing is still awkward with one good hand. And Christmas trivia—well, that's just trivia to me."

"Rather interesting to think there's anything trivial about Christmas." She resumed her search for Golden Yellow.

"Oh, they'll be naming Santa's reindeer and trying to remember who made the first recording of 'Jingle Bells.' That sort of thing, I imagine." He pulled up another stool and sat at the end of the table where he could study her face in the gray light coming through the window. Her soft, thick brown hair hung to her shoulders. He wanted to touch it, to tuck it behind her ear so he could see her profile. Her eyes were warm and brown like her hair, and her eyelashes were thick and heavy.

"Beatrice's impromptu performance set me to thinking about the power of art and stories," Emily explained as she rummaged. "And I just wanted to draw. I had some ideas about my children's book. I want children to know there's always hope." She pushed the box of pencils away and began to sketch.

"So, tell me about this children's book. Or is it some secret that I'll have to wait and see?"

"Well, it's about a little girl named Daisy who loves flowers and playing in her garden all day long," Emily said as she drew. "She has conversations with the blossoms and the butterflies, and one day she asks her friend Sunflower what she does during the night all by herself while Daisy is asleep. Sunflower tells her that she hangs her head because the sun is gone."

Kent pulled his stool closer and looked at her drawing. "That doesn't look like a daisy or a sunflower to me."

"That's good, because it's not." She smiled pleasantly at him. "This flower is about the rest of the story."

"You're not planning to leave me in suspense, are you? Tell me the rest."

"Well, Daisy talks to her mother, Rose, and tells her she doesn't like the nighttime anymore and that she's only happy when she can see her flower friends."

"And what does Daisy's mother tell her?" Kent was almost hypnotized by the movement of Emily's pencil, watching an unusual flower appear on the page before him.

"Her mother tells her to have another conversation with Sunflower about why she hangs her head. And Sunflower explains it's because she's been turning her face to the sun all day, because that's what sunflowers do. And she's just resting and waiting for the sun to come back." She stopped and looked into Kent's eyes, which were nearer than before. "And then her mother hands her some seeds to plant right outside her bedroom window."

"Seeds, huh? This is getting suspenseful."

"Yes, seeds. And every day, Daisy waters the seeds and watches a vine grow up to her window. And she begins to see tiny white buds. But they won't open. Finally, one evening, Daisy is lying in bed next to her window and looking out at the stars when she smells the sweetest fragrance."

Kent stood up. "I know. Daisy smelled cookies baking in the oven."

Emily pulled him down again with a laugh. "Stop it. I smell the cookies too. But you're about to miss the best part."

"So, what does she smell?"

"Daisy smells a flower she's never smelled before. She jumps out of bed and goes to the window to see a large, fragrant white blossom smiling in the moonlight—her moonflower."

"A moonflower? Is there such a thing?"

"Oh yes, they're lovely, and my back garden fence is covered in them, and they only bloom at night." She showed him her drawing.

"And the moral of this story is?"

"The moral. Hmmm." She paused to think. "I'd say the moral is that nighttime comes, and we should plant seeds of hope in the day- time so that we'll have sweet-smelling blossoms in the darkness."

"And kids will get this?"

"Of course they will—especially when I'm finished. I gave you the condensed version. You haven't heard the conversation with Moonflower and Mariposa and Tulip, but Daisy learns that without the darkness, she'd never get to see the stars or gaze at the moon or watch the fireflies down by the stream. And better than all that, the children will remember the story."

Kent got up and went to the window and looked out at the gray- ness. He was quiet. "I've seen the desert in Iraq, barren with noth- ing growing, but never have I seen stars like I did in those wide-open spaces in that vast darkness." He paused. "My parents planted seeds in my soul when I was a kid. They taught me that life wasn't always fair, but they taught me there was always hope. I learned that truth when I was a child, and it was like water to my soul in that dry, parched place." He turned back around to Emily. "My parents taught me well, but never so beautifully as your story. You must finish this book. And I'd like to buy the first copy."

"What if I wanted to give you the very first copy?" She stood and walked to him at the window. They stood side by side, her hand barely brushing his.

"Then I'd gladly accept it, especially if you'd sign it. Of course, you'd have to give me your address so that I could come and pick it up."

She spoke quietly. "Two twenty-two Meadowlark Lane. It will be the house with the teal-blue mailbox with sunflowers on it."

Facing the window, he took her hand in his. "I still have some work and some healing to do when we get home, but Emily ... do you think we could see each other after this trip?" He paused. "But maybe I should ask first if there's someone else in your life?"

Emily squeezed his hand and turned to him. "I'd really like that. I did just give you my address. And no, there is no one else in my life outside all those cute fellows in my class of kindergartners."

Kent faced her and looked intently into her eyes. "Christmas, the season of miracles, and the most beautiful girl in the world has just agreed to see me again." He pulled her close and bent to bury his face in her soft hair before gently kissing her. "You're my moon-flower, Emily. My fragrant blossom in the darkness."

She looked up at him and was about to speak when Lita popped her head through the doorway. "Oh, you two, you make my heart sing. I should have told you this place can cast quite a spell on young lovers. You keep on enjoying this place and each other. I'm just here to bring you some warm cookies right out of the oven and to warm up your cups of apple cider." Lita set the plate of cookies down on the art table, and poured hot cider into their cups. "Like I said, no better place on earth and no better time of the year to find love—right here at Grey Sage."

Kent winked at Lita. "I'd say that's true. And the moonflowers that grow around here are beyond spectacular."

Lita looked puzzled, shook her head, laughed her heartiest laugh, and walked back down the hallway.

Emily sipped her cider. "Do you think maybe we should join the group now?"

"Oh, please don't make me. I'm terrible at figuring out my Scrabble score even with my three-letter words, and I'm worse at trivia of any kind." He moved his stool once again to the end of the drawing table. "Could I bother you for a sheet of drawing paper and a couple of charcoal pencils?"

"Do you draw?"

"A little." They sat comfortably and quietly with only the sound of their pencils against the paper disturbing their silence. More than half an hour passed, and Kent put his pencil down. "My afternoon's masterpiece." He handed his drawing to Emily. "A study in darkness and light."

She took the paper. The likeness was surprisingly well executed—her profile against stark darkness with a myriad of tiny bright stars encircling her head. Most prominent was the moonflower in her hair.

Chapter Thirteen

Lita stirred the pasta sauce, taking another spoon to taste for seasoning. Laura tossed her salad. "Lita, I can't believe all these years I've made salad and never made homemade salad dressing. You've made it so easy, I may never buy dressing again."

"Salads are great. A mixture of greens is like one of Maude's blank canvases, and you can add a splash of this and a smear of that, and soon you have a work of salad art. I'll wager our guests will be very surprised this evening at what you have created."

Lita walked by and patted Laura on the shoulder. "Tell me about Ted. You've told me about your family, but not his."

Laura was chopping black olives now. "Ted grew up in Ann Arbor, too, but we didn't know each other until college. When his family wasn't traveling the world, he grew up in their basement with his chemistry set. He says as he grew, so did his lab. Chemistry and research have always been his passions, and maybe I should add art to that as well. After our first date, we just were comfortable and never dated anyone else."

Lita added more Parmesan cheese to her sauce. "A chemist and a musician? Seems like an odd match to me."

"I suppose we were, but we were both only children with highly educated parents, and our parents were older than most of our friends' parents. And they had high expectations of their offspring. We just understood each other." Laura sprinkled the large bowl of greens with sunflower seeds.

"So your parents must be gone since you're not with them at Christmas?"

"Yes, all of them are gone, died years ago. So now we live on the family estate where Ted grew up, and we inherited their art collection. Since we have no heirs, we're making arrangements now to transfer the collection to the University of Michigan."

Lita knew she might be touching a spot that would cause an eruption or a shutdown, but she felt it needed to be asked. "What about children?"

Laura was slow to respond. "That's a deep sadness in my life. We tried when we were much younger, but things didn't work out for us. We spoke about adoption, but Ted wasn't so keen on that idea, and his parents abhorred the thought. So I gave in, and we decided to give our lives to our work and invest ourselves in a few students along the way—students who needed financial help to get through school."

"That was a generous and unselfish thing to do. I can imagine you still get visits and calls from these students."

"We do, and we're even godparents to two of their children." She paused. "Basically, Ted and I are alone in the world, rambling around in a historic mansion surrounded by beautiful things and manicured gardens. But I'd trade it all for a Doli or Catori." She wiped her hands on her apron.

"I'm sorry about that, Laura. I think you would have been a wonderful mother. But you and Ted have made quite a nice life for yourselves. I can imagine you have interesting friends, and you've seen places I've only read about." Lita poured the pasta from the boiling water into a colander. "Enough sad talk. I'm about to mix this pasta and sauce together, and you need to finish tossing that salad. These folks will be whining like hungry babies if we don't get them fed on time."

As she worked, Lita imagined Ted and Laura's life—academia, art, architecture, eccentric friends, catered meals, lectures, and travels. A life that suited them. But apparently nothing about their life suited them for Christmas. Lita preferred her adobe house, with its rough-hewn beams and tile floors and pictures of her grandchildren on the refrigerator, and cooking large pots of deliciousness to express her love for her family. Thoughts of leaving home at Christmas were beyond her.

At six fifteen, Lita and Laura, with Maude's help, were ready to serve the meal. Every member of the Unlikely Christmas Party was seated in the seats Lita had assigned them for their very first meal on Tuesday evening.

Before the serving began, Kent requested, "Miss Lita, I've been waiting all afternoon to see you standing at the head of the table, announcing the delicious fare you prepared for us. We've already sampled your cookies this afternoon. You really spoil us, ma'am. I've been eating in the mess hall so long that just hearing you describe your food is like a fanfare and makes my mouth water. So, would you please tell us what we'll be eating this evening?"

Lita, remembering the scene in the studio, said, "You two were so busy this afternoon. I hope you had time to sample the cookies."

"Yes, ma'am, we did." Kent nodded, looking grateful she had kept their secret.

Lita began. "I must tell you, Laura made the cookies. I could never have pulled off cookies and dinner without her help. She also made the salad with a variety of greens, chopped olives, sunflower seeds, sliced mushrooms, and shredded jicama with her homemade vinaigrette with my secret ingredient. And for the second course, we have made pasta with a green chili and corn cream sauce with grilled chicken strips."

Maude and Laura began the procession and delivery of salad plates.

"This meal could be called Hopi-Italian-Lita fusion. The Hopi part, of course, is the green chili cream sauce and something special that Laura has made—Indian fry bread."

Laura put two heaping baskets of hot bread on the table. Maude came behind her with two small pitchers of honey and dishes of butter.

"You may enjoy the fry bread with butter as you would a roll, or you may enjoy it like a sopapilla with honey at the end of your meal. Either way, I think you'll find it slightly crispy on the outside and oh-so-soft in the middle, and you should be thanking Laura for its perfection."

Lita raised both hands, inviting them to eat. "Bon appétit, my friends."

Conversation around the table ranged from Henry's fascination with Alo's ways of predicting weather to Silas's report of more snow blowing in to Lily's whining over how unfair the Christmas trivia game had been.

Beatrice stopped Lily mid-sentence, interrupting the table with her raised voice. "You're just angry because you were losing. You didn't even know the answer about the Sugar Plum Fairy after I practically performed it the other night. And then you left and spent all afternoon on the telephone. I can't imagine who you were talking to all that time. You're not very easy to talk to, you know."

Eyes narrowed, Lily rescued the conversation and asked if everyone had seen *The Nutcracker.* They all began naming the cities where they had seen the ballet, and Lily tallied them up. "You people must love the ballet. Altogether we've seen the ballet in nineteen cities across the country. Since most of have lived in Chicago all our lives, we can thank Bea for dancing her way across America."

Beatrice beamed.

Lily stood up. "Now that we all have full and happy tummies, what do you say, Party people, shall we make our way to the gathering room? I think Alo has a roaring fire. And since Beatrice has already shared a story about a Christmas in her past as a ballerina, why don't we each share about a memorable Christmas in our lives?"

The group obliged and pushed away from the table to make their way into the gathering room, which looked entirely different tonight. Lights blinked on the Christmas tree, candles glowed in the windows and on the mantle, and the smell of pine and cedar wafted through the room. There was even a scattering of Beatrice's tagged Christmas gifts under the tree.

While Alo waited for the guests to take their seats, he and Lita stood near the tree and looked out the window. Shaking his head, he whispered to Lita, "Did you bring your nightgown? I'm thinking we should just stay the night here. Not a blizzard, but getting close. The snow's blowing sideways out there. Hard to tell if it's coming down or if the wind is blowing the loose snow from the ground up." He noticed the frown on Lita's face.

"I think you're right. Trying to get home and then back again in the morning if it does this all night might be more trouble than it's worth. I'll borrow a gown from Maude."

Alo watched the colonel take his seat in the wing chair next to the fireplace and pull out his pipe. He played with it as though it were a ritual that relaxed him, like Alo sharpening his knife.

Lily turned to Henry. "Colonel, I don't think it would embarrass you if I said that you've seen more Christmases than anyone else here. I was hoping that you would tell us about a Christmas in your past, one that was especially memorable."

Henry's chuckle was low pitched and gravelly. "No embarrassment at all, Lily. At my age and with what I've seen, I'm not certain even you could embarrass me." He removed the leather tobacco pouch from the inside pocket of his tweed jacket, filled the bowl of the briarwood pipe, and tamped it down. "Well, like all of you, I've had many Christmases with my family in our family home—Christmases like they were meant to be, like the one Bing Crosby sings about." He paused. "But I think I'll tell you about the Christmas of 1944. I remember more about that Christmas than I care to, and since many of you weren't even born then, I know you haven't experienced a Christmas like that one."

Alo was too young to have memories of those somber days during the war's holiday seasons, but he remembered reading about them and hearing his parents discuss those times. He had never heard a firsthand account from someone who had fought in the war.

Lily sat down next to Beatrice on the sofa. "Oh, please do, Colonel. Sounds most interesting."

Henry tamped down more tobacco in his pipe before striking a match on the stone hearth. He lit the tobacco, took a smooth draw, stared into the fire, and began his story. "Well, I was a young captain in the army in 1944. Our unit had about eighty men—fifteen officers with about sixty-five enlisted men, mostly from Kentucky and Tennessee. Just good old mountain boys. Our small unit was one of several in charge of the air defense of Paris, and our job was to deploy anti-aircraft artillery battalions. Compared to our frontline infantry, we had it pretty good. Our headquarters was a six-story château northwest of Paris."

He took another long draw on his pipe. "We arrived there about a month before Christmas, so we had time to establish communications and settle in." He looked back to the group. "Now if you know your history, you'll remember that the Battle of the Bulge was raging during Christmas of that year, and our American boys were taking the brunt of that siege. Our unit was extra busy at Christmas. We didn't have a chaplain, so there was no service of any kind. We didn't have time for a service anyway." He rubbed the stem of his pipe across his lips.

"But what I do remember about Christmas was the longing for home and the way we were just all a bit nicer to each other—for a day or two anyway. And I remember our Christmas dinner. No C rations or K rations that day. Some of the locals offered us food, and we were glad for it—roast turkey and dressing, mashed potatoes, peas and carrots, and apple cobbler for dessert. Strange that I would remember that detail, but I do. They even brought us some kind of nuts. I guess it had something to do with the way the French eat at Christmas.

"I remember that meal, and I remember having a hard time swallowing it because I knew what was going on a couple of hundred miles north of us. Our boys were fighting hard, lying in the snow and taking fire from the Germans."

The colonel paused. "Not much Christmas on the battlefield. But as I told you, those enlisted men in our unit, well, they were just fellows from the mountains of Tennessee, and they had good hearts. I don't know how they did it, didn't need to know, but those boys cut down some puny-looking tree and put it in the great hall of that grand château. Had to decorate the spindly thing with bits and pieces of tinfoil. No lights or colored bulbs, you know. It was a sight, not so much for my eyes as it was for my heart, because it said something, something important. It said there's a longing and a need for Christmas in all of us."

Henry continued. "Oh, did I miss my family that Christmas! Guess it was a good thing we were working so hard. Kept me busy. Two days after Christmas, we were reassigned to Heerlen, Holland. Took us three days to make the move in some mighty cold, snowy weather, kind of like we're seeing tonight. Drove so close to the Bulge that we could hear the artillery fire.

"We got to Holland, and the conditions weren't so good as in Paris. We set up our command center in a school there in the middle of the little town, and we shared housing with the Catholic priests and nuns who lived down the road. They were gracious to us. The first floor of that building was where they kept their animals—some cows and pigs. As I recall, they had a donkey, and of course some chickens. Then we lived upstairs. Only came there to sleep and clean up."

Thinking of their own comfortable surroundings, Alo glanced around the room. None of the listeners moved even a muscle. They were totally engrossed in Henry's detailed recounting of decades ago.

"But New Year's Eve was something. The priests invited us officers to dine with them. Don't remember much about the meal, but I do remember sitting in their quarters hearing Hitler on the radio after we ate. One of the priests translated. Something very different about the way Hitler spoke that night. We could hear it in the tone of his voice and in what he said.

"The next day, New Year's Day, Hitler unleashed hell, filling the air with German airplanes. Our anti-aircraft battalions took down over three hundred German planes in one day, but it wasn't without loss on our side. There was no Happy New Year for those men that day."

Henry leaned forward in his chair. "One of the pictures I still have in my head was of the Germans a few days later. They were encamped on the east side of the Ruhr River, and we were just across the river to the west. We used scopes to watch what they were doing. Interesting. They were doing the same things we were, walking around, eating, huddled together in small groups around a campfire. We all had our jobs to do, the Germans too, and not a one of us really wanted to be where we were or doing what we were doing. But duty called us all.

"Yet it was hope that kept us going. Hope that one day soon this war would be over, and we'd be back home with our families again. Somehow, I think that's what Christmas is all about, giving us hope that one day we will be home, really home, the home we were made for, and we'll be with the one who made us and the ones he gave us to love."

He looked at Kent, who was staring intently back at him. "Son, you've been there. To war, I mean. Wars were fought differently sixty years ago. No such thing as calling home or seeing your family on the computer like you can now, and so many of our wounded died before they could be treated. But war is still hell, no matter where or when it's fought."

The colonel looked back at the fire, its flames dying down. "I wish I had a happier Christmas story to tell you, but this was one that needed telling."

No one spoke because no one had words. Only Kent dared break the silence. "Yes, sir, Colonel. It needed telling, and we needed to hear it. You're so right, sir. Our war is different, but it is still hell. I don't want to take anything away from what you told us, sir, but with your permission, I'd like to talk about my last Christmas."

Henry looked at Kent and nodded his head. "Sounds like there's another story that needs telling. Go ahead, son."

Kent cleared his throat. "I was serving in Iraq this time last year. My unit served with a medical team outside Baghdad, and I remember the grime—the sand and dirt, sweat when it was hot, and there was always the smell of something burning. You probably think of the desert as being hot all the time, but it was bitter cold. And nothing to stop that bitter wind last Christmas."

Kent felt the growing distance between him and the others as his memories ushered him back to Iraq. "There is always this intense longing when you're on the battlefield—knowing that you're in this hellhole and you don't belong there. And you long for this one place where you desperately want to be, and you're not there, and you can't get there. Seemed worse at Christmas—"

A sudden popping sound from outside startled Kent into silence. A distant rifle shot. He looked around the room, noting from the puzzled expressions that others had heard it too. But the sound didn't repeat, so he continued.

He looked at Henry. "Don't know if you experienced this, Colonel, but seemed to me there was more bonding among the troops during Christmas or any of the holidays. We always shared that same aching and longing. Oh, we expressed it a little differently, but it was still there. Some looked for ways to make things better—like sharing something they received from home they wouldn't normally share or being extra kind. Or decorating like your mountain boys did. Or talking about their families and past Christmases.

"We didn't have a meal like yours, sir. We still had our cafeteria food, but the servers wore Santa hats and laughed a lot, and maybe if you were lucky, you got a bigger slice of cake on Christmas. We turned on some Christmas music while the VIPs walked through on Christmas Day and shook a few hands, trying to encourage us. Oh, and we got to talk with our families back home, and Skype, but somehow that made things even harder. It made that place where we wanted to be seem so near, and yet it was a whole world away from us and we couldn't get to it." He looked at his mother, whose brow showed the pain of reliving these experiences. "I'm not sure how it was for my folks, but I don't imagine it was much easier for them either.

"Our enemies didn't know or care if it was Christmas. The snipers were still at it, blowing up anything that crossed their paths, and we were being mortared constantly—thirty or forty times on that Christmas day. I just remember thinking no one should have to die on Christmas."

Kent cleared his throat again. "Our enemies were different than yours. Friends one day and enemies the next. Our medics would treat the wounded Iraqi civilians, and they would survive and praise us and thank us for our help. A month later, they'd be brought in as prisoners because they were trying to blow up our makeshift hospital. It's hard fighting an enemy you don't understand." Kent wiped his eye and reached for his wallet in his hip pocket. "You're right about hope, Colonel. It was all that kept us sane, and kept us getting up every morning and putting one foot in front of another and looking out for each other."

He pulled a worn piece of paper from his wallet. "I carry this with me. One of my best buddies was a doctor. He was a good man. We found time once in a while to ride bikes around the base together and just do simple, stupid stuff. We needed to do that. He had a wife and a little boy at home, but he didn't make it back. He wrote this after a really hard day when he lost a patient—a little village boy about the age of his own son. Guess it was his way of coping. He gave it to me when one of my best buddies didn't make it after a roadside bomb incident. My doctor friend had a way of making things real and simple, and he could always say things better than I could. He died himself about a month after he gave this to me. If you don't mind, I'll try to read it.

Notes on the death of a child
Blond hair, like my son.
His eyes already looking beyond me,
His strength had passed.

I met him on his journey to somewhere else.
I wish I had seen him before this,
Known him as two-year-olds are supposed to be,
Loud, wild, crazy, brash, bold, messy.

We were there in the valley of the shadow of death together.
He got there before I did.
I had to leave him there by himself.
Dark, cold, alone, completely alone.
I was much too late.
The battle was lost by the time I saw him.
We forced his body to pretend to be alive.
We just couldn't accept his fate.
As we pumped on his chest,
We gave him medicine to keep his heart going,

Put a tube in his throat to make him breathe,
Searched for blood in his belly,
Air outside his lungs.
The whole time we knew it was his head.
His brain was swelling, and he was dying as he came to our door.

Kent felt his chin quiver as emotion overtook him. His voice cracked. He rested the paper on his knee and wiped his eyes with his shirtsleeve, praying for the strength to continue. But when he tried again, he found he simply couldn't. With a shaky breath, he handed the paper to Emily, asking her with his eyes to finish the reading.

She held the paper with her right hand and his hand with her left. She squeezed hard as she read.

We lost him when he was struck by the car.
A bumper smashed into his skull, and his brain began to swell.
We lost him when his parents lost track of him just for a moment.
We lost him when his country fell into chaos.

We lost him when war was chosen over peace, death over life.
We lost him when sin entered the world,
When self was chosen over God.

What I ache in part, his parents feel in full.
There, oh death, is your sting.
The worst kind.
But you will not always rule.
You have been defeated before, and you will be wholly defeated again.
On that great day, we will stand with him triumphant.
You have had your day, but not forever and always.

Someday, baby boys will not die like this.
To God be the glory, that someday, boys will not die like this.

Emily released Kent's hand and folded the paper neatly as it had been, and gave it back to him.

He took it and held it in his hand. "I guess what I'm trying to say is not everyone's having a beautiful Christmas like we are. I'm feeling guilty that I'm sitting in this room with all of you when the troops that I lead are dodging mortar shells. My buddies are still there in that hellhole, still with that same longing and aching to be somewhere else tonight." He raised the piece of paper for them all to see.

Greg rose and went to his son.

Kent stood and embraced his father. No one could speak.

Maude looked at Silas, sitting in stillness like a marble statue, his chiseled silhouette against the lamplight. She squeezed his hand. *I know what you're thinking right this minute, Silas. And I always knew. I knew the moment you walked through the door in the evenings. Your face showed the brutal loss of a patient, especially when you lost a child. Especially Elan. I wish you didn't have to know these things.*

A ringing phone broke the silence. Maude looked at her watch.

Ten fifteen. I had a feeling that gunshot was trouble. It's late for a medical call since Silas retired and no more emergencies. So something's up.

She watched as Silas excused himself to take the call. A moment later he returned, his face tight, and motioned for her. Her heart accelerating in sudden dread, she followed him to the kitchen with Alo close behind.

Silas wasted no time in explaining. "It's Beth. She's frantic and needs our help. Jedediah went out to check on the animals and had Shep with him. All she knows is that the wolves attacked Shep and Jedediah is hurt. She doesn't think she can't get him back inside by herself."

"Oh, no," Maude breathed, suddenly weak with worry. She felt tears threatening to overflow.

Silas hugged her. "Alo and I'll take care of it. Let me get my black bag." He left for his study.

Alo headed for the mudroom to get his jacket. "What about the gunshot?"

"She said nothing about a gunshot," Silas said as he hurried back into the kitchen, rummaging through his bag. "But I heard it too. We all did. Can't be coincidental?" Obviously not finding what he wanted in his medical supplies, he shook his head and disappeared again toward his study.

Kent entered the kitchen. "Excuse me, but I've spent too many nights in combat, and I can smell trouble. I came to help."

In spite of the situation, Maude couldn't help but feel grateful for the offer. "Oh, Kent, the neighbors have an emergency and need Silas. Alo can get him there. You don't need to—"

But Alo interrupted her. "Get on your warmest clothes, son, but make it fast. We can use your help. You have instincts, and that can help in situations like this one. We'll be on foot."

Kent walked with purpose out of the kitchen.

Maude was surprised. "What? You're not taking the truck?"

Alo put on his gloves. "No, too unpredictable. It's probably twenty degrees and near blizzard conditions. Assuming we could actually see in front of us to drive, there could be a tree down. And we'd have to turn around and come back and go on foot any way. No time to waste. Go get Lily's whistle. Could come in handy."

Maude did as Alo instructed. She and Kent returned to the kitchen together. Silas was already there. "We're walking?" he asked as he stuffed everything into his bag.

"Yes," Alo replied. "It's safer. I want to stop at the barn and get a piece of rope. We'll each have flashlights, but we have to stay close and together. We can cross the footbridge and be there in ten or fifteen minutes. Maude, call Beth. Tell her to turn on every light in her house and anything that makes a racket. Music, an alarm—anything that makes sound. It'll help us and keep the wolves away."

Maude handed Alo the whistle. He put it around his neck and stuffed it under his muffler.

Silas handed Kent a wool hood. "Here, young man, keep your head warm. You wearing warm gloves and good shoes?"

"Combat ready, sir."

Maude looked at Silas. "What do I tell the group? They're already asking questions."

"Tell them what you know. We'll call you with an update as soon as we can. And tell them to pray." Silas grabbed his bag. "When you talk to Beth, tell her to pile the blankets on Jedediah. And you keep the lights on over here too. All of them." He looked at Maude the way he had looked at her a thousand times through the years when he made emergency, middle-of-the-night calls.

Maude said tearfully, "Stay safe, my love. I'll keep the lights on for all of you."

Chapter Fourteen

Silas, Alo, and Kent opened the mudroom door to face biting winds. Alo stepped in front. "I'll lead. Silas, you stay in the middle, and Kent, bring up the rear. We're stopping at the barn."

They pulled their mufflers tighter around their necks and headed to the side door of the barn. Once inside, Alo grabbed two pieces of rope. He quickly took the ten-foot piece of rope and made three loops, one at each end, and one in the middle. He handed Kent the end of the rope. "Loop this around your wrist." He handed Silas the middle loop, and he took the loop at the other end.

"Kent, we have a fairly steep descent down to the creek, but amateurs hike it all the time, so just stay with us. We'll cross the creek on the footbridge, and then it's a climb to get up to Beth and Jedediah. No rock climbing or ledges. Just steady zigzagging up another steep hill."

Alo took the shorter piece of rope and turned to Silas. "Give me your bag. You'll need a free hand." Alo took Silas's medical bag, looped the rope through its handles and slid his arms through the loops in the rope. The medical bag was safely strapped to his back. "Stay together and stay vigilant."

They tightened the loops around their wrists and headed out of the barn. Alo closed the barn door. "Keep watch for the wolves. I'll be blowing this whistle. They hate loud noise, especially shrill, loud noises. Let's go."

They walked around the west side of the barn. The wind was fierce with near whiteout conditions. The moon was almost full, but nearly invisible through the thick grayness. It was backlighting for the low-hanging blanket of clouds, giving off an eerie and fading incandescent light across the sky.

Alo knew every inch of this property, but rarely had he seen it under these conditions. As they started their descent, he shined his flashlight, searching for the cedar rails he had built in places where the path was steep. Maude had insisted on those railings after one of her guest artists had fallen and broken her arm several years ago hiking.

The snow was about knee deep, and its depth made every step an effort. The North Star was not to be seen. If Alo could round this curve in the path and get through the cedar brake, he would be able to see the Klingmans' lights. House lights would become his compass.

Alo felt his heart pounding, not so much from tromping through the snow, but from the sense of urgency to get to Beth. He preferred not to think about what might have happened and what they would find.

Maude stood at the kitchen window as the men left the barn. She quietly watched until she could no longer see their flashlights as they faded into the gray oblivion. She dialed Beth again. No answer.

Oh, please God, not on Christmas. Please make this right. Take care of Jedediah. And Beth, Lord. I heard the panic in her voice. I know that panic and that frantic helplessness. Please protect my Silas and Alo and Kent. Let them do their job and return. I'm begging, now that Christmas has returned to Grey Sage, please, please don't let it be accompanied by another tragedy, another sadness to snatch Christmas away again.

Maude's prayerful thoughts were interrupted with a hand on her back. Lita stood shoulder to shoulder with her at the window. She heard a faint whistle.

"Tell me, Maude."

"First, let me try Beth again."

Still no answer.

Maude told Lita what she knew. "Silas said we must tell the guests. I hate to spoil their evening. I know they will just worry."

"Of course they will worry, but they can pray. Let's go, Maude. No need for them to worry about what they don't know. After all, one of their own is with Silas and Alo."

Maude and Lita walked silently down the hall to the gathering room where the group sat in wringing-their-hands silence.

Iris was the first to speak. "My boy, he's gone again to help someone?"

Maude moved closer to where Iris and Greg were seated on the loveseat. "Yes, he's with Silas and Alo." She looked at Laura. "Laura, I believe you were the only one to meet the Klingmans when they delivered our supplies this morning. They are our closest neighbors, and Jedediah's been hurt. They need Silas."

Lita interrupted. "Excuse me, Maude. I'll keep trying to call Beth." Lita left for the kitchen.

"What happened?" the colonel asked. "I heard the gunshot."

Maude hesitated. "We're not sure. All Beth said was that Jedediah had taken their dog Shep out and had gone to check the animals in the barn one last time before turning in. Apparently a wolf attacked Shep, and we don't know what happened to Jedediah. We just know that he's been hurt, and she's worried about getting him back inside."

Iris commented, "But I didn't see the car lights down the lane when Silas and Alo and Kent left."

"They left on foot," Maude responded. "It's close to three miles on the road, and Alo was worried about road conditions and falling trees in this wind. It's a bit less than half a mile across the creek. They felt it was faster and surer to walk it."

The colonel leaned forward in his chair. "I remember cold like this, but a half mile isn't that far."

Maude looked at Emily, her face wrinkled into a heap of worry. "Yes, and Alo knows this land, and he knows how to be safe. He won't let anything happen to Kent or Silas."

Greg patted Iris's hand. "Our boy has been in lots worse than this. He'll be fine."

He stood and moved in front of the fireplace. It had been center stage for Beatrice's performance earlier and for Alo's Christmas story; now it would become his. "We feel helpless because of what we don't know and what we can't do. But I know someone who is not helpless. Nor is he asleep, and he knows and cares. The one thing we can do is talk to him. Let's ask God to put a hedge of protection around Jedediah, for his sweet family, and for Silas, Alo, and Kent. Why don't we bow in silence and each pray in our own way for a few minutes?"

Maude agreed. "I think we can all find some comfort in praying."

She saw Lita coming down the hall, shaking her head.

Still no answer. Something else to pray about.

Jedediah lay in the snow, blood staining the white powder around his head. Young Daniel crouched at his father's feet with a gun poised and ready to shoot. His eyes nervously searched the woods around them. With only the outside barn lights and the houselights, the visibility was low.

Beth knelt beside Jedediah and leaned over him. "Jedediah … Jedediah …" Her gloved hand smoothed the bloody curls from his forehead. She didn't know much about wolves, only that they traveled in packs and attacked the head and neck areas of their prey, but she knew of no reported wolf attacks in New Mexico. "Come on, Jedediah, wake up."

"Mom, we have to get Dad inside. And I have to find Shep."

"Your dad's breathing, but I think he hurt his head, and I can't wake him up. We can't pick him up, but we have to move him. Hand me the gun, and run to the barn and get the sled."

He handed Beth the shotgun and was gone before Beth could hand him the flashlight.

Beth's eyes moved from her husband to the wooded area around them to the barn lights. In a matter of minutes she saw a form coming toward her. "Daniel!" she cried out. "Daniel, is that you?"

Daniel yelled back, "Yes, Mom, I'm coming." He appeared next to her with his sled in his hand. "I'll help you put Dad on the sled, and we can pull him to the house."

"Yes, we must get him out of the cold. By then Silas should be here." She put the gun down, and they carefully maneuvered Jedediah's body onto the makeshift stretcher. Beth made certain his head was supported. She grabbed the rope and gave it a tug. It was easier than she thought.

She stood up. "Shine the light here, Daniel. I'm putting the rope over my head and around my waist." As soon as that was done, she asked for the flashlight. "I'll try to choose the smoothest way."

He picked up the gun and hung back as she started forward, the wind howling around them.

"Daniel?" she hollered over her shoulder. "You know you can't go after Shep right now!"

"I'm not, Mom. I'm right behind you, but I'm watching for the wolves." He took up a position behind her, guarding their backs.

They trudged through the snow, inching closer to the house. After a moment Beth turned around to Daniel. "What was that? I heard something."

They both stopped, motionless and straining to hear. Daniel held the gun at his shoulder. "It sounds like a whistle, and I see three lights over near the bridge. They're coming to help us, Mom."

Beth looked in the direction of the creek bed. "It's Silas. They're coming by foot. Let's hurry and get your dad to the house. I can see the lights."

"Yes, ma'am. Pull, Mom."

Alo had led them through the pines and cedars to the creek bed. Snow had already covered most of the rocks along the creek's edge, and he was certain that areas of the creek would be frozen. They hung on to the railing and crossed the creek on the footbridge. Once across, he turned to Silas and Kent. "We're over halfway. Just the climb up now. Are you okay?"

"Yes, I'm fine," Silas responded.

Kent agreed. "Let's climb, and I'm here to push."

"We'll zigzag, but always heading west. Their house lights should be visible in the clearing shortly. Let's go." He started the ascent, blowing the whistle rhythmically every fourth step. He used his flashlight to spotlight landmarks in the distance, a particular tree or rock that he remembered.

A forty-five-degree incline stared at them as they trudged, facing a strong headwind that whirled snow around them at times. Alo felt a sudden jerking on the rope in his hand. He looked back. Silas had fallen, but Kent was already there, preventing a nasty slide back down to where they'd started.

The drifts were piling up, and it was getting harder to pull their feet out of their knee-deep tracks. Silas shined his light so that he could step in Alo's tracks. The Klingmans' barn lights were visible now.

As they reached the backside of the barn, Alo spied something in the snow. He kept his flashlight on it until they reached it. They stopped.

"Shep, the Klingmans' dog. Wolves got him. Something scared them off, but they'll be back." He motioned for them to keep moving.

Kent yelled over the wind. "Want me to get Shep? I can carry him. It's not far."

Alo paused. "No, not now. We need to take care of Jedediah. It's too late for Shep. Don't mention the dog when we get there."

They kept slogging toward the house.

"We made it, Mom." Daniel propped the gun against the outside wall of their adobe house.

"Let's get him inside. I couldn't do this without you, Daniel. You're such a brave boy." Beth removed the rope from around her waist. "Get the door."

Daniel opened the kitchen door as wide as it would open and turned to his mother.

She handed the rope to Daniel. "It's been fairly smooth across the snow, but we have to be careful over the threshold. No jarring." They moved in unison and dragged the sled carrying Jedediah through the kitchen door. "Over in front of the kiva. The floor will be warm there until Silas gets here." They continued pulling until they had crossed the kitchen and into their living space, where an adobe fireplace sat in the corner.

When they had pulled him close to the fire, Beth said to Daniel, "I'm so proud of you, son. I couldn't have done this without you. Now, please go and get me a warm washcloth."

Sending Daniel off, Beth knelt on the floor and looked at Jedediah. His face was pale. She called his name and patted his cheeks. No response.

Daniel returned with the warm cloth and handed it to his mother just as the phone rang.

"Answer it, Daniel. It's probably Maude."

Daniel answered the phone. "Mom, it's Miss Lita."

"Tell her we're inside and safe."

Daniel reported to Lita. "Yes ma'am. We're inside, but Dad's not waking up." He paused. "I think they'll be here in a few minutes. We saw their flashlights in the distance and heard a whistle." He paused again. "Yes, ma'am, I'll have Alo call you when they get here."

They said their goodbyes.

"Now could you get me a bowl of hot water?" Beth began bathing her husband's face and noticed his eyes fluttered. "Jedediah. It's Beth. You're safe. Would you talk to me? Please talk to me."

Just as Daniel returned with the bowl of warm water, her husband opened his eyes.

The Unlikely Christmas Party sat quietly in their chosen seats in Grey Sage's gathering room, each praying, some with their eyes closed and others staring into the fire. Lita entered.

"Finally got through and spoke with Daniel. He and Beth were able to get Jedediah back inside, but it sounds like he's unconscious."

Maude immediately asked, "What about our men?"

"Daniel said they had seen their flashlights and heard the whistle, so they must be near."

Ted, who had hardly said a word all evening, asked, "What about getting him to a hospital? If Alo chose to go on foot, then he must think getting the injured man out of here by vehicle is impossible, and I don't think airlifting him would be a possibility either in these winds."

Lily grasped her shawl and pulled it tighter around her shoulders. She stood and paced in front of the fireplace. "Oh my, what if I have brought this group here and something terrible happens?"

Maude was reassuring. "Silas will handle it, Lily. We're used to emergencies in these parts, and we're accustomed to handling them. And besides, it can't snow forever. We can check the roads at the first sign of light."

Ted persisted. "But if it was a wolf attack, then they'll need specialized medicine and time is of the essence. I doubt Silas carries those medicines in his black bag." He stopped short of using the word *rabies*.

Lita responded. "We don't know if it was a wolf attack, but having lived in these parts for the last forty years, Silas is prepared for most anything."

Greg intervened. "Sounds like progress is being made and we have something else to pray about."

Beatrice stood up from her place next to Reba on the sofa. "I don't like this. I don't like it at all. I'm headed to bed. I just cannot bear to think about such things anymore. Tomorrow is a new day, and everything will be better. I'm absolutely certain of it, and I'm not certain about many things anymore." She moved blithely across the room and disappeared into the hallway.

Maude said, "Let's hope Beatrice is right. We should hear word before long."

Silas, Alo, and Kent removed the looped ropes from their wrists, dusted off the accumulated snow on their jackets and hoods, and stepped through the kitchen door.

Alo called out. "Beth, it's Alo, and Silas and Silas's guest Kent are with me." He removed the makeshift backpack and handed Silas his medical bag.

"In here, next to the kiva."

Silas removed his jacket, his eyes already making a visual assessment of his patient. "Has he come to yet?"

"Just opened his eyes a minute ago and closed them again."

Silas knelt beside Jedediah and make a quick physical check. "Good. You have him in a warm spot right here. Doesn't seem to be in any noticeable pain." He quickly assessed Jedediah's legs for broken bones, and then his arms." His alarm grew when he saw the red-tinged water in the bowl. "Where's the blood coming from?"

Beth pointed. "Right here on the side of his head."

Silas looked more closely. "I see the gash." He looked up at Alo. "Help me, here, and let's get his gloves and jacket off."

Alo quickly stepped in, and they removed the jacket and gloves with minimal movement.

Silas never moved his eyes from Jedediah but asked, "So, do we know what happened?"

Beth answered. "I was in the kitchen putting some dishes away, and Jed wanted to check on the animals in the barn one more time, and Shep went with him. It couldn't have been more than two or three minutes before I heard horrible barking and howling, and then I heard Jed scream." She put her arm around her son. "And Daniel was thinking faster than I was. He grabbed his dad's gun and ran out the door. A few seconds later, I heard the shot. Before I could get my jacket on, Daniel yelled that his dad was hurt. That's when I called Maude. I knew we would need your help."

Alo turned to Daniel. "Hey, Daniel, can you fill us in on your details?"

"Yes, sir. I heard the barking. It was loud. Then I heard my dad shouting. Dad didn't tell me when it happened last week, but I knew the wolves got the barn cat, so I figured the wolves were back and they might get into it with Shep. I grabbed my dad's gun and ran outside. I couldn't see too good, but the outside barn light was on, and I ran toward it. The sound was really scary. When I got to my dad, he was already on the ground next to the tree. He had dropped the flashlight, and it was still shining. I saw three of them and Shep. I fired the gun and started screaming, and the wolves ran off. Shep went after them, but he didn't come back."

His duty done, Daniel started to cry.

Alo calmed him. "It's okay, son. You're only seven years old, and you did the job of a brave warrior. Looks like your quick thinking saved your dad."

"But Shep. Where is Shep? I couldn't save him." Daniel's tears rolled from his cheeks.

Leaving Alo to handle the boy, Silas reached in his bag for his stethoscope. He checked Jedediah's pulse before listening to his heart and lungs. "Respiration's good. Pulse is a bit slow, but that's to be expected given the time he's been in frigid temperatures."

Jedediah roused again.

Silas touched his forehead. "Jedediah, can you hear me?"

Jedediah opened his eyes and tried to lift himself up.

Silas kept his hand on his Jedediah's chest. "Not just yet, buddy. I need to check you out."

Jedediah rolled his head a bit and grimaced. "I'm fine, just have a bad headache. I want to get up."

Silas looked at Alo, who returned quickly to kneel beside Jedediah. "I think we can help you with that. Alo and I will help you sit up first. Then maybe we can get you to bed." Silas turned to Beth. "Can you get the bed ready? He's rousing, but he'll need to lie down for me to examine him."

Silas and Alo raised him up to sit.

Jedediah asked, "What am I doing on your sled, Daniel?"

"That's how Mom and I got you back inside."

Jedediah squinted his eyes from the pain and to focus. "Smart son I have."

Silas asked, "Can you move your arms and fingers?"

Jedediah lifted his arms and wiggled all his fingers.

"That's good." He turned to Alo. "Can you get his shoes off?"

As soon as his shoes were removed, Silas asked, "Now how about your legs and toes?"

"All good, doc. All my parts are moving." He looked up at Silas and smiled.

"What about pain? Do you hurt anywhere?"

"My head." Jedediah lifted his hand to the gash in his head.

"Do you remember what happened?" Silas asked. The rest stood waiting to hear.

"Yeah, I remember. I was headed to the barn to check the animals. Shep was with me. He started barking like there was no tomorrow. Then the wolves ..." He paused. "The wolves—I think two ... no, maybe three—came out of nowhere. One jumped me, and I fell back real hard. He must have been eighty to ninety pounds of pure force. And then I don't remember anything until a few minutes ago."

"That's good, Jedediah. That's real good." Silas knew that wolves went for the victim's head and neck, but he had less fear of that now. He needed to see the wound for a firm diagnosis. He had no rabies serum if needed, and that was a concern. "I'm thinking you must have hit your head on something when you fell. A tree limb or a rock, something that has given you a concussion. But I need to look. It's good that you're awake and you can remember. But you'll be having a headache like you've never had before." Silas motioned for Alo and

Kent. "Okay, men, let's get this cowboy to the bedroom and get these heavy clothes off him, and let me check his hard head."

They moved Jedediah slowly into a standing position. Once to his feet, Jedediah was able to hold himself upright. "I can walk, fellows." He tried a step and wavered a bit. Kent and Alo gave quick support.

"Where's Shep?" Jedediah looked at Daniel. "Where is he, Daniel?"

Daniel began to cry again.

Silas took Jedediah's arm and directed him to the bedroom. "Beth, would you make us a pot of coffee? I'll check Jedediah's head, and then I need to check Daniel's hands and feet for frostbite. He was in the cold without a coat or gloves."

A few minutes later, Jedediah was lying down, and Silas had pulled the stool from Beth's dressing table and was beside the bed. "Let me see what we have here." Silas pulled on his latex gloves and began the examination. "Well, I was concerned the wolf might have gotten you here, but it's as I thought. Just a nasty bump. I think a few stitches and a cold compress off and on through the night will do the trick."

Silas went to work, opening the wound and cleansing it multiple times before suturing it. "Your son and Shep saved your life, friend. Daniel heard the commotion, grabbed your gun, and found you. By the time he got to you, you had been attacked and were out cold. Amazing that wolf didn't get to you after he knocked you down. Daniel saw a bit of the struggle with the wolves, but fired the gun and they ran."

"And Shep?"

"Sorry, friend, but Shep didn't make it. We found him on the back side of your barn down the hill a ways. Shep was a good friend, loyal to the end. Without him, we'd be looking at something very different here tonight." He continued the suturing with precision. "Oh, and we haven't told Daniel about Shep yet, but the boy's smart about such things. I think he's already figured it out. You two did get that rabies vaccine I recommended last summer, didn't you?"

"Yes, sir. Daniel and I both got it when you told us we should. And the vet took care of giving it to Shep too. We roam these woods, you know, and we're always running into wild animals."

Silas finished the suturing and cleansed the wound one final time before putting on the bandage. "That's good. You'll be fine until the weather clears, but we'll want to get you to the hospital for a booster as soon as we can just to be absolute certain. But you're not to worry. The only thing you should worry about is whether or not Beth has a bag of frozen peas."

"Frozen peas?" Jedediah rolled over onto his back to look at Silas.

"Either peas or an ice pack. That'll help with the swelling. Oh, and don't plan on getting much rest for the next several hours. No sleeping through the night. You have a concussion. You can take some short naps, but one of us will be waking you periodically to check on you."

"Did you and Alo walk over here? And who's the other guy?" Jedediah fluffed up his pillow and lay back down.

"Yes, we walked. We were afraid we couldn't get here if the roads were too bad. And when Beth called, she didn't really know what had happened. We just knew to get here fast, so walking was the most expedient thing to do. And the other guy is Kent. He's one of our guests. You'd like him. He's a fine young leader just home from serious injuries in Iraq."

"Please thank him for me. And thank you, too, Doc. I'll have to find some way to repay you for your kindness when I can get moving again."

"Oh, we'll think of something. We'll be staying the night. Weather's too bad for us to get back home, so the three of us will be here to talk your ears off."

Silas got up, pulled off his gloves, and went to the bathroom to wash his hands. That done, he went to the kitchen and gave a report to those who waited. Relief replaced the worried looks on their faces.

"Now, let me check out this young hero."

Daniel shyly came to Silas. "Mom says you want to see my hands and feet. I had on shoes and socks, but no gloves." He held out his hands to Silas.

Silas looked at his palms and the backs of his hands, then checked his fingers and his ears. "Looks good. A little on the red side, but just a mild frost nip. Nothing that a warm soak for a few minutes won't fix. I'll give your mom some ointment that will help too." Silas looked at Daniel's feet, and they appeared normal. He instructed Beth on how to prepare a warm bath for her son's hands.

"Alo, how about giving Maude and Lita a call, and let them know what's going on over here. Be sure to tell them it's too bad they didn't get invited to the spend-the-night party we're having. Tell them we'll see them in the morning, and that all is well."

Maude returned from the kitchen with Lita and Lily. She knew her broad smile gave instant relief to her guests. "It seems that Beatrice was right. All is well." Maude gave them a full report of the incident with an update on Jedediah and Daniel. She recounted how Silas, Alo, and Kent had fared on their eleven o'clock hike across the creek in an almost blizzard.

When she finished and the gaggle of listeners had expressed their thanksgiving that all had ended well, Lily extended her arms, looking like a winged creature as her royal blue, fringed shawl spanned her arms. "To bed, people. It's been a long day, and it's almost tomorrow. We can sleep soundly knowing that we're safe and warm, and we've already had two Christmas miracles. Tomorrow is another day, and it will be Christmas Eve. Good night, my friends."

With a chorus of goodnights, the guests followed Lily down the hall to their rooms.

Maude and Lita headed to the kitchen. Maude made sure the lights were on and candles were burning in the windows. Lita began unloading the dishwasher. "Maude, I need to borrow a nightgown. I had no idea we'd have such an eventful day, and I didn't come prepared to stay the night. Although I think you could hang me on a nail and I could go to sleep."

"I'm fresh out of nails to hang you on, but I've already put everything you need in the O'Keefe Suite. I think we can both sleep now that we know all is well."

"I have one more thing to get ready for in the morning, but it won't take long. You go to bed. It's been a long day." Lita put away the last of the clean dishes and walked toward the pantry.

Maude walked slowly down the hallway to her bedroom. *I had no idea when I woke this morning how this day would turn out, but thank you, Father, for taking care of us all.*

This will definitely be another Christmas at Grey Sage to remember.

Chapter Fifteen

The weather was kinder on Christmas Eve morning. The fierce winds had calmed, and the blowing snow fell gently now. Silas stood with Beth at the kitchen window drinking coffee. "It's been a long night, but I think Jedediah will be just fine. Just give him the medicine I gave you for his headaches."

Alo and Kent joined them in the kitchen. "Just talked to Lita. Breakfast will be served in a half an hour. Think we can make it?"

Silas took a big gulp of coffee. "If we made it during a blizzard in the dark, I think we'll be able to skip home this morning."

Alo put on his jacket and pulled his gloves out of his pocket. "Wouldn't be skipping on the roads though. Just heard the news— snowdrifts and trees down from here to Santa Fe. My guess is that's it's worse farther up in the mountains. Unless it warms up, it'll be days before the roads in the mountains will be passable."

Kent turned to Alo. "I could use a little help here getting this jacket zipped up over my bad arm. And by the way, I'll take the snow over sand any day of the week."

Silas checked on Jedediah one more time before grabbing his bag and following Alo out the door. He turned to Beth as they left. "Sounds like you might need to change your Christmas plans. I know your folks live up in the mountains, but it might be futile to try to get there. Grey Sage is open to you, friend. We'd love to have you spend Christmas with us. And I could keep an eye on Jedediah too, if he's at our house."

Alo led the way again, this time without the rope and flashlights.

In less than half an hour, they were removing their jackets in the mudroom at Grey Sage and were welcomed in the kitchen by all the cheering guests.

Maude's arms wrapped around Silas seconds after he walked through the door. She held his face in her hands. "I kept the lights on and all the candles burning for you," she said. He kissed her cheek and embraced her, suddenly inordinately glad to feel his wife in his arms.

Alo hugged Lita as well. And Kent, abandoning previous caution, went straight to Emily and held her.

"You mean this is all there is?" Silas joked. "No ticker-tape parade or marching bands? After all, we walked half a mile to get here for breakfast!"

Kent added, "Oh, but Lita, I'd have walked twenty miles for your breakfast this morning."

"Young man, I know exactly why you would have walked twenty miles to get here this morning." She winked at him and reached for the whistle still around Alo's neck. She blew it hard. "Breakfast is served. And aren't we mighty glad we're all here and safe and together this morning?"

After breakfast, the guests scattered. Silas, Alo, and Kent left for hot showers and a nap. Greg challenged Ted to a game of backgammon, while Lily determined it was time to teach Iris and Reba how to play poker. The colonel and Beatrice joined them, but Beatrice insisted they use the wrapped cinnamon candies stashed in her bag for their wagering.

Emily sat quietly sketching by the window and waited for Kent to join her. Maude turned on the Christmas music before heading to her office to make her traditional Christmas Eve calls to her nieces and nephews.

Lita was in the kitchen making lentil soup and baked ham for lunch when Laura found her.

"Oh, good. You're all by yourself," Laura exclaimed.

Lita, standing at the stove, smiled at the difference in Laura's expression, almost like she'd had an instant facelift. "Yes, but I'd be glad for some help. You willing?"

"I'll be happy to help, but I think I have this really great idea." Laura stepped closer to Lita, looked around the kitchen to make certain no one else was around to hear. "It's something I've always wanted to do, but I never had the opportunity. I know there aren't any children around, but I still think it would be fun, and I think that Maude would love it."

Lita was intrigued. "So what is it you've never done that Maude would love?"

Laura handed her a piece of paper. "See, I worked on this last night, and I think I have it all figured out. But obviously I need your help. What do you think?"

Lita beamed. "I think it's a fabulous idea, but the hardest part will be keeping this under wraps. We'll have to do most of the work in the laundry room. Nobody will be bothering you in there."

"Do you really think we can do this, Lita? I mean, with everything else you have to do?"

"I think you can do this. You've already done it in your mind. So yes, you can do this! I'll get you started, and I'll cover for you with the group. I'll tell them you're indispensable in the kitchen and to please excuse you from the fun and games." Lita chuckled.

"Oh, this will be more fun than anything else I could possibly do today. I haven't even told Ted. He can just entertain himself. He does a lot of that anyway."

Laura went to the pantry and returned with her apron from yesterday. "I'm ready to help you. Just no more fry bread. I'm still treating grease-spattered speckles."

Kent showered and tried to sleep, but knowing that Emily was somewhere inside these adobe walls kept him awake. Sleeping was at the cost of irretrievable time with her. He wouldn't waste the opportunity, especially on Christmas Eve.

He wished now he had purchased the necklace she liked in the Railyard District. At least he'd have something to give her for Christmas. He sat on the edge of the bed and thought of what he could come up with that she would like. Then it hit him.

He dressed for the day and left his room to find Maude. He saw Emily's silhouette at the window as he passed through on his way to the kitchen, and hoped she didn't see him.

"Lita, do you know where I might find Maude? And by the way, I never had baked oatmeal in my life, but that was the absolute best. If you ever teach cooking lessons here, I'll return to be your first student. Now, about Maude? You think I could speak to her?"

"She's in her office down the south hall."

Kent followed her pointed finger. "I've never been to a place that had halls for every direction on a compass and then all kinds of rooms in between. Thanks, Lita."

Kent walked down the south hall until he saw an open doorway and heard Maude's voice. He stood at the door, seeing that she was on the phone and unwilling to disturb her. But Maude acknowledged his presence and motioned for him to come in. When she finished her conversation, she swiveled her office chair around to face him.

"So, Kent, your face—especially the wrinkles in your brow—show urgency. How may I help you?"

"You can tell all that by just looking at my face?"

"Of course. Remember, I'm an artist. I study detail, especially in faces. Can't you tell things by looking in faces? Especially Emily's face?" She smiled as his face softened.

"About Emily ... I have this idea, and you're the only one who can help me. But you must keep it a secret." He moved closer to Maude's desk and told her what he was thinking.

Maude scribbled some notes on her notepad. "I think that is

splendid, and of course, I will help you. And how fun to keep it a secret! I haven't had to keep this kind of secret in a very long time." She looked at the clock on her desk. "Could you give me maybe half an hour?"

"Yes, ma'am. Thank you so much for helping. I really want to give Emily something special for Christmas."

Before he left Maude's office, Kent looked at the painting over the fireplace. "Miss Maude, did you paint that?" He pointed to the portrait.

Maude stood and joined him in front of the painting. "Yes, I did. There was a time when I painted a new work to be unveiled every Christmas. This was our son, Elan, when he was between six and seven years old. He was a beautiful boy, and if he had lived, he would have been a beautiful man—like you, Kent." Her heart twinged as she followed the lines and planes of her son's face.

"Why, thank you, ma'am." She felt him watch her as she stared at the painting. "I hope my asking didn't bring sadness to you," he said carefully.

"Well, honestly, it did a bit, but it also brings some joy too. My memories of him are so sweet now. You would have liked Elan, especially as he grew older. Why, he could draw and swipe paint on a canvas and then go on emergency house calls with his father in the middle of the night. At fifteen, he read Tolstoy and listened to Tchaikovsky, yet he lived so close to the earth—Alo made sure of that by always teaching him the Hopi ways. They both knew every square foot of this mountain, walking the forest floor without making a sound. Elan could trill like a hermit thrush, and I saw him catch fish in the creek with the most primitive contraption you can imagine. Alo taught him how to find his way in the woods and how to survive if he was ever lost." Maude paused. "But all of that goodness is gone."

Kent attempted to console her. "I'm so sorry, ma'am. I can tell he was a most unusual young man."

"He truly was. He was like his name said—a friend to all who knew him and to this mystical place that was his home. I wonder sometimes what an incredible man he might have become. Oh, and did he love Christmas! It was our favorite holiday. Our relatives from

West Texas would take up residence for a week in all the extra bedrooms. The smell of mulled cider and cedar would float through all these rooms like the smoke from the fireplace drifts through the pine grove. And Christmas mornings, oh my, well, the gathering room would be knee deep in wrapping paper, and we'd have to hopscotch through the room to avoid stepping on Elan's electric train. It was a tradition every year to add a car or two to his collection, and Silas and Elan would set it up to circle the Christmas tree in the corner."

She sighed. "Oh, those Christmases at Grey Sage were magical. Until 1983, when they were no more. It was in the autumn of that year that Elan fell while rock climbing, attempting to rescue another climber ..."

Realizing she'd trailed off, Maude cleared her throat and turned to Kent, who looked as though he regretted mentioning the painting. "Enough about that. We were talking about sweet memories." She looked into his eyes. "And we're about to make some sweet memories, aren't we?"

"Yes, ma'am, with your help."

With a grin, Kent left the room and walked back down the south hall, a very satisfied man. This time he went straight for the silhouette in the window next to the Christmas tree. "Good morning, again." He sat in the chair opposite Emily.

"I thought you'd still be sleeping." She didn't appear too sad that he wasn't.

"And why would I want to sleep when I can enjoy watching you draw? Besides, it's Christmas Eve. Never could sleep on Christmas Eve. Too much excitement."

She stopped drawing and looked at him. "I hope you don't mind, and I don't want to spoil your exciting Christmas, but between the wreck in the van and last night, I've had about all the excitement I need. Oh, that was so unnerving. And then you decided to go with Alo and Silas, and it became downright frightening for me."

"Really, you were afraid something might happen to me?" Something warmed under his ribcage.

"Well, there were wolves involved. And let's not forget the whole blizzard thing and climbing an unfamiliar mountain in the dark. For a kindergarten teacher, that's high drama. Weren't you afraid?"

"Of snow and wolves and the dark? No way. A kindergarten class? And my knees turn to Jell-O."

They laughed together. He asked, "So what would like to do today within the sprawling confines of Grey Sage Inn?"

"Oh, I'm happy to draw or just sit and get to know more about you, like why you have this need to rescue everyone. I watched you do it when we were stranded on the bus, and then I heard your stories about Iraq last night and taking care of your troops. And when Beth's call came, you were the first to put your jacket on. What is it about you that makes you want to do that? Step in to rescue someone in need?" She closed her drawing pad and sat in anticipation.

"That's a legitimate shrink question. Sounds like you're more of your mother's daughter than you think." Kent paused. "I never gave it much thought. It's more like a natural reflex, and I suppose if I understood where natural reflexes come from, then I could answer you."

"Fair enough. I guess it's just who you are. So, I know you're still healing, but have you thought about your future after that?"

"I have, but my future depends on getting the full use of my arm back. I'm still in the military, technically on medical leave, and honestly, I had planned on making a career of that. It suits my skills, and I'd like to think I could make a difference." He moved to the edge of his chair, nearer to Emily. "Hey, I just stopped by to see how you want to spend the afternoon. We're getting into the demilitarized zone in this discussion."

Emily's cheeks flushed. "Oh, I'm sorry. I really didn't mean to pry into things you're obviously not ready to talk about. I hope I didn't offend you."

"Neither, ma'am. I'm taking it that you're interested in my future because it might have something to do with yours. Could I be right?"

Shyly, she said, "I think I did give you my address."

"You did, and I'm looking forward to my first visit and seeing how you live. I want to know how well I'm imagining your life." He stood up. "Look, it's Christmas Eve. Now it's still bitter cold and snowing, but the wind isn't so terrible. I thought about taking a walk."

"A walk? In this?"

"Well, maybe not a walk, actually, but I had an idea of making snow angels. I know it's kind of funny since one of my wings has been clipped, but I haven't done that since I was a kid. I have my camera. Maybe we could take a couple of pictures."

Emily was on her feet in an instant. "What do you say we go back to the studio and work until the weather clears, and then take a walk?"

He grinned at her and took her hand. "Sounds like a plan. All I need is a plan."

The afternoon passed slowly with more games and more conversation. Lita was busy with her traditional Christmas Eve dinner. She felt as though she and Laura were railcars, coming and going from the kitchen to the laundry room and back.

Maude joined her in the kitchen. "You and Laura are like ants, constantly moving. What can I do to help?"

"It's all under control. Venison's in the oven. Did you get the table set?"

"I did. Fiestaware on the table tonight to honor your traditional Christmas Eve meal, which I've not eaten in twenty-three years." She stepped into the butler's pantry. "Looking for red napkins," she called. "Don't we have red ones?"

"Yes, bottom shelf in the cupboard on the left in the back. We only use them on the Fourth of July if we have guests. And it wasn't my choice that you didn't have my venison for the last twenty-three Christmas Eves, but I can tell you, it will make me happy to see you and Silas eating it this evening."

Maude returned with the napkins. "I can almost taste it now. Oh, I hope that deer had a big rump because I set three more plates at the table tonight. Beth called. They're stuck here for Christmas, and I invited them to come share our meal and spend the night."

"What about Jedediah? Is he able? And Daniel? Won't he be upset not to be at home for Christmas morning?"

Maude counted out forks, knives, and spoons and began wrapping them in the red napkins. "Beth said Jed could make it, and they'd go back home in the morning. I guess Santa will have come while they're away."

Lita sliced the jicama and red onion. "Maybe Alo should go and see if they need any help. He's really good at helping Santa, you know."

"Good idea. And I saw the green napkins in the cupboard. We'll use those tomorrow evening with our Christmas china for our Christmas dinner. Your prime rib can only be served on the finest." Finished, Maude walked toward the dining room with a basket of silverware wrapped in bright red napkins. "Where's Laura?"

Lita stammered, wondering how she was going to cover. "Oh, she's in and out. I think she must have a bladder infection or something. Can't seem to stay in here very long at the time. But she always manages to come back just when I need her."

Apparently she'd covered well enough. With nothing more than a shrug, Maude exited the kitchen.

Moments later, Laura entered with a puzzled look on her face. "I just ran into Maude in the dining room. She told me she hoped I would be feeling better soon. Do you know what that was all about?"

Lita laid the Bibb lettuce on paper towels to dry. "I do. I told you I'd cover for you, and Maude noticed you had been coming and going in the kitchen all day. So I did as promised and told her you had a bladder infection."

The only thing that could have thrilled Lita more than seeing Laura bent double in laughter at that moment would be to see Catori and Doli come walking through the door.

"A bladder infection?" Laura laughed out loud. "You're a quick thinker, Lita. Quicker than I am at what I'm doing. But you must come and see. I don't know if I can do this or not, but it's not from lack of wanting to or trying."

The scattered guests barely heard the dinner bell over all the music and laughter. But once again, they gathered around the large dining table, noticing the seats were a bit closer together and there were four extra places at the table. Before they could take their seats, Alo entered the room with the Klingmans.

Silas moved toward the couple and turned to the other guests. "Friends, I'd like to introduce you to Jedediah and Beth and little Daniel Klingman. They are our neighbors, the ones you prayed for last evening. They've walked over to join us for Christmas."

Jedediah spoke first. "Please let me say thank you for your prayers. Silas and Alo and Kent were good to come and take care of us. And you were so good to pray. We're most grateful." He turned to Beth, who chimed in.

"Yes, we are, and we hope we're not crashing your party. Since we can't get out to join our family up in the mountains, Maude invited us to join you. So thank you for allowing us to celebrate Christmas with you."

Lily stepped up beside Silas. "Yes, you have joined the most Unlikely Christmas Party ever. Such an unexpected Christmas for all of us. And I must say, we'll be telling stories about this one for a spell."

The rumble around the room was proof of everyone's agreement with Lily.

Silas motioned for the Klingmans to have a seat, and joined Maude as everyone found a place at the table.

Lily looked at the number of settings at the table and turned to Maude. "Maude, are you expecting someone else, or have you lost the ability to count?"

"Well, sometimes, my counting is not as good as it used to be, but tonight I counted correctly. And to answer your question, no, we are not expecting another guest this evening. But we'll have a place for the Christ Child—or maybe someone else if a stranger happens by." She looked at Greg. "Greg, would you please express our gratitude for the day, and for the food, and for being together, and most especially for the miracle of Christmas?"

Greg stood at his place. "Maude, I think you just did that, but it will be a privilege to say it again. Thank you for asking."

Once Greg had prayed and taken his seat, the guests awaited the announcement of Lita's Christmas fare. She stood behind Kent's chair with her hands on his shoulders.

"This is just for you, Kent. Laura and I have prepared for you this evening our traditional Hopi Christmas Eve dinner, beginning with a Christmas salad of Bibb lettuce, pickled beets, prickly pears, pine nuts, red onions, and sliced avocado, dressed with a vinaigrette with my secret spices." She pinched Kent's shoulder. "For your main course, I hope you'll enjoy a venison rump roast that has been marinated and slow cooked in more secret spices. A medley of roasted root vegetables with sweet potatoes, parsnips, leeks, carrots, and onion will accompany the venison and will be served atop a cheesy polenta. And of course, dessert—Mexican Hot Chocolate Trifle. Need I say more?"

"All this just for Christmas Eve? Oh, Lita, you're too good to be true." Kent reached up with his good hand and squeezed Lita's hand on his shoulder.

With the music of Christmas in the background, the room soon filled with the clatter of silverware and the sounds of many hungry diners digging in. Conversations continued around the table throughout the meal, along with laughter. Gazing around the table, Silas thought back to the last time this room had been filled with Christmas Eve cheer. So many years gone by. When he caught Maude's eye, he knew she was thinking the same thing. Her eyes glistened, and he gripped her hand a moment in acknowledgment before diving back into his meal.

When everyone was finished and the table was cleared, Lily stood for her evening announcements.

"Listen, people. I'm sure you'll agree this meal was nothing short of fabulous. So why don't we let the cooks know?"

Their applause and twirling of their napkins in the air put smiles on Laura's and Lita's faces.

"I also think we can agree that we would enjoy our dessert a little later, maybe after something Maude has planned for us. And while I have your attention, tomorrow is Christmas, and truly we could not be any happier at the Broadmoor than we are here at Grey Sage. We're indeed having a most splendid Christmas holiday. I'll keep an eye on the weather and give you plenty of warning for our departure. But we will spend tomorrow and tomorrow evening right here.

"Lita has informed me that coffee and a continental breakfast will be served at your leisure from seven thirty until eight in the morning. So, let's move to the gathering room to see what she's planned for this glorious Christmas Eve."

With a chorus of conversations and jostling, everyone made their way to the adjoining room. After everyone was comfortably seated and Alo had the fire blazing, Maude orchestrated the storytelling once again, asking each guest to tell of one special Christmas. She then took her place beside Silas.

Ted told of exotic travel to Bethlehem during one of their Christmas breaks, but nothing of a childhood Christmas. Laura told of her sixteenth Christmas when her grandmother gave her an heirloom locket that had been in her family for six generations. The reverend entertained them with funny stories of his church's Christmas pageants. Iris added her soft humor and detail to his renditions.

Reba recollected a Christmas when she was called away for an emergency to talk one of her patients "off the ledge," but her best memory was of returning home to her husband and to Emily dressed in her Christmas nightgown. Emily added that it was a tradition for her to get a new Christmas nightgown every year. Reba had tucked every one of those gowns away in a cedar chest, and now Emily just added to it. She was saving the gowns for a daughter she hoped to have one day.

Silas sat quietly listening, but watching young Daniel as he sat on the floor at his father's knee, totally captivated by all their stories. Silas couldn't forget that the boy had just lost his dog, his best friend. He also didn't like looking at the near-bare floor under the Christmas tree. Without Beatrice's bags of candy, the floor would have been stone-cold, bare Saltillo tile.

When Emily finished her story, Maude stood up. "You people are walking treasure chests of beautiful stories, and I'm certain we could go on all evening. But for now, I have something special in mind. We have two pianists in this party, and I think it's time for some music. While you were playing poker and backgammon and drawing pictures this afternoon, I was searching for our Christmas music book and these booklets." She went to the piano and picked up a stack of green booklets and began passing them around. "So, Silas and Laura, what must we do to get you to play for us?"

Silas held up his hands. "Have you looked at my hands lately, Maude?"

Jedediah retorted quickly. "They did a mighty fine job of stitching up my scalp last evening, and I can imagine they still do a mighty fine job of tickling those ivories."

Silas looked at Laura. "I think we must, Laura. Come join me, please?"

Maude sensed the entire room taking a breath, as if waiting to see how Laura would respond. They'd not forgotten her dismissal the last time she'd been asked.

They needn't have worried. With a smile, Laura joined Silas at the piano, both of them sitting on the bench side by side.

Silas turned to the guests. "Here's how this works. We only take requests, and then you must, and I mean must, sing. No singing? No playing. Understood?"

The guests began flipping through their song booklets, calling out their favorites. Silas and Laura took turns accompanying as everyone dutifully lifted their voices in song. Lily's, not always in the same key as the others, could always be heard. She sang with the same exuberance she applied to painting or to blowing her whistle. Ted stared at her in disbelief, but Lily never knew. Maude held her breath when Beatrice rose and started to sway to "Silver Bells." But after allowing her a moment, Henry gently coaxed her back to her seat. There would be no stumbling tonight.

After a hearty round of singing, Lita, with help from Iris, began serving coffee and chocolate trifle in crystal goblets. No sweeter time could be had as dessert replaced the music. Maude came from her seat and stood in front of the fireplace.

"Thank you, Laura and Silas. You have given us a grand evening of beautiful music." She looked at Lily. "Well, it was beautiful most of the time."

Ted's laughter could be heard above the rest.

"And thank you, Lita, for chocolate!"

Silas and Laura begin to move from the piano. Maude stopped them. "Could you wait at the piano, Laura? But Silas, you may return to your chair and have your dessert."

Laura sat back down.

Maude squeezed the book in her hand. "Many years ago, it was our custom to read the Christmas story from the second chapter of Luke at the end of our Christmas Eve family gathering right here in this room. With your permission, I'd like us to continue that tradition. I have asked the colonel to read this evening. And then Laura, you played "Silent Night" so beautifully—would you play a quiet medita-tion for us that would be our benediction to quite a lovely evening?"

Laura smiled and nodded in agreement from the piano.

Maude handed her worn leather Bible to the colonel, took her seat next to Silas, and reached for his hand.

The room was quiet and warm and resonating with good things—sweet memories, warm light, and satisfied faces. The colonel opened the Bible and began to read in a voice that could only be had by a gen-tleman who had lived long, in the voice and cadence of one familiar with this story, and with the conviction of one who could attest to a faith that had sustained him through pain and pleasure and ordinary days.

Sitting beside her, Silas knew Maude was reliving many Christmases in a matter of moments. As was he. His teary eyes followed every movement of young Daniel again, sitting at his father's feet. He remembered how his boy Elan had sat with him to hear his grandfather read the same story. He remembered how much Elan had loved Christmas and how he'd spent what seemed like hours just staring at the tree and counting the gifts under it and then retelling the Christmas story with the olive-wood nativity set on the hearth.

His thoughts returned to the tree. Not one box wrapped in red foil and tied with a gold ribbon. Not one intriguing bundle awaiting discovery. Nothing but bare floor and an embarrassingly few bags of candy, which somehow made the floor look emptier and sadder and colder.

The colonel finished the reading. After a brief moment of holy hush, Laura mesmerized them with an ethereal and haunting improvisation of "Silent Night." It was the soulful end to a perfect day at Grey Sage.

The guests said their "Merry Christmas" goodnights and trailed to their rooms—all except Emily and Kent, who didn't move from the love seat. The roaring fire was now embers, and the house was quiet again.

Maude and Silas walked hand in hand to their bedroom. While Maude readied herself for bed, Silas built a small fire in the kiva in the corner. Only moments passed before they snuggled under the covers, enjoying the fire's glow and the afterglow of a perfect evening. They recapped the day, then lapsed into silence, smiling to themselves about how good it felt to have the inn filled with a few old friends and many new ones. Silas felt a bit sorry that he had grumbled about having guests for Christmas. He was growing attached to a few of them.

Sleep was sweet.

Chapter Sixteen

Sunday, December 25

Christmas morning. No need to set the clock. Maude's internal timer had been working precisely for decades, and this holiday had brought enough unexpected excitement to rouse her early. "Get up, Silas! It's Christmas."

Silas rolled over. "So you say it's Christmas? Do you think they're having a Christmas like this in Curaçao?"

Maude chuckled. "Don't be facetious. We'll still go to Curaçao one day. I'm just not certain when it will be."

Silas was up now, and they made the bed the bed together. "I am."

"You are. You're what?"

He reached over to his nightstand, took up a piece of paper, and walked around the bed to Maude. "I know when we're going." He offered her the handwritten note.

She read it out loud. *"Coupon good for ten days of sailing to* Curaçao. *The ship, with us on it, will embark from Fort Lauderdale on February second. Merry Christmas from your Traveling Companion."*

She looked up at him. "Is this what you were up to last night when you got up and left the room? Silas, you are the dearest man in all of time. We're going to Curaçao."

"We are indeed going to Curaçao, and Merry Christmas, my joy!"

With an exclamation, she embraced the man who had shared all but nine of her Christmases. "Thank you. You still know how to put a smile on my face. Let's get dressed."

Maude had laid out Silas's shirt and sweater and her Christmas Day attire the night before—black wool slacks, her finest white blouse, the forest-green wool sweater Silas had bought for her in England a decade ago, and her favorite Christmas scarf, dripping in holly leaves and red berries. She dressed quickly, brushed and braided her long white hair, and coiled it into a bun high on her head. In a matter of minutes, they were decked out like the mannequins in Macy's Christmas window and were walking arm in arm down the hall.

The smell of pine filled the hallway. Normally, the aroma of coffee and cinnamon buns would lure them to the kitchen, but Silas escorted Maude and took a detour through the gathering room. The Christmas tree lights were on and the fire had been started. Even though daybreak was sending rays of morning light through the glass panes, Alo had already lit every candle in every window and on the mantle. But what caught Maude's eye was underneath the Christmas tree: No more bare floor.

She squeezed Silas's arm as tears filled her eyes. "So that's what you were up to last night when I thought you had indigestion from the secret spices in Lita's vinaigrette."

Silas kissed her cheek. "Well, it wasn't exactly mischief I was up to, was it? Just trying to get rid of my Scroogey reputation."

Maude smiled at him, trying to remember if there was ever a time she could have loved him more. There was no one in the world like her Silas.

There was no one in the world like his Maude, Silas thought as he embraced his wife. He'd worked on his surprise not for his Scroogey reputation, of course, but to see the look on her face just now. If he'd had any doubts about his plan, they were gone now.

He gave her a squeeze and a peck on the cheek. "Now, I need to check on Jedediah, to see how he is and to orchestrate the surprise this Christmas morning. Suppose you get us some coffee?"

With a last brilliant smile, she wiped her eyes and headed off while Silas tiptoed down the hall toward the Klingmans' room. He lightly tapped on the door.

Jedediah answered, already dressed and looking like he needed a cup of coffee.

Silas motioned for him to come out into the hallway and close the door. "Still have a headache? Not feeling so good this morning?"

"Oh, no, sir, not me. I'm fine. I had to tell Daniel about Shep yesterday. He cried hard when I first told him. I think coming over here distracted him some, but when we got back to our room last night and things got quiet ... Well, I think he had held it in as long as he could. Had a hard time consoling him and getting him to sleep. It was a long night."

"Well, let's go get you a cup of coffee." They walked down the hallway. "I know about a boy losing his dog. We had a similar experience with our son, but at least it wasn't on Christmas."

"Yes, sir. And I need to find Shep and take care of things. I looked around when we walked by the barn yesterday afternoon, but I didn't see him. I figured the wolves came back. I just don't want Daniel finding him."

Silas stopped just shy of the kitchen. "That's already taken care of. You can thank Alo. He gave Shep a proper burial even with the snow. He'll take you to the place when the time is right."

"There's no one like Alo. He's good to me and to my boy, always teaching us so much about this land and living on it. He respects all living things, that man."

"He's good to us all." Silas paused. "Now, I hate to switch subjects so quickly, but time is running out. I know you've already taken care of Santa Claus for Daniel, and you'll be going home for that later this morning, but I wanted to do something that just might take Daniel's mind off losing Shep for a little while. I hope it's all right. Let me show you." Silas led Jedediah to the gathering room. "It was something I needed to do. See?"

Jedediah's face lit up as his eyes took in the sight before him. "Oh, wow, Silas. You're right about keeping his mind off losing Shep. I have no words right now, sir."

"That's because you haven't had your coffee. Let's go get some.

We can talk later. I just need you to keep Daniel in your room until I come and get you. I want everyone to see his surprise. Christmas just isn't Christmas without a child around, and we are blessed to have one in the house this morning."

Silas poured Jedediah a cup of coffee and one for Beth. "I'll come and get you when everyone's up and in the dining room. I don't think it will be long. I've already heard folks moving around."

Lita and Laura bustled about the kitchen, dressed in clean aprons. Laura stirred the fruit medley while Lita placed her sticky cinnamon buns on a large silver tray. Maude was also there, mixing up her special cream concoction to flavor the coffee.

Coming in ones and twos, guests gathered in the dining room, helping themselves to steaming coffee and fruit juice.

Lita heard them arriving. She wiped her hands and quickly stepped into the dining room. "Breakfast will be served in just a few minutes, but I think I heard someone ask about what's underneath this." She pointed to the green velvet cloth that Maude used for years of unveiling her Christmas paintings. It now covered something on the oak sideboard. "What can I say? It's Christmas, and Christmas always comes with a few secrets and surprises. This will be unveiled at just the right time, but it is rigged to disappear if anyone takes a peek."

Aahs went around the room.

Lita turned to walk away. "I wasn't kidding. And the culprit will be sent to bed without Christmas dinner." She sashayed out of the dining room, her apron strings trailing in the wind behind her.

A few moments later when everything was on the table and Lita stood ready, Maude said to Silas, "You might get the Klingmans and bring them in here now."

Maude then turned to the group. "We have a real surprise this morning, so the plan is the surprise first, and then you're free to get your breakfast and coffee at your leisure, and we'll do our nibbling in the gathering room."

Lita stepped forward as Silas brought the Klingmans into the dining room. "Now, many years ago, it was tradition in this house to have an unveiling on Christmas. Maude always had a new painting of Grey Sage to show the family. Well, she thought she'd be in Curaçao on this lovely Christmas morning, so there's no new painting. But I know you've been wondering about what's underneath the green velvet cloth, and I think now is the time for you to find out. I must tell you that this was Laura's idea and her creation. She worked all day yesterday and into the night to make certain she would finish."

She pointed her finger at Laura. "And she is offering this to all of you as her Christmas gift." Laura stood near the sideboard, smiling shyly. "And Maude, Laura did this to say thank you for opening Grey Sage to a group of strangers for Christmas, and she thinks you'll really love it. Laura, would you like to unveil your masterpiece?"

"Would you help me with that end of the drape, Lita?" Laura and Lita charily lifted the cloth and dropped it to the floor.

Maude's eyes grew wide, and she stepped nearer to examine the gingerbread replica of Grey Sage. "Laura, this is absolutely a work of art. It's Grey Sage, every wing, every door, and every window— all in gingerbread and candies. How in the world did you do this? Lita's right, it is a masterpiece. And you're right, I really love it." She hugged Laura.

Laura responded. "I always wanted to build a gingerbread house, but I never did. Why, I'd never made a cookie until three days ago, and Lita is so amazing that she has made a cook and a baker of me. I never could have done this without her help. She gave me the cookie recipe, and the icing recipe, and then helped me gather the other candies and items for the detail. And she stayed up with me until it was finished. I truly hope you like it. It was great fun!"

The guests gathered round to see the replica. Reba remarked, "Are those marzipan trees? And the glass panes—are they made of sugar?"

Laura answered. "Yes, cooked to the perfect temperature and then allowed to cool. And pretzels for tree trunks. Even the ceilings for all the covered porches are made of strips of cookies. And of course royal icing tinted just the right muddy color is the mortar holding all this together, and the white icing dripping from the roof top looks so much like icicles, don't you think?"

Lily touched the candy-cane lamppost. "Why, Laura, you could really start a business doing this you know! You even drew the design yourself?"

"Yes, but you must know adobe houses are easy. If it had been a Victorian, like the one we live in, I'm not sure I would have attempted it."

Maude hugged her again. "Well, we are so glad you attempted this one. May I suggest we enjoy looking at it for a few hours before we start with the demolition."

Lily spoke up. "Translated, that means, 'Everyone keep your eyes on Beatrice.' She's the one we'd have to worry about."

Beatrice frowned and shook her head. "Not I, Lily. It's Christmas. No misbehaving."

"You'll have your fill, Beatrice. I made a whole tray of gingerbread cookies too." With a last grateful smile at Lita, Laura picked up the green velvet drape from the floor and moved away so everyone could gather around and examine her creation.

Silas stood in the archway leading to the gathering room. "This morning has already started with such a delicious surprise, but that's not the only surprise." He looked around the group. "Where's Daniel?"

Daniel raised his hand. He was still in his superhero pajamas and fur-lined moccasins. His curly blond hair looked smeared all over his head.

"Come here, son." Silas put his hand on Daniel's shoulder. "Just want to remind everyone what a hero you were night before last! It was amazing thing you did for a young boy your age. And I'm sorry you didn't get to be with your grandparents for Christmas. But we're so glad that you're here with us."

Daniel's cheeks reddened from the attention. "Yes, sir, thank you."

"Now I know Santa made a stop at your house last night and you'll be leaving soon to go and check it out. But I think you'll be glad to know he made a stop here after he left your house. His ruckus woke me up. I wasn't expecting him here, but when I came out to check on the noise, Santa told me he almost got stuck in that kiva of yours, so he needed a big chimney to deliver this gift. Why don't you go look under the tree?"

Daniel looked up at Silas. "Santa delivered something here for me?" The boy practically slid through the dining room, his felt-bottomed slippers skating across the tile floor. The guests followed quickly to see.

In the gathering room, Daniel made a quick survey, then turned to Silas. "Did you mean these little bags?" he asked curiously.

Beatrice interrupted quickly. "No, no, not the bags, young man. They already have names on them. I would have gotten you a bag, but I didn't know you were coming."

Silas moved to where Daniel stood. "Have you never seen an electric train, son?"

"No, sir, never. Is …" He hesitated, unsure but hopeful. "Is it for me?"

At Silas's nod, Daniel skidded across the room to where the train was running, crossing bridges, and entering and exiting tunnels. "Wow! I can't believe it. Mom! Dad! Santa brought me a train. A real electric train. Can I move the track?"

Silas chuckled. "Of course, you can. But I think you'd better stop it first. And it'll be up to you to keep those train cars polished, and you can add all kinds of things to an electric train set—new train cars, more bridges and scenery … It'll be fun, and you and your dad can build a special table for it."

Silas stepped back, joined Maude, and put his arm around her. He knew they were sharing the same memories, the same bitter tears, and the same budding joy. He knew it was time for the train to be out of its black bins and in the hands of a little boy.

"I like it. I like it so much. I promise to take care of it, Dad." He got down on the floor to see all the moving parts. "I have a train, a real electric train, and I didn't even know I wanted one."

The whole room broke up in laughter.

Greg, being the theologian he was, obviously couldn't allow this opportunity to pass on Christmas morning. "Well, Daniel, that's just like Christmas. When Christmas came, we didn't know to even ask for Christmas because we didn't know we wanted it or needed it. But we did, and God was good to see our need and give us the best gift ever: himself. Merry, Merry Christmas, everyone."

With a smile at Silas, Maude turned the music on and let Christmas happen.

The day was filled with conversations, more backgammon, picture taking, more piano playing, and a few brave soloists who knew they couldn't be heard about the chatter. Lita and Laura kept the table filled with snacks and began working to prepare a traditional Christmas Dinner to be served at five o'clock.

The Klingmans went home, but not before Daniel promised to return before Christmas dinner to see his train later in the day. He wanted to know when he could take it home. Silas promised to pack it on Monday, and as soon as the roads were clear, he would deliver the train to Daniel's front door.

The day was still bitterly cold, but the wind had subsided, blue sky replaced the thick gray clouds, and the sun made its appearance in the afternoon for the first time in days. Kent and Emily joined the Christmas trivia game for a while, but at the first available stopping point, Kent stepped away. Being the grand champion of Christmas trivia was not high on his list of things to accomplish. "Keep playing, friends, but I'm going for a snack. So don't wait for me."

Emily followed him to the dining table for another round of Lita's morsels.

He took a piece of cream-cheese-stuffed celery from the tray. "This is my third one of these. They're good. Raisins and cream cheese. Interesting. But Lita probably has some secret ingredient in this too." He paused. "What do you say we take that walk we didn't take yesterday?"

"A walk sounds inviting. I love this place, and I'm not at all getting cabin fever, but fresh air sounds wonderful."

"Get your warmest gear. The sun may be shining, but it's still cold out there."

Emily smiled and saluted him. "Yes, Corporal. Or Sergeant. Or … I don't even know your rank."

"I'll settle for captain, ma'am."

"Yes, sir, Captain." She quickly went and retrieved her jacket.

They moved through the kitchen into the mudroom, putting on hats and gloves as they walked.

"I love you, Lita," Kent said to her as they passed her at the stove. "And I'm coming back to be your sous chef someday soon. Or maybe you can teach me to cook first. But I want to cook just like you, and then I'm certain everyone will love me."

Lita gave him a significant look. "Someone loves you, Kent. Enjoy the sunshine. There'll be hot chocolate and some leftover Hot Chocolate Trifle when you get back." She turned to Laura, who was crumbling cornbread for the dressing. "Budding love. Nothing in the whole world like it. Especially when they're not so young, and those powerful feelings aren't wasted."

Emily blushed.

"Come on." Kent led her out. "I want to walk down to the bridge. We crossed it the other night going to Jedediah's, but I couldn't see anything beyond Silas, and I couldn't see much more on the walk back home yesterday morning. This terrain must be something in the light of day. I just have a feeling about it."

He took her hand, and they walked beyond the barn and took the path. Once they reached the pine brake, he pointed out the bridge down below to her.

Emily struggled to keep up with him as they descended to the creek. "It's not so easy walking in this powdery snow. It's above my knees, and my legs aren't quite as long as yours."

"Then, let's not walk." Kent stopped in his tracks and fell backward into the pillowy snow, feeling like a tall pine that had been felled.

Emily gasped. "Are you all right?"

Kent's laugh came from somewhere deep inside, a place that had not been rattled with laughter in a long time. "More all right than I've been in quite awhile. You said it was hard to walk, so just lie down. We wanted to make some snow angels anyway." He rose up on his elbow. "Come on, turn around and just let go. The snow will catch you, and it's soft."

But Emily was pulling off her gloves and reaching into her pocket for her camera. "Not until I take your picture. Do your snow-angel thing!"

Kent lay back down, imprinting the snow with his head and limbs. He moved his legs in and out and his right arm up and down to create one good wing. Emily snapped several shots.

"Now, it's my turn." She turned around and fell into the snow beside him and made her snow angel, giggling like a schoolgirl. "Too bad there's no one to take our picture. My students wouldn't believe this."

Kent pushed himself up with his good arm, careful not to disturb the imprint of his snow angel. "Hand me your camera. I'll take your picture." He took several and then extended his arm to help her up. When she was upright, he pulled her close to him and kissed her on the cheek. "Now, you take a picture of our snow angels, and I want a copy." He looked at the blanket of snow. "Never thought of an angel with one wing. Come on. We have to get to the bridge."

They plodded on, laughing and talking about what a surprising Christmas it had been. When they reached the bridge, it was as he'd thought—unbelievably beautiful, with a trickling creek through a stone bed. "When the snow melts, this creek will swell. Can you imagine what it would look like in April?"

Emily stood, holding on to the bridge railing and straining to see. "Oh, to be here in the spring. I've visited lots of places, but this is one of the most enchanting. It's like my soul is home here. I love everything about it."

Kent reached into the inside pocket of his jacket and pulled out an envelope. "Emily, I wanted to get you something for Christmas. No … it was more like I had a need to give you something, and it just happens to be Christmas. So here it is."

"Is it the drawing of me you did, the one with the moonflower in my hair?"

"No, that's for me. Just look."

She pulled the paper and a brochure from the envelope. A note was typed on Grey Sage letterhead. "*This is good for a week of your choice at an artists' or writers' retreat this spring. You choose the date, and if my new assignment allows, I'll meet you here. We'll return to the bridge together and see it in springtime. Always, Kent.*"

Her arms went around his neck as though that's what they were made for. Kent leaned to kiss her and held her close with one arm. He was passionate and yet gentle. "The next time we're on this bridge, both my arms will be around you, Emily Sutton. I'm counting on it."

"Me too. This is the best Christmas gift I have ever received, Kent. You've given me not only time here with you, but you've given me happy days from now until April, days filled with anticipation for being here with you."

He looked deeply into her eyes. "Thank you for being my moonflower, and for giving me some hope in my darkness, Emily." He kissed her lips. "But I'll be seeing you before April."

"Then I'll have even happier days." She stretched to kiss him again.

Christmas day was like a stocking full of surprises—Silas's coupon for Maude's trip to Curaçao, Laura's gingerbread house that no one could bear to touch, Silas's gift of the electric train to young Daniel, Kent's "Return to Grey Sage" trip for Emily, and Beatrice's bags of candy—which she handed to recipients with the unashamed declaration that if they didn't like the contents, she'd gladly take them back.

A traditional dinner with Lita's prime rib was served and enjoyed by every guest. There was nothing missing, and no lack of joy at Grey Sage this Christmas.

After the evening's last story, Lita served coffee and slices of her traditional Cold Christmas Cake that Laura had made. Lita told the story of how her ancestors had chilled the cake in the creek for two days, but she assured them Laura had chilled hers in the fridge.

"Speaking of Cold Christmas Cake …" Lily stepped in front of the fireplace, not to warm her backside, but because that had become the designated spot for announcements, readings, storytelling, and even impromptu ballet moves.

"Listen up, you Party people. It's time to say thank you to our hosts, so don't go back to the kitchen yet, Lita. Let's see … Maude guided us through Santa Fe, down Canyon Road, through the Railyard District and the Loretto Chapel. Lita has fed us food fit for the gods. I didn't always know what I was eating, Lita, except that it was absolutely delicious, and thank God for refrigerators. Alo has kept us warm with blazing fires. And aside from being a gentlemanly host, Silas has proven his medical skills on more than one patient.

"In addition to all that, we managed to wreck the van and spend a day stranded in the edge of a snow-covered forest. We escaped the terrors of howling wolves. We've sung Christmas carols and heard stories that I still don't believe, and we've had more surprises today than I can list. Young and old, we've had a grand time."

She paused and gestured dramatically. "And now, Alo and Lita, will you come forward please?"

Alo and Lita, still in her apron, joined Lily. Lily handed them an envelope. "You two have kept the fires burning and such good food on the table. We wanted to say thank you, so we've arranged a Couples' Day Treat at one of the spas in town just for you. All you need to do is tell them who you are, and you will be treated as royally as you have treated us this week. Thank you so much."

Alo responded first. "It has been our pleasure. Lita and I would have had the loneliest and quietest Christmas without you good people. We will miss you as you travel a new road tomorrow."

Lita joined him. "Yes, you have made me hand-clapping happy as you enjoyed my meals. And I have such a good new friend. Laura, you have been so wonderful to help me. I hope you will all return to Grey Sage. Our doors are always open to you."

The guests applauded.

Lily took center stage again. "Now stay right here, Lita, Alo. Maude and Silas, will you come up?"

Maude and Silas joined the three of them.

Lily turned to Maude. "Maude, we've been friends almost forever, since that first time I saw you on the street corner in Chicago in our university days. I love you, my friend. I know it was your tradition for many years to buy something special for Grey Sage every Christmas. And ... I saw you eyeing a beautiful piece of hand-blown glass on Canyon Road. You know, the one with red-and-yellow spirals like a giant lollipop. Now I couldn't get back there because of the weather, but I've made arrangements for you to pick it up at your convenience. This is our Christmas gift to you and Silas and to Grey Sage. And I want you to know, I missed two hours of poker playing and my chance to beat Henry because I was on the phone trying to locate this piece. Do you know how many galleries there are on Canyon Road?"

"Oh, my, Lily." For a moment, Maude couldn't speak. "I will cherish it, and I know exactly where it will hang. The light coming through that piece will be red and yellow, bright colors that will always remind me of the color this group has brought back to Grey Sage, thanks to an unexpected snowstorm. So thank you, so very much."

Bea interrupted. "So that's where you went yesterday when you left the trivia game? I suppose I need to apologize. I really didn't think you could find anyone who would talk to you. Certainly not for that long. I stand corrected."

Silas spoke up. "But wait. One more gift."

Beatrice continued as if Silas hadn't said a word. "Don't forget there were gifts under the tree for everyone from me. And I do hope you remember, Maude, that I gave you and Silas and Alo and Lita your gifts the morning we left. I would have gladly left them under your tree, but you didn't have a tree. Oh, and that was the dreadful morning that I almost died from—" There was a quiet scuffle amongst the nearby guests, and Bea abruptly subsided.

Silas took center stage again. "Oh, we remember, Beatrice, the sweet gifts you gave us and how you returned to us for Christmas. We wouldn't forget, and we wouldn't forget this one more gift." He pulled a small gift-wrapped box from the pocket of his sweater and asked Lily to step forward. "Lily, I have something very special for you. I hid it once and returned it. We used it to keep the wolves at bay, and now that you've announced you're leaving tomorrow, I'm giving it back."

Lily unwrapped the gold-foiled box and removed her sterling silver whistle on its sterling silver chain. She unfolded the handwritten note inside and read it aloud for all to hear. *"Lily, we welcome you back to Grey Sage anytime, whistle and all, especially if your Unlikely Christmas Party on Wheels will come with you. We have enjoyed each and every one of you. Remember your nights here are our gift to you. Thank you for making our Christmas one we'll never forget—a Christmas when an unexpected storm made friends of strangers and truly brought Christmas back to Grey Sage. Merry Christmas, Silas and Maude."*

Maude woke early the next morning. "Silas ... Silas, I know you're awake. I can tell by your breathing. We must get up. There's much to do this morning. The roads are cleared and our guests are leaving. I know Lita's already up and making a fabulous last breakfast."

"Maude, do you ever think how often you wake me with instructions about getting up?"

"Not so much."

"Well, you do. And one of these mornings, I'm just not going to listen to you. But it's not this morning." He rolled to his side and climbed out of the warm bed.

In short order, they were dressed and headed for the kitchen.

Only minutes passed before the guests began stirring. Some were busy bringing their luggage and other bags to the front door, and others were enjoying the last morning in front of the fire when Maude entered the room and gently rang the bell. "It's breakfast. Your last morning at Grey Sage."

When they were gathered around the table, Kent voiced the question on everyone's mind: "What's for breakfast, Miss Lita? It's not that I care, because I know it'll be good. I'm just dying to know, and I like how you say it."

Lita stood behind him at the table and squeezed his shoulders one more time. "This morning, you're having an open-faced bacon-and-tomato sandwich served on toasted sour dough bread. The tomatoes have been roasted, and the bacon has been covered in maple syrup and baked to a perfect crispiness. And it's topped with a fried egg. Then you'll find a green chili-avocado sauce on the side and a bowl of citrus fruit this morning. For those of you wanting lighter fare, I have baked oatmeal with fresh, stewed apples. I don't want anyone leaving hungry. But in case you're still hungry after breakfast, I have to-go bags with cookies. You can thank Laura for all that goodness."

Kevin twirled his napkin above his head. "No secret ingredient this morning?"

"Young man, there's always a secret ingredient around here. Check out the green chili-avocado sauce."

"I'll be back in April to put the apron on, and I'm not leaving without the secret ingredient."

Bea stood up from the table. "Breakfast was wonderful. Now let's go. I must see my family."

Maude and Silas had been sitting quietly at the end of the table, enjoying the morning's conversation. Maude responded. "Bea, I really do hate to see you go. You've been nothing short of delightful."

"Yes, I know. But please tell me we're not going to have to do that ritual thing again with the paint on our hands this morning. Are we?" She rolled her tiny blue eyes. "If we do, I'm taking my shoes off to put my footprint on your wall. It's much more famous than my hand."

The members of the Unlikely Christmas Party all laughed, but Silas laughed the loudest.

Maude spoke. "No ritual this morning, Bea, unless you'd *like* to leave your footprint. But I must say again, each one of you has made a wonderful impression on us, and we are grateful that you brought to us a most unforgettable Christmas. What do you say we do it again next year?"

Everyone clapped as they rose from the table. Lily moved next to Maude and pulled out her whistle. "Don't make me do this, people. But I will and I can. We're leaving in ten minutes. I think Gordy and Alo have already loaded the van."

In less than ten minutes, Maude, Silas, Lita, and Alo stood at the door bidding farewell and safe travel to each member of the Unlikely Christmas Party. They lingered to wave as Gordy drove the Party down the snow-lined lane. They were about to close the door when Maude heard the horn and noticed the brake lights. "Wait, they're stopping. Maybe someone forgot something."

They stood, watching and waiting.

Then Lily appeared, hanging out of the side door of the van. She blew the whistle as loud as she could and yelled, "If I don't see you before then, we'll all be back next Christmas. You can count on it."

Christmases in Passing

*W*hen Maude and Silas returned their Christmas decorations to the storage closet in 1982, they had no idea there would be no Christmas at Grey Sage for twenty-three years. But Christmas returned when Lily arrived with her Unlikely Christmas Party on Wheels in 2005.

And when those unexpected Christmas guests sat around the fire in the gathering room during that holiday, no one regretted being stranded by a snowstorm or thought that a new Christmas tradition might be beginning. Or perhaps that this Christmas was the rebirth of some treasured old traditions.

For the next several years, Lily brought her entourage, as Silas called it, to the Grey Sage Inn—folks who had no family or nowhere to go or who didn't want to be alone for Christmas. The returning guests always seemed to remember their seats at the dining table and their favorite chairs in the gathering room. And they always requested their same suites. Even though some of the guests returned year after year to the Christmas traditions, there were always a few new ones who showed up for reasons of their own.

Lily led the group for the next ten years. Each time, she'd show up in her shaggy Mongolian lamb vest, always with her whistle around her neck. Lita continued threatening to set Lily's hair on fire every year, but she never followed through.

When Lily's health no longer allowed her to travel, Maude began a new tradition of visiting her in Chicago. On one such trip, Lily sent a small, gift-wrapped box back to Grey Sage for Alo. It was her silver whistle with a note that read, *"This whistle is to keep the wolves away.*

I'm counting on you to keep my friends, Maude and Silas, safe. Always, Lily."

Beatrice Caldwell and Colonel Henry Walton attended the Grey Sage Christmas gatherings for several more years until, after serving as Bea's escort as faithfully as he'd served his country, the colonel died in 2009. He was given a hero's burial in Arlington Cemetery. Captain Kent Martin, dressed in his army best, attended the burial ceremony.

After the colonel passed away, Beatrice went to live with her daughter. Bea's changing realities made it unsafe for her to live alone, but there were some constants in her life: her delight in being alive and her love of dance and chocolate. And she never lost her ability to captivate an audience.

Ted and Laura Sutton never missed a Christmas at Grey Sage, and they always headed to Canyon Road to purchase a whimsical piece of art to go in the new gardens Laura designed for the estate—gardens that included beds of fresh herbs for her newly found passion. Laura resigned from her position of teaching music theory at the university and enrolled in culinary school. She spent a year planning and remodeling her kitchen in the historic Sutton mansion and enjoyed entertaining Ted's colleagues and baking birthday cakes for friends and neighborhood children. Ted continued teaching and spending time in his lab in the basement while Laura concocted recipes just above his head.

Maude was right when she told Laura she could start a business making gingerbread houses, but Laura was content to bake. She gave much of her time to volunteering at several neighborhood schools. When her vegetable and herb garden was established, she invited classes for field trips to their home to see the gardens and enjoy the kinetic art.

Laura shared her new recipes with Lita every Christmas as they spent time in the kitchen together, preparing sumptuous meals for Grey Sage's guests. And on Christmas morning, there was always a newly designed gingerbread house under the same piece of green velvet on the oak breakfront in the dining room. And of course, there was always Lita's Cold Christmas Cake for Christmas dinner.

Greg and Iris Martin returned to their home in the Chicago suburbs, where Iris hung her stained-glass iris in her kitchen window and Greg displayed his cactus on his desk in his office. As Greg had predicted, the piece of art initiated many a conversation, including an occasional homily on the hidden meanings found in the prickly plant. Every Christmas, they brought home enough cactus-pear jelly to last until their next visit, which was often a couple of times during the year.

Reba returned to her therapy practice, wearing her dragonfly ring to remind her that every day was a new beginning, a resurrection of sorts. She continued to enjoy taking art classes with Lily, and she used what she learned with her clients. On occasion, she was known to let her hair down. She would often accompany Greg and Iris for midyear visits back to New Mexico.

And Emily and Kent? Now that was a love story. When they returned to Chicago, Kent made the weekly drive to visit Emily a hundred miles away, always encouraging her to finish her children's book. They returned to Grey Sage in late April of 2006 to fulfill his Christmas present to her. Emily spent her days in the studio, studying with Maude and working on the illustrations for her book. Kent, continuing his therapy for a couple of hours every morning, was regaining the use of his left arm. That made him happy because he could cook alongside Lita in the kitchen while Emily was in the studio.

On the Friday afternoon of that week in April, late in the day, Kent persuaded Emily to take a walk down to the bridge. The snow had long since melted, and the trees along the creek bank were every shade of green. Water cascaded over smooth stones. He embraced her with both arms, just as he had told her he would when they ventured to the bridge that snowy afternoon in December. And after he kissed her, he bent down on one knee, pulled a ring from his pocket, and asked her to marry him.

They were wed in a ceremony on that same bridge on a Saturday evening in August, under a trellis covered in moonflowers—Kent's surprise for Emily. The entire Unlikely Christmas Party, along with other close family and friends, filled Grey Sage in celebration. And when they left for their honeymoon, Kent carried a jar of Lita's secret ingredient.

Kent and Emily found time every year to drive up to Grey Sage, and Christmas there became their tradition, even after the birth of their daughter three years later. Emily unpacked her cedar chest to find the gown her mother had purchased for her first Christmas nearly thirty years ago, and brought the gown with them to the inn.

Kent continued his military career, and Emily became a full-time mom and a writer of children's books. For years, Emily retrieved their mail from her sunflower mailbox.

The Klingmans continued to be good neighbors, checking in on Maude and Silas and Alo and Lita almost daily. Daniel and Jedediah built a special table in the barn for Daniel's electric train. He frequently invited Silas over to see the newest addition. When Silas felt Daniel was old enough to know, Silas told him the story of his own love for trains, and how he had given this train to his own son, Elan, on his sixth Christmas.

The time came when Maude and Silas and Alo and Lita made arrangements for the continued running of Grey Sage. Alo and Lita's daughter Catori accepted their invitation to run the inn. Alo oversaw the construction of another adobe casita on the property, where Catori and her husband and two boys would live.

Through the years, many strangers passed through the halls and portales of Grey Sage—artists, writers, travelers looking for a cup of coffee, and others who needed an open door to the real comfort and friendship they found at Grey Sage.

But Christmas was predictably more than special. The fireplaces were always ablaze, the table always full, and candles were always lit in every window. Music and stories and laughter echoed through the halls. Maude was right on that snowy Christmas Eve in 2005 when she told Silas, "Christmas is the time when strangers become friends."

Cold Christmas Cake

Ingredients:

1 pound box vanilla wafers or graham crackers
1 cup pecans (or walnuts), chopped
1 cup walnuts (or pecans), chopped
2 cups shredded moist coconut
1 pound raisins
1 regular can sweetened condensed milk
Candied cherries, optional
Whipped cream

Directions:

+ Crush the vanilla wafers or graham crackers in a food processor.
+ Chop the nuts or grind in a food processor. If you prefer, you may use 2 cups of chopped pecans or 2 cups of walnuts rather than 1 cup of each.
+ Combine the cookie crumbs with the chopped nuts, coconut, and raisins, mixing well.
+ Pour in sweetened condensed milk and work through with hands so that dry ingredients are thoroughly saturated.
+ Press the mixture tightly into a spring-form pan.
+ If desired, you may use candied cherries to decorate the top. (I like to cut red cherries into shapes of poinsettia petals and used chopped green cherries for leaves.)
+ Refrigerate for two days before slicing and serving with a dollop of whipped cream.

Native American Fry Bread

Ingredients:
  2 cups all-purpose flour
  1 tablespoon baking powder
  1 teaspoon kosher salt
  1 cup steaming tap water
  Vegetable oil for frying

Directions:
- Mix dry ingredients well.
- Add water and stir until a dough forms.
- Grease your hands and shape the dough into a mound.
- Cover the dough with a towel and allow it to rest in a warm place for thirty minutes.
- Pour about 1 inch of oil into a pan and heat on medium-high. Test by dropping a dusting of flour into the oil to see if it sizzles. The oil should be hot so the bread is not soggy or greasy.
- Spoon a ping-pong-sized ball of dough into your greased hands and flatten it like a cookie. They should be between four and five inches across. Poke a small hole in the center like a donut.
- Place the dough in the hot oil and allow it to brown on one side before turning (approximately two to three minutes per side).
- Drain on paper towels before serving.

Note: I like to dust powdered sugar on these for dessert with a bowl of my favorite ice cream. My husband loves them with butter and honey, like sopapillas. And they're especially good with a piping hot bowl of homemade vegetable soup or chili.

Acknowledgments

I want to thank you, the reader, for taking a few hours of your time to visit Grey Sage. It is only when you read it scene by scene that the story comes to life—when characters' voices can be heard, when icy winds can be felt, when warm cider can be smelled, and when what you read makes you feel, or remember or think about something differently. So, I thank you for allowing this story and these characters to live with you for a while.

Without a few good friends who shared an unforgettable experience, there would be no *Christmas at Grey Sage*. The idea for this book was born the night when a sudden and most unusual thunderstorm stranded our traveling group at an inn in downtown Santa Fe. That storm dazzled us with spectacular lightning, made us jumpy with its thunderclaps, and created an evening to remember. Downtown dinner plans and all electricity were washed away with the floodwaters, and we found ourselves making do in the darkness and sharing what we had with strangers who quickly became friends. You, my traveling companions, could not have known as we all sat around the roaring fire, sharing stories and laughing with abandon, that I was studying faces, listening intently, and storing memories. You know who you are, and I thank you for an incredible evening.

Maybe your life experiences have taught you that Christmas can be a tender time for some, especially those who are away from people they love at Christmas. I am deeply indebted to two very special and unusual men who served our country on the battlefield and spent Christmases away from their families. Their Christmastime experiences in a war were six decades apart. How their wars were fought was different, but the hearts of the soldiers were the same. Charles Walker, I am so proud to call you my friend. Thank you for reliving your World War Two experiences while telling them to me in amazing detail and then for allowing me to chronicle them in this book. You are at the top of my list of heroes. And, Dr. Andy Muck, you are nothing short of remarkable. Together, we've served the least of these in Guatemala. Serving alongside you was a joy and an inspiration. Thank you for sharing your experiences in Iraq as a doctor taking care of the most critically wounded and for allowing me to use your most poignantly penned memory of losing a child-patient on the battlefield. Thank you for how you live your life, relieving suffering, calming the frightened, and teaching young doctors in the field of emergency medicine.

I am so grateful for the highly professional and yet truly kind team at Gilead Publishing. Dan Balow, you understand in this "universe of word matter" that words really do matter. I am grateful you love a good story and that you would allow me to tell this story. Becky Philpott, you are omniscient and omnipresent when it comes to publishing a book. Jordan Smith, you live in a world of technology and social media, and you navigate it with such ease. Thank you for being so patient with this Luddite and for bringing me along. And Kristen Gearhart, you're a fantastic hand-holder and spinner of so many plates. You all are top in your class of professionals, and yet you're always personal and kind, made so by our Father's Spirit who lives in you. Then there is Leslie Peterson whose editorial work helped me deliver this book to you. It is a better book because of you, Leslie. Thank you.

I am always indebted to my husband Bill, the love of my life and the one who never, and I mean never, lets things get boring. He understands why I write and why I must write. He was unbothered when I rose in the middle of the night because a character was nudging me to work. He asked no questions when I told him I needed to return to Santa Fe to see and feel and smell and walk those streets again. He loaded the Jeep, and off we went. He never complained when he was served Indian fry bread for days until I perfected the recipe so that it was worthy of Lita, the innkeeper at Grey Sage. Thank you, Bill, for being my leader and my cheerleader, and for being my home while we walk Home together.